SHADOW OF OZ

By Nick Damon

To Mary -
Thanks for keeping me healthy!!
Love those Acai Bowls!
N Damon 2013

Secret Origin Press

For more information about the author, visit
www.ndamon.com

FOR MOM & DAD

CHAPTER 1
LOST

ZO.

Z and O.

Those two simple letters gnawed at her. Taunted and tugged at her mind. Would often send her thoughts drifting at the sight of either one of them. When seen next to each other, she found herself… somewhere else.

Somewhere dark and empty.

She was there now.

The two letters hung together in midair while she pondered them. The world around her was a black void.

The letters reminded her of something. Something just on the tip of her tongue. Something important.

She couldn't look away. In fact, the harder she stared, the bolder the letters became.

A jarring sound, a ringing, crashed out of the emptiness, startling her.

The starless world around her shattered like glass, falling away in sharp fragments, letting in blinding light.

Fluorescent light to be more precise. Life crushing, soul sucking, fluorescent light. The bane of all who spend their waking hours trapped beneath them. A blue white glare that sapped precious energy while others outside enjoyed the natural glow and warmth of the sun. The fluorescent flickered, giving out a brief electric crackle like a bug zapper.

Dorothy Gale blinked.

In front of her was a computer monitor. Her hands resting on the keyboard. A cursor blinked on an unfinished word: ***Horizo-***

She added the final letters finishing the sentence— ***Far Horizons.***

It was the name of a company whose ad campaign she was working on. She had been writing up a proposal for them when her mind decided to take a vacation.

Feeling slightly dazed, Dorothy glanced around at her surroundings.

She was sitting in a sparse office cubicle. No personal items decorated her claustrophobic walls or plastic desk, just sticky notes here and there reminding her of tasks that she didn't want to do. On her dull gray desktop, next to her computer monitor, were stacks of folders and paperwork awaiting her attention.

A maze of identical cubicles boxed her in. A grim honeycomb crowded with lethargic workers performing their mundane routines. At the edge of the office labyrinth, large windows gave a grand view of the New York city skyline. Unfortunately for all of the office workers, the cubicle walls prevented any chance of enjoying this wonderfully impressive sight.

The phone buzzed near Dorothy's left hand. That was the sound that had snapped her out of her trance.

She looked down at it with contempt. She hated that phone. Its piercing ring signaled another conversation that she would have to fake. False enthusiasm and energy that was becoming harder and harder to muster.

She was feeling disconnected again.

She had always felt unattached to the world around her, going through the motions like some sort of zombie. Never quite fitting in. Play-acting a role imposed by the machine of life. If she didn't, she felt that somehow they would discover she was a fraud. An impostor. Whoever '*they*' were.

Lately though, she was finding it harder to maintain the charade. Unconsciously, her habits were changing. She had been able to fake social conversations with co-workers in the past, but now it had decreased to a point where they forgot she was even there.

The actual work had always been a chore, now it was unbearable. Every sentence typed, every phone call received, every meeting attended, was agonizing and seemed to take forever. Endless minutiae debated and broken down until what little spark the idea may have had was dead and buried.

She had even stopped trying to look and dress the part. Instead of wasting time styling her long auburn hair, she wore it in a simple tight ponytail. She still wore a blazer and slacks, but a month ago she had abandoned dress shoes and started wearing sneakers. She had also traded in her blouse for black t-shirts.

Each day a black t-shirt with a different logo graphic. Today's was an MC Escher drawing of the infinite stairs. The logos didn't really mean anything to her, she just needed something different.

She needed to be different.

Otherwise she felt she might just disappear.

She began to click her heels together. A nervous tic that she had developed when thinking about wanting to be back home. To be away from work. Away from everything.

The phone rang again. The high pitched annoying sound seemed to intensify as if it knew it was being ignored. Dorothy answered before it could cry out again.

"Emerald Designs, Dorothy speaking." Her voice was pleasant and upbeat, part of the zombie's routine. "Yes, Mr. Martinson. Of course we value you as a client. You should have the plans on your desk by tomorrow—" She paused to listen. "Yes. We will. We—"

A dial tone cut her off.

Her jaw tightened in irritation. Her temple throbbed.

The constant smell of coffee permeated the room, giving her the beginnings of a headache. Coffee was the lifeblood of the zombies. The only thing that kept them moving. Her gaze dropped down to her own cup growing cold.

She suppressed a shudder.

She looked up at the clock. Ten fifteen. Only six more hours to go. She could make it through today. She could do it. The next day, though… and the one after that…

She closed her eyes. The zombie's battle was getting harder to fight.

* * *

That evening, Dorothy trudged into her apartment carrying her chinese take-out. She shrugged out of her jacket, kicked off her shoes, dropped her keys and purse on the table near the door, then flopped onto the couch with her food.

Her apartment was small and empty, and like her cubicle, furnished without any hint of personality. No knickknacks. No flowers or plants. No paintings or photos. Just a large mirror hanging on a wall. It had been there when she moved in and she hadn't bothered to take it down.

She flipped on the TV and sighed.

"Happy Birthday," she said to herself as she nudged her noodles around with chopsticks. "You made it through another year."

She was twenty-five today. Her gaze traveled across the blank slate of her living room. *Twenty-five years old with nothing to show for it.*

The place was temporary, she had told herself. After a year, she would move into something bigger. Something better. One year turned into two. Then five. Now the drafty little place was her sanctuary away from… from what? She didn't know.

Always on the tip of her mind. Just out of sight. Sometimes when thinking about something else, she'd almost sneak up on the errant thought and latch on, but it would vanish before she caught it. It was an irritating game that her mind played on her. One she was used to. Had learned to ignore it. For the most part.

Off to the side, in the hanging mirror, the glass shimmered. A reflection formed—a face, cast in shadow. It was facing toward Dorothy, almost appearing to be watching her.

Dorothy stopped chewing, suddenly feeling paranoid. Noodles still hung from her lips.

The hairs on the back of her neck stood up.

In her peripheral vision, she thought she saw movement in the mirror. She turned toward it, spooked, but there was nothing there. She stood up to get a better look, sucking in the dangling noodles.

She saw only herself staring back—green eyes, light spray of freckles across the bridge of her nose, thin lips. She was attractive, but the zombie's routine had sucked the life out of her.

She looked older.

Lonelier.

Lost.

CHAPTER 2
SIGNS

The next morning, Dorothy walked the last block to her work, trying not to think about the monotony that awaited her.

She shivered, watching her breath cloud in front of her.

Winter was on its way.

It was sunny, but there was a brisk wind that cut right through her dark green jacket and into her bones. Her contoured jacket was sporty—which is why she wore it—but it was thin and did little against the November chill. Luckily, she had thought to put on leather gloves and a red scarf, so she was able to retain at least some of her body heat.

She stuffed her hands into her coat pockets as she passed by a row of leafless trees that lined the street.

A stray branch caught her sleeve, yanking her back.

She stopped and tugged on it. It was snagged pretty good,

caught up in the tree's twisted branch. She fumbled with it, her gloves making the simple job difficult.

Suddenly, another tree branch whipped down and caught itself up in her jacket.

She gasped, flinching away from it. She could have sworn that branch had moved by itself.

Then the entire tree bent toward her, its trunk cracking and creaking, all of its branches angling down, clawing at her.

Dorothy let out a panicked cry, clamping her eyes shut and waved her arms wildly, swatting the gnarled, twig-fingers away. She could feel the rough, bark covered limbs wrapping around her arms and waist. Her ribcage felt like it was being crushed, making it hard to breathe. The branches were on the verge of pulling her apart.

She let out a final, shrill scream for help.

With her eyes still squeezed shut, she heard her scream echo faintly in the distance, bouncing from building to building. She could hear her own heavy breathing.

And people whispering.

She stopped struggling.

The pressure was gone from her ribs.

Opening her eyes, she saw that everything was normal again.

The tree was in its original state. Her coat was still snagged on the one branch.

People were stopped on the sidewalk, staring at her with wary, disapproving eyes, muttering to each other and shaking their heads. None of them were looking at the tree.

Because there's nothing wrong with the tree. Something's wrong with **me**, Dorothy thought to herself.

The way people looked at her as they passed, confirmed her

worst fear—she wasn't '*normal*'. Not one of '*them*'. She was a foreigner in disguise and her mask was slipping.

What's happening to me?

With hesitant hands, Dorothy carefully unhooked her coat and backed away from the tree. She slowly turned and continued on her way to work, trying desperately to blend in.

She was starting to tremble, not from the cold this time, but from the icy fear that she was losing her sanity.

* * *

Inside the safety of her cubicle, insulated from the outside world, Dorothy sat at her desk, numb.

The tree had moved. Or she was going mad. It was one or the other. Unfortunately, neither choice was good.

The phone rang, startling her.

This time she was almost thankful to answer it. It would distract her from thinking about her deteriorating mental state.

"Emerald Design, Dorothy speaking. Yes, Mr. Martinson. Of course." As she listened to him yammer on, her attention was drawn to a newspaper on her desk. It was positioned so that she was looking at it sideways. She could still read it, though.

The headline read: ***"NEW ZONING LAWS IN EFFECT TODAY"***

Mr. Martinson was still talking, but his voice was a million miles away to Dorothy. She was being drawn toward that headline.

Dorothy folded the paper on both sides so that only the word ***"ZONING"*** was visible. She folded it again so that it read: ***"ZO"***. She was transfixed by the letters.

She absent-mindedly finished the phone conversation.

"We're glad you're pleased. We will. Goodbye," she said faintly, hanging up, while keeping her eyes glued to the newspaper.

Looking at it sideways gave her a new perspective. She turned the newspaper upside-down and felt her stomach drop. The world around her seemed to stutter and slow down, becoming silent as she read the word aloud… "**OZ**."

THUMP!

The deep, hollow sound snapped Dorothy out of her trance. *What was that?* Her heart was racing. She was having trouble focusing with the word "OZ" still ricocheting inside her skull. Had she imagined the sound?

THUMP!

She shot up, peering over the cubicle walls, scanning the room, trying to identify the source of the mystery sound. Her gaze landed on the windows.

She saw a big black bird falling away from where it had struck the glass. It left a mark, a dark blotch, on the window. There was a similar mark above it.

It was just a couple of birds hitting the window. She was about to sit down when another one collided into the glass. It caught her by surprise, making her flinch.

It was a crow.

Another one hit a half second later. Then another and another. They kept coming.

The thumping sound grew in rapid succession as hundreds of crows slammed into the window with incredible machine-gun like force.

The glass began to crack under the assault. Sharp snaps echoed in the room as the fractures lengthened across the window.

Dorothy's eyes widened in horror. Her mouth hung open. She was frozen, unable to look away.

The window finally surrendered, shattering into thousands of jagged pieces as the crows flooded into the office.

Dorothy sucked in a breath and stepped back. The crows streamed right toward her. They swirled around her in a tornado of feathers and beaks. The cawing and shrieking was deafening. She screamed, cowering down, swinging her arms wildly, trying to bat them away.

The birds closed in on her, smothering her in darkness. She couldn't breathe anymore. All she could smell, taste and feel were feathers. Fetid, greasy feathers.

She let out a howl of anguish, hoping someone would save her.

And then… all was quiet.

No fluttering of wings. No squawking. The air was still.

They were gone.

A phone rang in the back, breaking the silence.

Dorothy cracked open her eyes and saw that the birds had vanished. She got to her feet. Her breathing was ragged as she nervously cast glances around the room.

The rest of her co-workers were all staring at her in shock. Their expressions identical to the faces she had seen after the tree attacked her—that she *thought* had attacked her. Suspicious expressions obviously indicating that she was insane.

Maybe they're right, she thought.

She saw that the large window was perfectly intact. She walked over to it and ran her quivering fingers over the smooth, cold glass.

What's happening to me?

It was the second time she had asked herself that question today.

CHAPTER 3
AWAKE

Dorothy sat in front of Ms. Rowen's desk, trying to regain her composure. After her nervous breakdown in front of everyone, she had been called into Ms. Rowen's office. Her boss.

Ms. Rowen sat behind her desk, studying Dorothy.

A no-nonsense woman in her late forties, Ms. Rowen ran a tight ship. She dressed in sleek expensive designer clothes—usually blacks or grays—that hugged her too-thin form. Her hair was too short, emulating a man's cut. Face pulled a little too tight from plastic surgery, trying to hide her age. A hint of the lizard lips. It couldn't hide the hard lines etched from the stress of the business, though—of keeping things running smoothly.

Dorothy realized Ms. Rowen was a zombie too. Higher up the ladder, true, but still part of the machinery. A cog. Still part of the routine.

This made Dorothy wonder if there was a point to it all. How far up did you have to go to be free of the machine? To experience joy? Ms. Rowen looked like she hadn't known happiness in decades. This made Dorothy think of her co-workers. They punched in and punched out, never showing any enthusiasm during office hours. Maybe they had wonderful, joy-filled lives outside of work, but Dorothy doubted it.

There was more to life than this. There had to be.

Ms. Rowen leaned forward. "You're one of my best people, Dorothy," she sighed, "If you need to take some time off, then tell me now. I understand. Sometimes the stress can get to you, but I can't have you breaking down like that again. Especially not in front of the others."

Dorothy nodded. "I'm sorry."

Ms. Rowen leaned back again and gestured toward Dorothy, waving a thin hand that had one too many rings on it. "I'm already letting you slide with the way you're dressing. You're young. I figure it's a phase. I'm *hoping* it's a phase."

"I know. It's just..." Dorothy trailed off, not knowing what to say.

"Go on. It's just what?"

Dorothy's head was swimming. Her thoughts were hazy and confused, yet some things were starting to become clear. She didn't want to end up like Ms. Rowen. It was a life with no destination. At least not for herself.

"I don't really know what I'm doing here. I mean I don't know how I... *got* here." And Dorothy realized with a start, that she really *didn't* remember.

How did she end up working here? For that matter, when did she move to New York? Had she ever had a boyfriend? Been in love? It felt like chunks of her memory were missing. Like she was waking from a dream.

Ms. Rowen pursed her lips and drew her waxed brows together. "I like you, Dorothy, but I can't have someone on my team that isn't focused. Take a few days off and get your head together. Then let me know if I need to seek a replacement or not. Do you understand? You've built a good life here," she folded her stiff fingers together and sniffed in a patronizing manner, "It'd be shame to throw it all away."

Dorothy nodded again and stood, already moving to the door. She had heard everything, but Ms. Rowen's voice was distant, almost muffled, pushed aside by the thoughts flooding Dorothy's mind.

In a mental fog, Dorothy navigated her way through the maze to her desk, gathering her coat and purse, then promptly stepped into the elevator.

She had questions about her own memories.

Questions with no answers.

By the time Dorothy left the building, she knew she would never return. She didn't even bother to look back. That chapter of her life was over. She had broken free and escaped the zombie world. It was exhilarating to feel alive again.

Now though, there was the nagging clarity that part of her existence was blank. Not hazy or foggy. It wasn't there at all.

She felt like she had just woken up and the past few years living in New York were part of some kind of strange dream. Dorothy remembered those years clearly, it was just that it seemed like someone else's life and not hers.

Dorothy also remembered her childhood back on the farm. Memories of living with her aunt and uncle in the middle of nowhere. Of waking up at the crack of dawn to do her chores. Of hiding away in her room and the shed to snuggle up with her books. They were her escape from the stale and mundane reality she was trapped in.

These earlier memories were much more vivid.

It was the in-between that was missing. She had no memory of leaving the farm and coming to New York. When she tried to remember that missing time, her thoughts would veer off to either before or after. The memory was slippery and elusive. Like her own mind wouldn't let her focus on it.

Dorothy was concentrating on chasing after the memory when a man ran by, his shoulder smacking into hers, nearly knocking her down. She glared back at him wondering what his problem was.

Then she looked ahead and saw it.

It was chaos.

CHAPTER 4
FOUND

People were running everywhere. In all directions. Ducking and screaming as big black things dived down at them.

Cars honked and screeched as drivers swerved to avoid hitting the crowds that were spilling into the streets.

Dorothy blinked, not believing her eyes.

The black things were crows.

They were diving and swooping by the dozens. Clawing and pecking at the crowds. Attacking. Just like in the office.

Looking up at the darkening sky, Dorothy saw a swirling mass approaching. Thousands of crows were coming. So many that they were blotting out the setting sun.

She couldn't run. She couldn't take her eyes off the sight.

No.

It was all too unreal and felt like it was happening in slow motion. *Maybe it's another hallucination,* she thought. *Maybe it will just go away.*

Something else caught her eye.

Something white was moving down the street toward her.

A horse.

With a man in green riding it.

The stallion moved with incredible speed and grace, maneuvering around the crashing vehicles with ease, while staying ahead of the oncoming swarm of birds.

The rider came right for her, pulling on the reins at the last instant, bringing the ivory horse to an abrupt stop. The horse snorted and shook its muscled neck from the effort of putting on the brakes.

Dorothy stared up at the rider and blinked again. *This was definitely an hallucination.*

The man appeared to be in his early thirties and was dashingly handsome. His strong face topped by tousled, shaggy brown hair that was attractive by it's sheer messiness.

He was dressed in a debonair green leather jacket with brass buttons running up the front of it, on the right side. The top button was undone, so that the corner hung down in a loose flap. Dorothy thought the jacket looked like it was out of a history book. The kind old pilots used to wear. His trousers were a darker shade of green that tucked into dark brown, polished leather boots. A white cape with a green stripe lining it, billowed out behind him.

The rider had broad shoulders and Dorothy could tell he had an athletic build underneath the uniform.

He looked down at her with piercing blue-gray eyes.

"Dorothy Gale," he said. It wasn't a question.

"Y-yes?" She barely got the word out. She was finding it hard to talk all of a sudden.

He held out his hand. "Hurry, M'Lady, they've found you!"

"What?" It was hard to concentrate on what he was saying. Her head was swimming again, though for different reasons this time.

The rider stole a glance up at the crows. "There's no time! We have to go!"

A crow swept down and clawed at Dorothy. She let out a cry of surprise, knocking it away and quickly took the man's hand.

He was surprisingly strong, lifting her with ease, swinging her up onto his horse so that she sat behind him.

"Hold tight!" he warned, spurring his horse forward.

Dorothy barely had time to wrap her arms around his waist as they took off.

The undulating cloud of crows veered after them in pursuit.

The horse galloped through the city streets at a frightening pace, rounding corners so fast that it was all Dorothy could do to hang on. She risked a peek back and saw that the birds were right behind them.

The rider leaned forward and shouted, "I can't shake them!" For a second, she thought he was talking to his horse.

The rider spotted people descending into a subway entrance. "There!" He yanked the reins to the side, guiding them toward the stairs.

Dorothy tightened her grip as the horse took the steps ten at a time, causing people to scream and dive to the sides.

They reached the platform below and came to a stop, circling, sending the crowd into a panic. The rider wasn't concerned with the spectacle he was making. His head was jerking from side to side. "Is there another way out?"

Recovering from her own fright, Dorothy looked around,

trying to get her bearings. Before she could answer, he spoke again.

"Never mind, I see it!" He fixed on something to her right.

Dorothy looked to where the rider had focused his attention. He was staring at the people on the other side of the tracks who were gawking at them. Behind the stunned crowd of onlookers was another stairway. She went pale, shaking her head. "Wait!"

The rider had already brought his horse around, putting some distance between them and the edge of the platform. He snapped his reins and sent them charging straight toward the gap.

"No!" Dorothy held on for dear life, terrified.

At the last possible second, they leaped across the subway tracks to the opposite side. The horse's hooves hit the slick tiled ground, sliding to a stop, nearly knocking a dozen people over.

Luckily, the sight of a huge muscled stallion hurtling toward them had made the crowd run for cover. Miraculously, no one was hurt. Including Dorothy herself, much to her surprise.

Angry screeches filled the underground tunnels, building into a wave of painful white noise. Crows were streaming down into the subway station behind them.

"Persistent things aren't they?" The rider spurred his horse toward the second staircase.

A train's horn made Dorothy turn. She watched as a subway train sped by, smashing through the cluster of birds. Hundreds of the winged beasts disappeared in an explosion of feathers that whirled crazily beside the moving train. The surviving crows on the other side could be heard squawking in a bewildered frenzy.

Cold air slapped Dorothy's face as the horse vaulted up the stairs and out onto another busy street.

The rider wove his way between cars without slowing down, giving Dorothy a series of minor heart-attacks.

Looking back, Dorothy saw the remaining crows were falling behind, scattered across the sky, disoriented and frantic. The steel and glass skyscrapers helped to hide their escape as they fled.

A nearby blaring horn brought her attention around to see an oncoming car heading straight toward them. She let out a short scream and gritted her teeth, preparing for impact.

Without hesitation, the rider launched his horse up into the air, over the vehicle, and landed behind it, all while never breaking the horse's stride.

Dorothy couldn't take anymore. "Stop! Please! Let me down! You're crazy!"

"Not until we lose the crows."

"Why are they after *us*?" None of this was making sense to her. It was madness.

He shook his head. "They're not after us. They're after *you*!"

"*Me*?" Dorothy was rattled.

"The Nome King has finally found you!" he yelled back to her.

"Who? What are you talking about?" Her head was throbbing. Too much was happening at once.

"He's tracked you down. Sent his forces to capture you." The rider yanked the reins, guiding his horse to turn a corner. "I've come to take you back!"

"Take me back where?" Dorothy asked, exasperated.

The rider glanced over his shoulder at her with a wry grin. "Back to the Land of Oz!"

She was speechless.

Oz.

The word exploded inside her mind. It pushed every other thought out of her head, growing and expanding until it completely overwhelmed the synapses in her brain.

Her eyes rolled back and her body went limp.

She fainted.

The last thing she saw was the rider's arm shooting out to catch her.

CHAPTER 5
THE EMERALD KNIGHT

"M'Lady."

The man's voice seeped into Dorothy's unconscious mind. She felt a warm hand caress her cheek.

Her eyes sleepily fluttered open. She looked up to see the rider kneeling next to her, concern etched on his face. Above him, branches of a tree rustled as a cold wind blew through, taking with it a dozen orange and red leaves.

The chill made her shiver. The cool, soft grass under her face and hands didn't help. *Trees? Grass?*

She abruptly sat up. The whole area was thick with trees. "Where am I?"

"We needed cover. I came upon this forest."

His horse was nearby and gave a short snort of disapproval.

The rider glanced at his steed, then turned back to Dorothy

with a smirk. "Alright, *he's* the one that found this forest."

"Forest?" She got to her feet, trying to clear her head. Past the treetops, she now saw skyscrapers with windows lit, jutting up into the evening sky. "This is Central Park."

He stood next to her, glancing up at the sky. "It won't hide us for long."

Dorothy took a step back, putting some distance between them. She was starting to take in the reality of the situation. The strange costume he was wearing. The fact that he was riding a horse in New York and thought Central Park was a forest.

He's obviously delusional. Probably escaped from an institution, she thought. *And now I'm alone with him in Central Park. At night. Stay calm,* she told herself. *Stay calm and keep your head together.*

"Who are you?" she asked.

The rider grinned and bowed. "Forgive my manners, M'Lady. Jasper Clayfellow, a Knight of Oz, at your service."

She shook her head and backed away a bit more. "Listen, thanks for helping me back there, but… I don't understand any of this. I'm going home."

As she turned to go, Jasper grabbed her wrist. "You can't."

Dorothy tried to yank her arm away, but his grasp was firm. Panic was beginning to bubble up inside her. "Let go of me!"

Jasper immediately released her. "Your life is in danger. Your home is no longer safe."

"Right." She was about to walk away as fast as she could when she heard it.

The cawing.

The crows were coming again. By the sound of it, they were a good distance away, but getting louder by the second. She spotted them. The birds were darting back and forth over the park, all of them moving as one. A rippling wave. They looked like they were searching for something.

For her.

Jasper took a step forward, his voice low, but emphatic. "Don't you remember who you are?"

Dorothy froze, dumbstruck by the question. Isn't this what she'd been wondering herself? She looked at Jasper, suddenly vulnerable.

"No. I… I don't." And it was the truth.

The white stallion shook its magnificent milky mane and approached, lifting its head slightly and to one side to gaze directly at Dorothy with one eye. Then it did something completely unexpected—

It spoke.

"You, M'Lady, are the Queen of Oz," it said in a throaty, friendly male voice.

Dorothy's legs started to wobble. She was on the verge of fainting again, but the sound of the crows flapping overhead drew her attention.

Jasper pulled her close against a tree, trying to get some cover. He whispered to his horse. "Chalk! Go!"

Chalk nodded and galloped away, kicking up clods of grass behind him.

The crows shrieked at the movement and gave chase, sweeping across the trees after the white stallion.

A few seconds later, the crows were gone, leaving Jasper and Dorothy in a quiet protective embrace. He was studying the skies, listening.

He was so close to Dorothy, she could feel his warm breath against her face. He was tense but calm, whereas her own heart was thudding. When he looked back down at her, she felt her heartbeat kick into a higher gear, thumping so hard, she thought even he must feel it. Her face flushed. She hoped it wasn't noticeable.

He gazed deeply into her green eyes. "I'm sworn not only to protect my kingdom, but you as well. I will defend you with my life. You have to trust me."

Dorothy's face was on fire. Her breath caught in her throat. The compassion and sincerity in his voice was real. He meant every word. He would *die* for her. She could only nod.

Jasper took her hand as he led her away through the trees. "We have to go. Chalk won't fool them for long. They'll be back."

"But your horse—"

He kept moving. "Chalk can handle himself."

Jasper was fast and it was hard for her to keep pace with his long legs. Within minutes, they had reached the edge of the park. He stopped and surveyed the area. She took the moment to catch her breath.

Jasper squinted, tracking the cars whizzing by. "If we could capture one of these carriages..."

Carriages? She gave Jasper a discerning stare. He wasn't kidding. Part of her wanted to laugh. The other part wanted to know everything about him.

"Wait here," she said, stepping off the curb. She flagged down a taxi. A moment later, a yellow cab pulled up next to them. She opened the door and hopped inside, gesturing for Jasper to follow. "Get in."

He climbed inside and closed the door behind him, examining the interior as he did so.

"Where to?" the cabbie said with not the slightest of interest.

Dorothy recognized the cabbie's tone. *Poor guy. Another zombie stuck in the machine.* Dorothy waved her hand forward. "Just drive."

The cabbie nodded. "You got it, lady." The cab jerked out into traffic, almost colliding into another taxi, setting off a brief war of honking horns.

Jasper was fascinated, observing how the cabbie controlled the vehicle with the steering wheel.

Dorothy was in turn, observing Jasper. Watching how his eyebrows furrowed, how intense his stare was as he absorbed his new environment.

She didn't think she had ever seen a man so attractive before. He wasn't pretty like today's heartthrobs. He was rough around the edges. Someone who had been on adventures. Survived dangerous circumstances, yet maintained a mischievous demeanor. Had a glint in his eye that offered fun and excitement on the horizon. *Get a hold of yourself,* she thought, *a second ago you thought he was an escaped lunatic.*

"You've never been in a car?" she asked.

"No," he said, with wonder in his voice. "They're extraordinary."

She chewed her lower lip, contemplating this. *How could someone in this day and age never have been in a car? Was Oz a foreign country? He sounded slightly British. Come to think of it, his horse did too.* Her mental gears ground to a halt.

His horse had talked. It had clearly spoken to her. Hadn't it? Better not dwell on that, she told herself. She was already having doubts about her sanity and thoughts like that would only make things worse. *Stick to the facts.*

"Okay, help me out here," she folded a leg underneath her to be able to face Jasper better. "This 'Oz'. Where is it? How do we get there?"

Jasper sat back, giving Dorothy his full attention. "Oz is very, *very* far away. And getting there is going to be a little tricky.

You see, how *I* got here was a one way trip." He hesitated, then smiled. "I was actually counting on you knowing the way home."

Dorothy was flabbergasted. She sputtered. "I don't know the way! How am I supposed to know?"

"Minor setback," He held up his hands, trying to calm her. "That's why I said it's going to be tricky. We thought you had planned a way back."

"Well, I guess you were wrong." She was feeling angry. She had hoped for answers. Instead she was finding only new questions. She was still adrift. Still without any form of an anchor of who she was and where she was supposed to be.

"Maybe. Maybe not." Jasper didn't seem to be worried or anxious about this problem. He reached inside his jacket and pulled out a pair of folded glasses. They were sleek and sturdy, yet elegantly designed, almost Victorian in style.

He offered them to her. "The General said you might need these."

Dorothy took the glasses, holding them gently up to the light for a better look. They were a bit heavier than they appeared. More like goggles than glasses. The lenses were tinted and when she slipped them on, she found that the tint was green.

She looked at Jasper, then the world outside the taxi. Everything now had a pleasant green hue, but other than that she couldn't see anything out of the ordinary.

She turned back to Jasper. "They're green sunglasses. What are they supposed to do?"

"He said they were yours and that you asked that they be returned to you when the time comes. Now is that time I assume."

Dorothy sighed as she removed the glasses and tucked them into her jacket. "Okaaay. That was helpful. Any other ideas, because we're not getting anywhere here."

Jasper rubbed his strong chin and thought a moment. "There is one possibility. The Wizard is being held captive on this side. If we could find him, he might be able to help us get back."

"The wizard?" Dorothy's mind balked again. It had blown a fuse. She was getting into dangerous territory, where one could easily end up in a straight jacket gibbering about wizards and talking horses.

She glanced at the cabbie. He had heard and was watching them with suspicious eyes. *Probably debating on whether to dump us out onto the street or not,* she thought.

Jasper continued unfazed. "The General's had some communications with him." He reached into his jacket again and dug out a piece of scrap paper from an inner pocket. He presented it to Dorothy. "I think it's some form of code."

She took the paper fragment and examined it. It felt rough and looked like vellum. Something from ancient times. The note was scrawled in rushed calligraphy. It read:

1900 Baum Street

Dorothy's brows knotted together. "This is an address."

Jasper sat forward. "You know it then?"

She shook her head. "I know *what* it is, but not *where* it is."

"It's in a place called…" Jasper closed his eyes struggling to remember. They snapped back open as the answer came to him. "Can-zis," he said, pronouncing it awkwardly.

The hairs on the back of Dorothy's neck stood straight up and danced. "Kansas? That's where I grew up."

Jasper snapped his fingers. "Then that's where we're going." He slapped the cabbie's shoulder, getting his attention. "To Canzis, my friend."

The cabbie growled and shrugged Jasper's hand off his shoulder.

Dorothy knew the cabbie was about to blow his top. She had to intervene. "Uh… take us to the airport."

What am I doing? Am I seriously going to do this? Dorothy paused, letting that thought linger. *Yes. Yes, I am.* She chuckled at how crazy this all was. Crazy and exciting.

When she looked back at Jasper, she realized how out of place he was. His outfit would draw too much attention. They'd never get past security.

Jasper noticed her scrutinizing gaze. "Is something wrong?"

"Yeah." She leaned toward the cabbie. "We need to make a stop first."

CHAPTER 6
THE DISTURBING DISGUISE

With Thanksgiving approaching, the airport was overflowing with travelers.

Everyone was distracted and rushing about, which made Dorothy feel better. She felt less conspicuous, though she realized, she wasn't doing anything wrong. She was only guilty of following a complete stranger to a place she'd never heard of, that was all.

She laughed to herself. It was thrilling to leave her old life behind and embark on an adventure into the unknown.

Dorothy and Jasper stood in line at the counter. She was surprisingly calm. It was Jasper who couldn't keep still.

He was fidgeting in his new uncomfortable clothes. A pair of Levi's, a long-sleeved *green* shirt (he had been a stickler on the color) and sneakers. He was carrying his Oz uniform in a shopping bag. They had made a brief stop along the way to pick up some normal clothes for him—ones that wouldn't make people ask questions.

He stuck a finger in his collar and adjusted it by stretching it out.

Dorothy saw the store tag dangling off his shirt, rubbing against his neck. She yanked it off. "That better?"

He relaxed. "Much."

The line moved an inch closer to the counter.

They were almost there. Dorothy took a deep breath. *They would just buy their tickets and they'd be on their way.* She opened her purse and fished out her wallet and driver's license, then stopped, staring blankly at the picture of herself.

She pulled Jasper close, whispering in his ear. "You're going to need an I.D." She held out her driver's license to show him. "I'm going to guess you don't have one, right?"

He shook his head. "No. Where do I get one?"

She pulled him out of line, anxious. "You can't." She led him toward the exit. "We'll have to find another way."

As they threaded their way through the mob of travelers, Jasper saw a balding, pudgy man talking on a cell phone while stuffing some money into his wallet. The man's I.D. was clearly visible.

Jasper watched as the man shoved the wallet into his coat pocket and fumbled with two suitcases, while still trying to hold the phone.

Dorothy felt Jasper slip free.

She turned to see him disappear into the crowd. Before she could say anything, he reappeared with a smile.

Jasper led her over to a wall and held out the man's open wallet, displaying the driver's license. "Will this do?"

"Where did you get that? Did you just steal it?" Dorothy whipped her head around guiltily.

"I borrowed it."

"You have to give it back!" She shoved the wallet away.

He pushed it toward her. "Time is against us. We do what we need to."

She slapped her hand to her forehead, feeling stressed. "It doesn't even look anything like you!"

They both looked down at the man's driver's license. The photo on it showed the balding, pudgy man staring back at them with a tired, unhappy expression.

Another poor zombie victim, Dorothy noted. When she looked back up at Jasper to explain to him why this wouldn't work, she almost fell over backwards.

Standing in Jasper's place and wearing Jasper's clothes was the chubby, bald man in the photo.

Dorothy's mouth dropped open and repeatedly tried to form words, but nothing came out. If anyone had happened to witness this, they would have thought she was doing an imitation of a fish.

The pudgy man leaned toward her. "It's me. Jasper." It was still Jasper's voice.

Her wide eyes doubled in size.

"You said I have to look like the picture." He pointed at the man's wallet in his thick, plump hand.

"But—how?" Her vocal chords had finally loosened.

He patted his chest. "I'm made of clay."

"What?"

"Watch. And please—don't panic."

The pudgy man pressed his hand against the side of his face and pushed. His flesh buckled and rippled like Play-Doh, his cheek overlapping his nose and mouth in a grotesque contortion. He let go and his warped features unfolded, oozing back into place.

Dorothy stood frozen, her eyes bulging in horror. "No," she said faintly, backing away.

He held out his hand, "Wait."

She shook her head, "No…"

"You said you trusted me."

"You're not even human!" She felt betrayed. The first man she had ever been truly attracted to and he was made of clay. Of dirt.

The pudgy man visibly flinched at her words. He stood proudly. His round body and face, still that of the bald man, but his demeanor and stance was that of a Knight. "I may not be flesh and blood, but I'm as human as you."

Dorothy could see she had hurt him. She could see the man under the disguise. But he wasn't real. Then what *was* real?

The question floated through her mind. *We rode a talking horse and now we're off to see a wizard. Why would a man of clay shock or surprise me?* She could feel herself calming down.

We're off to see a wizard.

That phrase somehow seemed familiar. She had to follow this to the end. She needed to know why she couldn't remember her past. And that meant she had to stay with Jasper—the man made of clay.

She held Jasper's plump hand. It felt so strange, his strong hands, now soft and spongy. The disguise was astonishing. "I'm sorry."

He clasped her hand between his. "No need to apologize—"

Movement caught his eye.

Dorothy turned and spied what had drawn his attention.

Long shadows flitted across a nearby floor and wall, moving in their general direction. The strange thing was that the shadows were traveling of their own accord, untethered by any person or object.

Jasper's round face tensed as he spoke. "Shades. Living shadows. Agents of the Nome King."

Dorothy huddled closer to him. "They know we're here."

He nodded. "We need to go before they see us."

She took his hand and led him toward the ticket counter.

CHAPTER 7
THE UNREMEMBERED SECRET

The plane rumbled through the darkness, its engines droning in the empty sky.

Above the thin layer of clouds, the night was clear, stars were bright and the crescent moon was nestled among them.

Jasper marveled at the beautiful view. He sat near the window, his disguise still in effect. He turned his gaze down to the sights below.

Dorothy sat beside him, uncomfortable and exhausted. The aisle seat next to her was empty. A small miracle that she was thankful for. Getting onto the plane had been stressful. Between worrying about airport security and avoiding the Shades, the tension had taken its toll on her.

The weather was on their side, giving them a peaceful flight. Hopefully it would last.

Out of the corner of her eye, she sneaked a peek at Jasper.

His altered face and body disturbed her. She trusted him, but it didn't change the fact that it was disorienting to be sitting next to a 'stranger.'

She winced. The jackhammer in her head was really going at it. Her head had been throbbing since they had taken off. She closed her eyes and rubbed her temples. There was just too much information to process.

Or maybe not enough. She couldn't decide.

"Those lights below. They're cities full of people?" Jasper asked with his ever present curiosity.

"Yeah." Reluctantly, she looked over at him and was startled to see he was back to normal.

He was no longer pudgy and bald. His messy hair, his sparkling eyes, his scruffy handsome face—all back in place. It was bizarre how she had already found herself missing that face. It was nice to have it back.

She found herself grinning at him like a schoolgirl. She didn't even notice that her headache had vanished.

"Reminds me of the Faerie cities in the Crystal Valleys." There was a nostalgic excitement in his voice that was hard to resist.

Dorothy leaned over to have a look. They had been traveling for awhile and she had no idea where they were. Through the gaps in the clouds, she could see the spiderweb of city lights passing by underneath them.

From this height, the lights did have an ethereal quality to them. It was easy to get caught up in the fantasy. She bit her bottom lip, imagining magical creatures flitting to and fro down there. A sense of wonder was washing over her.

She suddenly realized Jasper was looking out the window

with her. She felt the warmth of his cheek near hers. Their faces were almost touching. She quickly pulled back, her face reddening.

"Sorry." Jasper smiled, amused at her embarrassment

"It's okay." She felt the heat radiating from her cheeks.

"You're blushing," he pointed out.

"I'm not blushing. It's just hot in here." This was a conversation she did not want to continue.

"Feels fine to me," he said.

"Well, it's hot over *here*," Dorothy said testily. She hated that she was being so defensive.

"Do you want to change seats?" he offered.

"I'm fine." She reached up and clicked on the overhead fan. Cool air blew in her face. "There."

He looked at her, smirking.

"What?" She laughed out the word, dissolving into giggles.

He laughed too. "As long as you're comfortable."

"I am." She was freezing cold now, but would never admit it.

Dorothy changed the subject. "So tell me about Oz. All I can remember is the name."

Still smiling, his expression grew wistful and longing. Dorothy could see how much he cared about his home.

"Oz is..." he struggled to think of an appropriate word to describe it and failed. "Oz is Oz," he said simply. "There are wonders everywhere you look." He gestured around them. "This world is so grey in comparison."

He paused, becoming solemn. "Well, that's not true. Not anymore." He locked eyes with her. "Things have changed since you've been away."

"Why did I leave?" Dorothy asked, having already forgotten

her embarrassment and was now concentrating on piecing together her puzzling past.

"The Nome King attacked and took control of Emerald City. You escaped and fled here."

Emerald City? That name jolted her. Sent a chill down her spine. It would explain why she ended up working for a company named Emerald Designs. *Must have been a subconscious choice,* she thought.

"Okay," Dorothy straightened, hungry for more information, "you mentioned this guy before. This Nome King. Who is he? And why is he after me?"

Jasper leaned closer to her. "He's an enemy of Oz. One of the oldest. A tyrant from the underground that's hated Emerald City and its rulers since it was first built. Every time he's attacked, we've driven him back to his caves. You actually helped win a few of those battles."

Dorothy shook her head. "I don't remember any of this."

"Well, he finally succeeded. He's taken over the land. But that doesn't mean anything unless he has the Ozma."

"And what's that?" She was on the edge of her seat, literally, leaning almost shoulder to shoulder with Jasper. This all sounded so amazing and exciting that she desperately wanted to believe it.

"The Ozma is the first emerald. A special one. The heart of Oz itself. Without it, the land will die. You hid it before you escaped. That was twelve years ago." He hesitated, "The land is dying."

"Where did I hide it?" She gnawed on her lower lip, enthralled by the mystery.

His voice was low, almost a whisper and he spoke with a grave tone. "You're the only one that knows. That's why you need to regain your memories—you're the only one that can save us."

Dorothy sat back, her excitement fading, replaced by dread. If any of this were true, then the pressure on her was overwhelming.

Over Jasper's shoulder, she saw something strange outside the window. The wing of the plane, visible in the moonlight, was slicing through the clouds and there was something moving in the air above its tip.

A dark form.

She could definitely make it out now.

It was the shape of a person, shrouded in shadow, hunched forward. The figure wore a pointed, wide-brimmed black hat and a flowing black robe and cape.

And even more bizarre—the person was riding a *broom.*

Like a witch, Dorothy thought to herself.

The figure's sinister gaze found Dorothy. They made eye contact, sending an icy chill down Dorothy's spine.

The witch's gnarled hand made a violent cutting motion in the air and the plane's wing suddenly ripped in half, sending a geyser of sparks shooting into the night sky!

Dorothy screamed as the plane started to shudder violently. It shook and tilted sharply. Luggage compartments popped open and suitcases tumbled out, banging into the aisle. The engines whined under the stress and then—

—Everything was fine.

The wing was undamaged.

The compartments were secure.

There was no witch outside.

"What's wrong?" Jasper was holding her shaking hands, looking out the window, then back at her.

She was still trembling. *Another hallucination.*

The other passengers were giving her dirty looks.

She pulled Jasper close, leaning against him and whispered, "I think I'm losing my mind. I thought I saw a witch outside." She felt his body become tense.

He looked out the window for a good minute before returning to Dorothy. He lifted her chin and she saw the truth in his eyes. His steady, compassionate eyes.

Jasper shook his head. "You're not crazy. Those are your memories fighting to escape. You just have to—"

He stopped as he saw a long shadow slide eerily across the wall of the plane.

"They followed us," he said in a low voice.

Dorothy had already traced Jasper's gaze and spotted it as well. "What do we do?" she said in a strained hush.

"They're toying with us. Letting us know we're being watched." Jasper sat back, keeping a vigilant eye on the rest of the plane.

Dorothy sank lower into her seat. "Why aren't they attacking?"

"Too confined in here. They know we'd resist. Shades aren't fighters, they try to avoid combat." His voice lowered further so that only she could hear. "When we land, we'll have to move fast."

Dorothy switched on the overhead lights. Whether they would help or not, she didn't know, but it made her feel more secure.

She squeezed closer to Jasper, keeping a watch on the creeping shadows.

CHAPTER 8
THE SHADOWS STRIKE

The Kansas airport wasn't nearly as crowded, but there were enough people to make life difficult if you wanted to move fast.

Dorothy and Jasper were having a hard time staying together as they hurried through the throng of commuters, keeping an eye out for their pursuers.

They had made it off the plane without incident. The Shades hadn't attacked. Hadn't made any kind of threatening move.

But they were close by.

Both Dorothy and Jasper could feel it. A prickly sensation of being watched. Of being followed.

A pair of individuals abruptly forced their way between them. One was an older, stocky businessman in a suit and tie, with thinning grey hair—the other, a young man in a red hooded sweatshirt and jeans. They both shoved Jasper backward, ramming him into a wall.

Two other strangers grabbed Dorothy and yanked her away into the crowd. The new pair of assailants consisted of a middle-aged man with glasses, looking every bit like an average dad wearing a t-shirt and slacks, while the other man wore baggy trousers and appeared to spend an exorbitant amount of time lifting weights.

Jasper saw Dorothy disappear with them into the bustling mass of travelers.

His attention was diverted by the fact that the young man in the red hoodie was gripping him by the throat. The businessman wasn't helping matters with his thick forearms pressing into Jasper's chest, holding him against the wall.

Red Hoodie grinned. "Be still, clay man. The girl is ours now."

That was when Jasper realized both of the men's eyes were *solid black.*

Jasper stopped resisting, meeting the young man's ebony gaze with his own unwavering stare. "I don't think so."

Red Hoodie's hand suddenly slipped through Jasper's neck. Jasper's flesh was becoming soft clay. Jasper's whole body was oozing downward, leaving nothing for them to grasp. The Businessman clawed at Jasper's clothing, searching for something to hold onto.

Before his clay mass hit the floor, Jasper began to reform, kicking the Businessman hard in the gut, sending him flying backwards.

Jasper then turned and swung for Red Hoodie. Jasper's arm was still reforming as it sliced through the air. The instant before impact, his fist solidified and smashed into Red Hoodie's nose, knocking the young man flat onto the ground.

Leaping over his attackers, Jasper raced after Dorothy, leaving a few shocked witnesses wondering what they had just seen. Moving on his own, Jasper slipped easily through the crowd and spotted the two men leading Dorothy away.

Closing the distance quickly, he grabbed the Middle-aged Man by the shoulder, spun him around, and decked him. The Middle-aged Man went tumbling to the floor, his ebony eyes closing in pain.

The Weight-Lifter turned and faced Jasper, towering over him, staring at him with solid black eyes.

Without hesitation, Jasper slugged the man in the jaw.

The Weight-Lifter let go of Dorothy and rubbed his stubbled chin.

A lightning fast right hook caught Jasper off guard, spinning him almost completely around.

"Jasper!" Dorothy wanted to run to his aid, but knew she couldn't help against this mountain of a man.

Jasper steadied his legs and squared off against the Weight-Lifter once more. "Let's try that again."

Almost immediately, the Weight-Lifter threw another lunging punch.

This time Jasper was ready and dodged out of the way. He then planted a powerful blow into the Weight-Lifter's kidney.

The Weight-Lifter doubled over in pain. Jasper didn't wait around. He slugged the man right in the nose.

The Weight-Lifter teetered on wobbly legs.

Not taking another chance, Jasper struck him again.

The large man hit the ground like a fallen redwood tree.

"Wow." It was all Dorothy could say. Jasper was far stronger than he looked.

Jasper gave her a cocky grin. "Shall we?" He held out his

hand.

She laughed and took it as they rushed out the nearby exit into the cold Kansas night.

Behind them, the Weight-Lifter sat up holding his throbbing, bleeding nose. He looked around, confused. His eyes were no longer black, but a more normal hazel. He watched, dumbfounded, as his shadow stretched out across the floor toward the exit, then detached and slid away from him.

Outside the airport, Dorothy suddenly stopped and jerked away from Jasper.

Reflexively, he tightened his grip. She frantically twisted and yanked her arm, trying to free herself.

For a moment, Jasper was baffled, then he saw her eyes.

Solid black.

She was a fighter. He wouldn't be able to hold onto her for long. He quickly scanned the area and spotted a shuttle waiting at the curb. He pulled her over to it and held her in the bright beam of the headlight. Dorothy fought, but he wrapped his arms around her, holding her still.

The black substance flowed across the surface of her eyes, leaving her body as inky tears, streaming sideways, trying desperately to escape the bright light. Dorothy let out a cry of anguish as she collapsed to the pavement.

Jasper saw the Shade streak across the ground away from Dorothy and into the nearest cluster of shadows.

Dorothy's eyes were clear.

"We have to go." Jasper released his hold on her and helped her to her feet.

She was dazed and shaking.

The shuttle honked for them to move, startling them both.

Jasper recognized a taxi nearby and escorted her over to it. He gently placed her inside and joined her. He waved his hand forward, imitating what Dorothy had said to the previous cabbie —"Just drive."

The cabbie nodded and swung out into traffic.

Jasper put a comforting arm around Dorothy.

She was still trembling. "What happened?"

"A Shade attached itself to you. Took control of you. The only way to get rid of one is to expose it to bright light."

She looked up at him, terrified. "I'm not crazy. This is all really happening. Everything you said is true."

He nodded. "I'd never lie to you."

Dorothy couldn't hold back the tears. "But I don't remember any of it! How am I supposed to help if I don't even know who I am?"

He held her close and spoke in a soft whisper. "Here's what I know about you. You've been visiting Oz since you were a little girl. You've had adventures that would tax the strongest of men and the smartest of scholars. You inspired so much admiration and love in the people there, that we elected you, an outsider, as Queen."

Dorothy's shivers were receding. Jasper's strong arm around her was providing a much needed sense of security. Her head felt heavy. She laid it against his shoulder and closed her eyes. "Thank you for believing in me, even when I don't."

He pulled a loose strand of hair away from her face. "Get some rest."

CHAPTER 9
OFF TO SEE THE WIZARD

1900 Baum Street.

It was a sharp-edged rectangular building that was about as architecturally bland as one could get. Composed of aging red bricks, the edifice had a cold, almost fortress-like presence. The exterior illumination was sparse and left the walls draped in long shadows. Against the night sky, its monolithic silhouette left one feeling small.

Dorothy and Jasper stood in front of the bleak, foreboding structure.

On the front lawn, planted deep in the withering grass, was an etched stone sign that read: **PLUMLY SANITARIUM**

Dorothy shivered in the cold Kansas air. Whether it was because of the chill or the creepy building they were about to enter, she couldn't decide. They left they're waiting cab and hesitantly approached the entrance.

She was about to knock on the wooden door when Jasper stopped her.

"If he's being held captive, we don't want to alert the guards," he said in a hushed voice.

"No, it's not like that. This is a sanitarium. Like a hospital." She saw he still didn't understand, so she simplified it. "Doctors."

He was still wary of the situation. "The General said he was being held against his will."

She sighed. "He probably is, but—listen, you asked me to trust *you*. Now I'm asking you to trust *me*."

For a brief second, she thought he was going to fight her on this, then he stepped aside, allowing her to take the lead.

Dorothy knocked lightly on the door.

No response.

She knocked a little louder. Again, no one answered.

Dorothy tried the doorknob and the door, surprisingly, creaked open. "Been in the city too long. Forgot no one locks their doors around here."

They entered a small waiting room with a front desk.

The furniture and decor seemed stuck somewhere between the fifties and the seventies, with a copper starburst-shaped clock on the olive green wall, curved burnt-orange plastic chairs with thin metal legs, and an old-fashioned wood-cased radio on a corner stand.

No one was present. It was deadly quiet, feeling deserted, aside from the lights still being on. They walked up to the desk, causing the linoleum floor to squeak with each step. There was no bell to ring and Dorothy was afraid to call out into the heavy silence.

A nurse walked by the office doorway and noticed them

with a slight double-take. She was a short, overweight African-American woman in her late forties and moved with a bouncy pep in her step as she slid behind the front desk. "Did I forget to lock that door again? Tsk, tsk. Ellie May, where is your mind at." She shook her head and chuckled. "Never mind me. Can I help you?"

"Um... We were told someone we know is here." Dorothy said, giving her a friendly smile.

The nurse returned the smile. "I'm sorry, visiting hours ended at eight, sweetie. You'll have to come back tomorrow."

Dorothy checked her watch. It was almost twelve-thirty. She hadn't realized it was so late.

Jasper placed his hand on the nurse's hand giving it a firm, but gentle squeeze. "We *need* to speak with him. It's an urgent matter."

The nurse considered them for a moment and Dorothy could have sworn the nurse was blushing. Dorothy could relate.

"Let me see what I can do for you." The nurse opened the log book, licking a finger as she turned a page.

Dorothy noted that there was no sign of a computer here. They still did everything by hand. The modern age really had passed them by.

The nurse flipped a few pages, then glanced up at them. "What's his name?"

There was an awkward silence as Dorothy shot a questioning look toward Jasper.

He shook his head. "I have no idea. We just know him as—."

Dorothy held out her hand to stop him. It would be better if she said it. Embarrassed, she faced the Nurse. "We don't know it."

The log book slammed shut, sending a few loose papers scuttling across the desk. The nurse gave them a curious glare. "Then how did you expect to find him?"

"This is going to sound really stupid, but..." Dorothy licked her lips, mustering the courage to finish the sentence, "he calls himself a wizard."

"Of Oz," Jasper chimed in.

"A wizard of Oz." Dorothy smiled, mortified. In the back of her mind, a fear arose that the doctors would end up locking her away in here. It *was* a sanitarium after all.

The nurse brightened and laughed. "That would be Mr. Zoroaster!"

It was not the reaction Dorothy had been expecting. "He's actually here?" She was dumbstruck.

"Oh my, yes. Oscar Zoroaster. Quite a storyteller that one." The nurse thought for a moment, "You know, he never has visitors. And he's a night-owl so I bet he's still up. Listen, I'll let you see him, but you can only stay a few minutes."

Dorothy nodded, amazed at their luck. "Thank you!"

The nurse led them inside and down a hall into a creaky elevator. She pushed a button for the second floor and the elevator squeaked and rattled its way up one level.

Jasper didn't like the sensation and steadied himself with a hand on the scuffed, metallic wall.

The light inside blinked when it came to a stop and Dorothy was scared that they would be trapped inside, in the dark. But thankfully, the light stayed on and the doors opened. She breathed easier when they stepped out.

They followed the nurse down poorly lit hallways, past rows of closed doors.

As nice as the nurse was, Dorothy still found the place to be claustrophobic and spooky. She could tell that Jasper felt the same way by how he walked. It was a subtle difference, but she could see he was on alert. Ready for action. *Ready to protect me,* she thought with a burst of exhilaration.

At room number 44, the nurse stopped and wagged a stubby finger as she instructed them in a whisper. "You have to keep your voices down. I don't want you waking the others."

Dorothy nodded again.

The nurse opened the door a crack and leaned in. "Mr. Zoroaster? You have some visitors. Would you like to see them?"

A voice came from behind the door that sounded old and frail. "Visitors?" There was an excited curiosity in his tone. "Please, please. That would be wonderful!"

The nurse ushered them inside.

The room was small, covered with faded, flower-patterned yellow wallpaper and had one tiny window that was too high, caked with dust and grime. An adjacent bathroom was off to the side, lost in the shadows. There was only one light source at the moment—a lamp on a nightstand, near a metal-framed bed.

Sitting up in that bed was Oscar Zoroaster. A feeble shell of a man. He looked ancient with wrinkles covering every inch of exposed pale flesh. Transparent plastic tubes ran from his arm, up to an IV stand at his bedside. He wore dark green silk pajamas and held an open book in his thin hands, which he lowered as Dorothy entered.

Tilting his head down, the old man squinted at them over his wire-rimmed glasses. "It's too dark. Come into the light."

He adjusted the lamp so that it brightened more of the room.

Dorothy and Jasper cautiously moved closer to him.

Mr. Zoroaster studied them for a second, then his eyes widened with a spark of recognition. A warm smile spread across his face.

"Oh my. Oh my, my, my. Miss Gale. It's good to see you again," the old man said.

CHAPTER 10
THE WIZARD OF OZ

Dorothy's mouth fell open in shock.

She didn't know what to say. This man remembered her. He was part of her past.

The nurse, satisfied that Mr. Zoroaster did in fact know them, patted her hand lightly on Dorothy's back.

"I'll leave you three alone." She then slipped out the door, shutting it behind her.

Mr. Zoroaster slowly shook his head from side to side. "You're all grown up, aren't you? I hadn't realized so much time had passed."

Dorothy couldn't help but smile at the way he spoke to her. Like a family member. Like a grandfather.

Her heart beat faster. This man had answers. Her mind raced, trying to formulate a question from the jumbled thoughts that were bouncing around inside her head.

Mr. Zoroaster turned his attention to Jasper, raising his eyebrows as he appraised the young man. "And who might you be, son?"

Jasper bowed with fluid grace, then stood tall. "Jasper Clayfellow, sir. A Knight of Oz."

"Oh! Splendid! Splendid!" Mr. Zoroaster clapped his hand against the pages of his book, then pointed a finger at Jasper, "I would caution you to not go around announcing that. They'll lock you up in here as well."

Jasper glanced around the room warily. He nodded, appreciating the old man's warning. "Not without a fight, sir."

Mr. Zoroaster laughed. "That's a good lad!" He leaned forward and spoke in a hushed tone. "I've managed to make contact with the General a few times using the mirror."

He gestured toward a mirror on the nightstand, next to the lamp. It was a circular five-inch mirror, sitting upright on a pivoting stand.

His skeletal fingers reached behind the bed and brought up a rod wrapped with aluminum foil. There was a ball of foil at the top end. Copper wire was coiled around the length of the rod.

He pointed to the loose end of the wire at the bottom. "You see, I attach the copper wire to the mirror and aim the top receiver toward the window."

Mr. Zoroaster propped the rod against the mirror and window to demonstrate. "Sometimes, usually during a thunderstorm, the signal gets through. I can only chance it at night though, what with these nurses bothering me every few hours with their medications."

The hairs on Dorothy's neck raised. She remembered the sensation of being watched in her apartment. Of a face in the mirror. Had it been real after all? Someone spying on her?

"In my apartment, I thought I saw a face in the mirror… was that you?" she asked in a soft voice.

"No, child. I've only had contact with the General." His bushy white eyebrows drew together, knotting into a mass of crinkles and creases. "Curious, though. There's not many alive that know how to use mirror transmission."

Jasper was kneeling, inspecting the rod. "Amazing."

Dorothy was less then impressed. The old man sounded like a complete crackpot. Aluminum foil! The mentally unstable were addicted to the stuff. She was surprised the old man wasn't wearing a hat made of it.

The fact that he knew about Oz and who she was, only confused her more.

Mr. Zoroaster grinned, his eyes twinkling with life. "Thank you, son. I do say, I'm proud of my own ingenuity. It's brought you two here to come and free me." He tucked the rod back behind his bed.

Dorothy winced. She didn't want to hurt the old man's feelings. "Well… not exactly."

"No?" Mr. Zoroaster looked up at her, puzzled.

She took a breath. "We need your help."

"Just like old times, eh?" Mr. Zoroaster chuckled. "Once again you seek aid from the great and powerful Wizard of Oz."

"Are you really a wizard?" asked Dorothy with a suspicious smile. She asked it as if waiting for the punchline to a joke.

Mr. Zoroaster eyed her with a scrutinizing stare, then motioned for her to kneel next to the bed. "Come closer."

She knelt down and looked up at him with searching eyes.

He put his shriveled, liver-spotted hand on hers and gave her a concerned look. "You don't know me, do you?"

Tears started to form, but she fought them back. "No. I don't remember anything about you. Or Oz."

He leveled a stern gaze at her. "You've been bewitched."

Jasper stood next to her. "Her own doing. To protect the Ozma."

Mr. Zoroaster rubbed his coarse chin and nodded knowingly. "Ah, I see. You've hidden it from the Nome King."

"That's what I've been told." Dorothy's breathing had slowed, becoming shallow. She was almost holding her breath, hoping this old man would give her something—anything—that would help her remember.

"Clever girl." Mr. Zoroaster leaned back, propping his balding head against the pillow. Wispy white hair ringed his temples. "To answer your question… am I a wizard? I didn't choose that title, but that's what they call me."

Dorothy leaned in, feeling foolish saying this out loud. "Do you have magic powers?"

He grinned. "One man's magic is another man's science, my dear."

If she wasn't so desperate, she would have laughed. His playfulness was contagious. "You don't like giving straight answers, do you?"

"Answers are funny little things. They don't like to be found easily and very rarely satisfy the person searching for them. I'm too old to go chasing after the critters. Better to just point in their direction." Mr. Zoroaster winked at her.

Hope was starting to dwindle in Dorothy. "Can you at least tell us how to get back?"

Mr. Zoroaster chuckled again, as if the answer were plain as day. "That part is easy. Your magic slippers will transport you there."

"Magic slippers?" Another mystery. Dorothy's heart felt like it was being crushed.

Mr. Zoroaster nodded. "Yes, yes. I would hazard a guess that you've hidden those too." He paused, taking a moment to think, then stabbed the air with confidence. "You're a sentimental girl. Start at the beginning. Look for them there."

"The beginning?" She had no idea what that meant.

"Just follow your heart, child. You always have." He said, warmly.

Dorothy was baffled. "If I find them, do I just put them on? I don't understand."

"Magic heels clicked thrice and a destination thought." Mr. Zoroaster tapped his temple. "The slippers will do the rest."

She laughed. "You're kidding, right?"

Mr. Zoroaster became deadly serious. "Those slippers are embedded with ancient magic. I would never speak lightly about them."

A little shaken by Mr. Zoroaster's intensity, Dorothy stood, ready to leave. "Is there anything else you can tell me?"

He grasped her hand, his expression grim. "Only this. When your memories do return, understand that they will be those of a child. Oz isn't the bright, cheerful world you thought it was. It has a darker side. Remember that."

Dorothy nodded, heeding his advice. "I'm sorry that we can't take you with us."

He waved a withered hand. "I'll be fine, my dear. I've been here so long, what's a few more ticks of the clock?"

"Thank you." She turned and headed out the door.

"Sir." Jasper bowed once more, then followed after her, leaving the Wizard of Oz alone in his tiny prison of a room.

Dorothy strode through the hallways, contemplating the

crazy information just given to her. It made no sense.

Start at the beginning.

It was frustrating that her life was blank with pieces of the puzzle seemingly within her grasp, yet staying just out of reach. She wanted to throw her hands in the air and scream. Scream at the world. At the universe.

It was a silent ride down in the elevator.

Jasper could see by Dorothy's attitude that she was in no mood to talk.

Start at the beginning.

What did that mean?

They exited the elevator and passed the nurse at her desk. Dorothy thanked her as they exited the building and walked toward the waiting cab.

Start at the beginning.

It was so vague, it could mean anything.

Then Dorothy stopped in her tracks.

Jasper almost collided with her. He was about to ask what was wrong, when he saw the change in her expression. He grinned. "You know what he's talking about, don't you?"

Dorothy knew. It had to be. When she looked at him, there was determination in her eyes.

"I'm doing what he said. I'm going back to the beginning."

CHAPTER 11
BACK TO THE BEGINNING

The cab sped down a lonely dirt road, spewing chunks of mud behind it. Its headlights cut into the night, carving a path out of the oppressive darkness.

The twin shafts of light offered only glimpses of what the surrounding area looked like—miles and miles of muddy abandoned farmland. A flat desolate void.

Looking out the taxi's windows, Dorothy was reliving her childhood in flashes. Remembering why she wanted to escape into her books. Into her imagination. There was nothing out here.

The car came to a stop in front of an old dilapidated farmhouse. The cab's headlights splashed across part of the house, leaving the rest to be swallowed by the night. The faded yellow paint was peeling and there were loose boards hanging askew.

Dorothy and Jasper got out of the car and walked toward

the front door, their shoes sinking into the wet dirt.

The cab had shut off its engine and with miles and miles of emptiness around them, it was noticeable that there weren't any animal noises.

No crickets. No stray dogs or coyotes or birds.

A dead zone. The silence was eerie. It made them move with care.

The door was locked. Dorothy looked down at a hefty rock, the size of a football, sitting in what used to be the front garden. She rolled the large stone over and exposed a rusty key.

She let out a quiet laugh. "It's still here." She snatched it up and unlocked the door. It groaned on its hinges as they entered.

The cab's headlights shined through the windows, giving them a sense of the room.

Disturbed dust particles swirled in the air, stirred by their presence. The place was layered with dust. Furniture and knickknacks still occupied their places, as if waiting for their owners to return and make use of them once more.

"This is where I grew up," Dorothy said in a whisper, though she didn't know why.

Jasper swept a hand across a shelf, displacing the caked grime. "You've been away a long time."

She felt a pang of guilt. "Too long."

As they moved deeper into the house, there was less light to see by and Dorothy more or less felt her way around. She guided Jasper into the kitchen and slid her hands across the counter, down to a series of drawers. "We had power outages all the time. I was taught to find this in the dark."

There was the sound of a match being struck, followed by a flame sparking into existence.

Dorothy lit three candles in a brass candelabra, which cast a warm glow across their faces. She pocketed some more matches and picked up the candelabra, holding it out in front of her as they made their way through the house.

"Where are your parents?" Jasper lowered his voice, which sounded too loud in the hallway.

"Never knew them. My Aunt and Uncle raised me." Dorothy paused, her voice becoming distant, "They both passed away when I was younger."

He looked over at her, getting a glimpse of the vulnerable little girl that she used to be. "I'm sorry."

She caught his gaze and straightened, squashing down that window into her past. "Nothing to be sorry about. Just the way it was."

The orange candlelight cast their flickering shadows against the walls. The old floorboards creaked under foot. With each dark room that they passed, Dorothy was becoming unsettled.

The place was so *lifeless*. The absence of her Aunt and Uncle was creating a ghostly vacuum in the house.

It had been a long time since she had thought about their deaths. Her Uncle Henry had died of a heart attack when she was ten. Auntie Em had died in her sleep a couple of years later. After that, her memory got hazy.

She came to the realization that she had never felt at home here either. That feeling of not fitting in had always been there. Since as early as she could remember.

Dorothy led Jasper into a small bedroom that held a bed with a frilly pink patchwork quilt covering it. On top of it were a few stuffed animals, their colors muted from age and dust.

In the corner was a bookcase and near the window stood a short dresser with a cracked vanity mirror. The walls were decorated with stickers of flowers and grinning suns.

She looked around wistfully. "My bedroom. Whatever we're looking for, it'll probably be here."

Jasper smiled as he took in the contents of the room. It was like a snapshot of her childhood. It made him feel closer to her.

She had grabbed a pillow and was busy patting it down, when she noticed his amused expression. She cocked a half grin. "Gimme a break. I was a little girl."

He laughed. "No, I like it. Very Queen-like."

She threw the pillow at him, laughing. "Shut up and search."

He caught it and chucked it to the ground, bowing with a grin. "Yes, M'Lady."

They searched the dresser drawers, under the bed, in the closet, and behind the dresser. They came up empty-handed.

As they were moving the dresser back into place, Dorothy thought she saw something out of the corner of her eye.

A shadowy face in the cracked vanity mirror, watching her.

A cold chill ran down her spine. She swung around to stare in the mirror and saw only her own reflection. That wasn't her imagination. She was sure of it. She gave the mirror a distrustful look.

Jasper stood beside her, appearing in the reflection with her. "You saw something?"

She nodded. "We were being watched."

Jasper frowned, his fists clenching. "That means someone knows we're here. We need to hurry."

Before she could give it any more thought, Dorothy's gaze shifted to the window, focusing on something outside.

"It's not *here*," She pointed toward the window. "It would be *there*."

CHAPTER 12
THE YELLOW BRICK ROAD

Jasper looked to where Dorothy was pointing in the window and saw a fairly large weather-beaten shed a few feet to the side of the house.

Dorothy rushed back toward the kitchen to snatch a keyring hanging on a wooden peg, then shot out the front door with Jasper right behind her.

She hurried toward the shed. The structure had once been a bright yellow, but time had stripped its vibrancy down to a dull grey.

She unlocked the heavy, weathered padlock that secured the shed's barn doors and grunted as she swung one side open, while Jasper effortlessly opened the other.

They stepped inside.

Two of the three candles had blown out in her dash between

buildings. She struck another match and relit them.

In the candlelight, they could see rakes, hoes, shovels, and other various farm equipment hanging on the walls. There were two small cross-paned windows on either side.

A smile crossed Dorothy's face. This was *her* space. "I used to spend most of my time in here. Reading. Playing."

Jasper scanned the walls. The hanging tools were sharp and dangerous looking. "Nice place for a kid."

She laughed. "My Aunt and Uncle didn't have much. I had to entertain myself."

They reached the back of the shed and she pointed to a frayed, worn out couch cushion that lay next to a red brick fireplace. "This is where I'd curl up with my blanket and get lost in my books."

Jasper could see the nostalgia welling up in her as she gazed at the spot on the floor.

"This must be it," he said with confidence.

Dorothy glanced over at him, snapping back to the present. "Hmm?"

He gestured toward the cushion. "This is where you would have hidden something."

She nodded. "It has to be."

Jasper dropped to one knee and started squeezing the cushion, feeling to see if anything was inside it.

Dorothy, however, was drawn to the fireplace.

"Uncle Henry knew this was my favorite spot. He built this to keep me warm and to give me light to read by." She stretched her arm up inside the fireplace, feeling around.

Jasper joined her. "Here, I've got a longer reach."

Dorothy pulled her arm out and brushed her hands together, removing the soot, while Jasper stuck his hand up inside.

After a minute, he shook his head and pulled his arm out. "Nothing up there."

She bit her lip, concentrating. "There's something about this fireplace. I can feel it."

Jasper felt around the exterior. "Then there has to be a clue." He started to run his fingers along its edges with an expert's touch.

While Jasper combed the fireplace for signs, Dorothy sat down on the cushion, cross-legged, and studied her environment.

This was maddening. *Why couldn't I leave easier clues for myself?*

She was becoming very irritated with the thought of her younger self planting this obscure trail. A brat making it difficult on purpose. Laughing, knowing that her future self would wander around like a buffoon, trying to piece it all together.

But Dorothy pushed that image out of her mind. She knew she wasn't that type of a person, even as a kid. She also knew she would have done the best that she could. She just had to look at this from her own point of view.

"If I knew I wasn't going to have my memories, why would I make it so difficult?" she wondered aloud.

"I don't know. You like challenges?" Jasper was now checking where the fireplace connected to the wall, seeing if there were a secret door or something.

"No. I wouldn't do that to myself." And that, of course, was the answer. She brightened. "I wouldn't make it hard! I would make it easy to find. I would hide it in a location that was only special to me and no one else. So we're in the right place."

She started glancing around, searching the room. "Next thing I would do is make it so that only *I* could see it."

She sat up straighter. She was on the right track.

"And how would you accomplish that?" Jasper could see she was onto her own trail. He knelt down, watching her puzzle out the mystery.

"I don't know. Maybe something that could only be seen from this exact spot." She craned her neck at different angles, but saw nothing out of the ordinary. "Maybe an arrow drawn somewhere that would glow in the dark or only show up with a black light or an infra-red camera or something.

"Can you do any of that?" he asked hopefully, not understanding what she was referring to.

"No," she said, frustrated. "That's the problem. I don't have those things. How would I know what I'd need?" She started talking to herself. "How would I know? How would I know?" And again the answer was simple. "I wouldn't know. Because I wouldn't be able to remember." She was close, she could feel it. She looked up at him. An electric chill coursed through her body. Goosebumps rose up her arms.

"I'd have someone give me what I needed when the time was right," she said excitedly.

"The glasses," they both said to each other at the same time.

"Whoever this General is, I trusted him to give me these." Dorothy said, pulling out the victorian style, green-tinted glasses that Jasper had given her back in New York.

She wasted no time in slipping them on.

Through the lenses, everything around Dorothy took on a green tint.

Everything, that is, except for one brick in the fireplace.

One brick was yellow.

It was so bright it almost glowed.

She gasped. "One of the bricks is yellow!"

"From the yellow brick road," Jasper said in a hushed tone,

"You must have saved a piece after the Nome King destroyed it."

Dorothy gripped the brick and found that it was loose.

It resisted at first, then with a firm tug, slid out, revealing a recessed nook behind it.

Inside the nook was an object wrapped tightly in cloth.

Carefully, Dorothy slid the object out. She removed the glasses and tucked them back into her jacket, so that she could better examine the discovery.

The cloth was checkered with blue and white squares. With a jolt, she recognized it immediately.

"Part of a dress I had when I was younger," she said in an awed whisper.

Ever so gently, she unwrapped it, exposing a pair of sparkling silver slippers.

Jasper and Dorothy both leaned in to admire their beauty.

"Slippers. Just like he said..." Dorothy ran a finger down the length of one. "Feels like glass, but soft."

She marveled how at first glance the slippers looked like polished silver, but when held at different angles, they would blossom with color— ruby red, then sky blue, then emerald green...

They were the most beautiful thing Dorothy had ever seen.

A sound outside made Dorothy jump.

Shrieking.

Like a mob of women and children crying out in pain. From out of the black night, the sound was downright unnerving and it was getting closer.

Dorothy was petrified.

Jasper rushed over to shut the doors. "Crows! They've tracked us down!"

Dorothy let out a breath that she hadn't realized she was

holding. He was right. It wasn't screaming, it was cawing. The crows—hundreds by the sound of it—had found them.

"Put the slippers on!" Jasper said as he slipped a shovel through the door handles, preventing the doors from swinging back open.

They could hear the birds' talons and beaks scratching and clawing on all sides of the shed, determined to get inside. The sounds echoed with each sliver of wood that was carved away by the feathered beasts.

Looking at the slippers, Dorothy saw that they were a child's size. "They're too small! They'll never fit!"

The glass cracked on both windows. The crows were pecking away furiously. They would be through those windows in seconds.

Jasper positioned himself near Dorothy, ready to defend her. "Make them fit!"

Dorothy kicked off her sneakers, standing in white socks, and started to force one of the slippers onto a foot.

She watched in amazement as the shoe elongated, sliding on with ease. She didn't question it and put on the other slipper which also resized itself.

The effect was immediate.

The terror and panic that was building inside her, faded away, replaced with a tingling, calming wave that washed over her. Her eyes were wide, in shock, as the sensation threatened to lift her off the ground.

Memories were flooding back to her.

Her first trip to Oz. The friends she made there—she could hear their voices. Remembered each of their quirky personalities. The laughter and fun they shared together. The adventures she had experienced. So many!

Her reaction to the news of being elected Queen. How proud she felt. Then soon after, the attack. The Nome King's assault on Emerald City.

Her preparation to protect the Ozma. The plan to hide herself in New York. To have Glinda weave a spell of amnesia on her after she put everything in its place.

Then—years of misery. Of being a blank slate. Of being a zombie. Waiting. Waiting for the moment to wake up.

And finally it had come.

"Jasper. I remember. I remember it all."

Jasper could sense the change in her. She was almost crackling with energy. "You know the way back?"

Dorothy's eyes gleamed. A wide smile spread across her lips as she held out her hand.

"Let's go." Her smile was warm and mischievous—full of adventure.

Jasper felt a bit unsteady which was unusual for him. Now he understood all the stories about Dorothy Gale. How a little girl could take on the likes of the Nome King, the Witches, or the Mangaboos and survive.

It was all right there in that smile. And it was the most attractive thing he had ever seen.

He took her hand and she laughed with delight. Jasper's throat went dry. Had the crows gone away? He couldn't hear them anymore. Or maybe he had just stopped paying attention.

Dorothy closed her eyes and clicked her heels three times. She smiled at the action. How many times had she clicked her heels at work, wishing to go home? A reflex memory from her childhood adventures.

She felt the stale air swirl around her in a whirlwind, blowing her hair across her face—the wind whistling past her ears. Faster and faster. Her feet lifted off the ground.

Dorothy couldn't help but to giggle. She was going home.

And there's no place like home.

CHAPTER 13
RETURN TO OZ

The air roared around Dorothy at phenomenal speeds—like she was caught inside a miniature tornado. Then just as fast as it began, it ceased.

Her feet touched soft earth with a solid thump. Her ponytail fell against her back, while loose strands fell forward against her face.

A cold brisk wind cut across Dorothy's cheek. The air no longer smelled of wood and dirt. It now had a hint of cinnamon and strawberries. It smelled sweeter. Familiar.

She opened her eyes and saw a wide open grassy field stretching out toward rolling hills. A brooding, cloudy night sky loomed overhead. The grass was overgrown and of a sickly color, almost black, giving the area a stark dreary appearance.

The sight made her stomach twist into a knot. This wasn't

Oz. Not *her* Oz. Where were the bright colors? And the animals that romped about? The musical songbirds darting from tree to tree? This was a wasteland of nothingness. It was all so muted as to be almost black and white.

Jasper was still standing by her side, holding her hand. He watched her react to the landscape and gave her hand a squeeze of reassurance.

Dorothy glanced around. "I tried to bring Chalk back with us. Guess it didn't work."

Thunder rumbled overhead and the winds picked up speed, whipping her ponytail to the side. The chill made her teeth chatter. She jerked her coat tighter, flipping up the collar to keep her neck warm.

Jasper eyed the gloomy skies with dread. "It's going to rain. We've got to find shelter fast."

Dorothy cast a puzzled look skyward, sensing fear in his voice, which was in turn making her nervous. "What's wrong with the rain?"

"I'm made of clay. I'll wash away to nothing." Jasper scanned the area, looking for somewhere to find refuge.

"Oh no!" Dorothy searched as well, seeing if there was anywhere nearby to seek shelter. The area was in bad shape and she couldn't identify any landmarks to guide her.

Jasper ran up the slope behind them to get a better vantage point. As he crested the top, he stopped cold. "The situation just got worse."

Dorothy hurried up, sliding a few times on the greasy grass. The slippers were magic and all, but at times like this, she wished she had held onto her sneakers. When she got to the top she froze.

Straight ahead was a magnificent walled city, constructed of emerald crystals and marbled jade. A majestic tower in its center—

the Royal Palace—rose up toward the heavens, a staircase spiraling up the length of it. Two lesser spires were on either side of the Palace.

In the past, the spires would have flown the flags of Oz, visible to all, flapping gloriously in the breezes. There were no flags today. The city was a solemn ghost town. Its colors dulled and faded. A shadow of its former self.

"Emerald City… it's dead." She felt nauseous. *How could this happen,* she thought. *How could everything have changed so much.*

Jasper nodded. "The Nome King is there. This is enemy territory now."

Thunder rolled across the heavens again.

He glanced up at the sky, paranoid. "You should wish us somewhere else. Quick."

Dorothy was still coming off the shock of seeing Emerald City. She was rattled and dizzy. "I can't think straight! I can't focus!"

An earsplitting crack of thunder boomed above them, making them both jump.

"No choice! I can't stay out in the open!" He grabbed her hand and they raced down the other side of the hill, toward the city. They ended up slipping on the oily grass, sliding most of the way down.

On the flatter ground, they ran through the fields. The grass was taller here, which helped to hide their reckless approach. Halfway to the city, the first drops began to fall. As soon as Jasper felt them, he was off like a shot, sprinting faster than before.

Dorothy somehow kept pace, though her chest was aching from the effort. Her breathing came in ragged gasps.

The only entrance to the city was through the main gate—two enormous doors carved with ornate decorative lines, looking very much like a sun with rays spreading outward. Nested inside the sun was the word "OZ" in gleaming golden letters.

On a normal day, they would have been greeted by two hawk-eyed Munchkins, the Guardians of the Gate, standing proud and noble, ever vigilant for intruders. Dorothy saw that they were missing and in their place were two Nomes.

The Nomes had grey skin and angular, craggy faces bearing permanent scowls. They wore dirty, tattered brown garments under crude dented armor and each carried a worn, chipped sword. Each also held a large green shield with the word "OZ" etched on them—obviously trophies from the city's original Guardians of the Gate, since no Nome could produce such fine craftsmanship.

Dorothy and Jasper were coming at the entrance from the side, so the two guards on patrol didn't see them until the last minute.

Jasper threw himself into one of the Nomes, tackling the guard before he knew what hit him.

The other guard, startled, took a tentative battle stance and shouted for backup. He swung at Jasper who was already rolling to his feet.

Jasper dodged the blade and drove his fist into the guard's stomach. The Nome doubled over. Jasper rammed his knee into the guard's face, sending him stumbling backward.

The first guard was starting to rise. Jasper grabbed the second Nome's fallen sword and made short work of both enemies with two quick slashes. Black dirt and rock sprayed from their wounds. Nomes had no blood to spill. They were magical creatures, stones brought to life. Minions of the Nome King. His slaves.

Dorothy was amazed at how fast and efficient Jasper was at

fighting. She joined him, huddling under the door's small alcove just as the heavy rain began to fall in earnest.

"Now would be a good time to wish us out of here! Someplace indoors!" He said, as he flattened himself as much as possible against the massive door.

She scrunched her eyes and tried to concentrate. This was all happening too fast. "Let me think! Let me think!" Where could she transport them? So much had changed, how could she know what was still standing?

The doors suddenly swung open. On the other side were a half dozen more Nome guards, each wearing a stunned expression of surprise at the sight of Jasper and Dorothy. The Nomes jumped back reaching for their swords.

Jasper charged into them, slashing away, not giving them time to properly defend themselves. He pushed forward, taking the fight into the Royal Courtyard.

Dorothy followed behind him at a distance, staying clear of his fierce swordplay. As she entered the courtyard and saw what had become of it, she felt like she'd been punched in the stomach.

Once a grand site, the Royal Courtyard was now filled with broken statues of Ozite heroes and a spectacularly lavish fountain that was overgrown with brown, dingy ivy and thriving black mold. The fountain no longer ran and the pooled water was a thick, dark soup covered in dead leaves. The smell of rotting vegetation hung heavy in the air.

It broke her heart to see Emerald City in such ruin.

A covered walkway ran from the main gate, splitting into two paths encircling the fountain, then rejoined on the opposite side, leading to the Royal Palace.

The rain hindered Jasper, restricting him to remain under this covered walkway as he fought. He dodged and parried, slashed and stabbed, managing to take a number of enemies down, but the noise had already drawn attention. A guard on a balcony blew a horn, sounding the alarm.

"M'Lady, take cover!" He shouted as more Nomes joined the fight.

Dorothy hid behind a jade pillar, watching Jasper do his best to protect her. She was so focused on Jasper's safety, that she failed to see two Nomes sneaking in behind them.

They moved in and seized her.

Jasper heard her scream and glanced back, nearly losing his head in the process. He felt the rush of air across his neck from the near fatal sword strike. It didn't phase him. Acting on pure reflex, he thrust his sword into the Nome, spilling its obsidian dust, then dove toward Dorothy.

The guards yanked her away into the rain.

Dorothy felt Jasper grab hold of her ankle, not letting her go. His strong grip was reassuring. She was sure he would free her, then she saw that his right arm—the one holding onto her—was out in the open, beyond the covered walkway, exposed and vulnerable. The heavy rain was drenching it, causing it to sag and lose its form.

She wanted to scream at him—to tell him to let go, to save himself, but the rough hand over her mouth prevented any such action. She couldn't even bite the guard's cold, hard fingers for fear of breaking her teeth on them.

With a final jerk, the Nomes snatched Dorothy from Jasper's sloshy grip and made off with her.

Through the pelting rain, as she was dragged away, Dorothy watched Jasper pull his arm back, clutching it to his chest. He met her gaze. The anguish of his failure was etched across his face. Witnessing how devastated he was made Dorothy want to cry.

Both for his pain and for seeing first hand how much he cared for her safety.

Jasper spun toward his enemies, letting out a primal scream of anger, ready to lash out and battle them all with his one good hand.

"ENOUGH!" The thunderous voice exploded over the courtyard, reverberating against the jade buildings. A voice like that of mountains crashing together.

The Nomes abruptly stopped in their tracks.

Jasper's head whipped around toward the Royal Palace.

A tall, robust figure stood in the Palace's doorway. Fury and power radiated from this man who wore a grimy, green royal robe and a tarnished crown.

Dorothy recognized the man and dug her feet into the mud, trying to fight against her two captors. Her memories had returned and she knew exactly who belonged to that intimidating voice.

Roquat Ruggedo.

The Nome King.

CHAPTER 14
THE NOME KING

In the past, Dorothy had fought with the Nome King many times in many battles and was fully aware what a despicable creature he was.

He was cunning and ruthless. Hungry for power. A vengeful tyrant that held onto grudges like they were precious treasures. Never wanting to let go. Obsessing over them, nurturing them, until, in his mind, they became personal wars. He would wait years, planning and gathering forces, then he would unleash his wrath upon the poor soul that crossed him.

Emerald City had withstood his attacks, turning him away again and again, each instance only adding fuel to his revenge. Until one terrible day, his anger was too great, the city too weak, and he conquered his most hated enemy.

Only he hadn't.

Dorothy, as Queen, had seen it coming and made plans to keep the Ozma out of his hands. All these years the Nome King had been deprived of final victory. And he blamed *her*.

The Nome King's eyes flashed with rage, locking onto Jasper, then over to Dorothy, whereupon his angry features melted into an expression of surprise, then pleasure.

His concrete colored mustache and beard parted as a smile oozed across his colorless grey face. A face similar to his minions with sharp angles and thick, heavy brows. Even his hair and beard were angular, as if carved from rock, though it moved with an unsettling fluidity. It was a visual contradiction that had always strained Dorothy's eyes.

The Nome King pointed to her. "Bring her to me."

The guards dragged Dorothy, kicking and swinging, up to their lord and master, presenting her like a prized wild animal.

Standing at seven feet tall, the Nome King towered over her. He grabbed her chin—a little too hard—and stared down at her soaking, dripping appearance, studying her face. She glared back with anger. This only amused him more.

"Time has certainly stolen your youth," he said, his voice sounding like a boulder being pulled across gravel. Yet it was also buttery smooth. Another contradiction.

Dorothy's jaw clenched, her teeth grinding together. Better to keep her mouth shut, lest she start throwing back insults, which would only make matters worse.

The Nome King chuckled, then his eyes gleamed as he spotted the slippers. "Ah! You've brought me a gift!"

He knelt down, holding Dorothy's legs still with his vice-like grip and removed the magic shoes. He stood back up, holding them with great care, stroking them.

The Nome King threw a sneer at Dorothy. "Imagine, after all

these years of searching, what a pleasant surprise to have you come right to my front door."

Dorothy couldn't hold it in any longer. "This palace isn't yours! You're a thief! A pretender to that crown you wear!"

He raised his stony eyebrows, feigning surprise. "*You're* the one that abandoned your throne. *You* abandoned all of Oz."

"You're wrong!" Dorothy growled.

The Nome King swung his long arm outward in a grand display. "Look around, child! The land is dying because of you."

His words were like a slap in her face. "No… I—I had to protect it from *you*."

The Nome King shook his head sorrowfully. "Selfish girl. I only want to *rule* Oz, not destroy it. You've done more harm than I ever could."

Dorothy felt weak. Her knees shook. She stopped struggling and went limp, supported by the Nome guards. *Was this all really her fault? Had she destroyed Oz?* Her thoughts ran together, making her lightheaded.

"Liar!" Jasper's voice echoed across the courtyard.

Dorothy looked over at him, his voice clearing her head.

The Nome King shot Jasper a scornful glare.

Jasper was still under the walkway's cover. He flexed his right hand. His arm was almost reformed. His voice was laced with bitterness and anger. "You'd remake Oz after your own kingdom! Where everyone is a slave to you! Where no green can grow!"

"Yet you sprang from that same land, my son." The Nome King glanced to a nearby guard and subtly motioned toward Jasper.

The guard nodded his head once and slipped away.

"Don't ever call me that!" Jasper snapped back.

Dorothy was confused by their exchange. She could see the hate boiling inside Jasper. But why? Why was he so furious?

The Nome King dramatically placed his free hand over his own chest. "You wound me. I created you and you show no gratitude. You never have."

"I owe no allegiance to my birthplace. Nor you—" Jasper spit out the next word, "—Father."

Dorothy's mouth fell open. Her mind reeled. The man that had rescued her—the man that she was attracted to—was the son of her sworn enemy.

"You're a fool." The Nome King lifted his hand and signaled to his Nomes.

A dozen of them came forward carrying pails of water, while another dozen held burning torches and oil.

Jasper took a step back, eyeing them warily.

"You've chosen your side," the Nome King declared. "Now choose how you will die. Washed away by water? Or baked by fire. Both deadly to a man made of clay."

Jasper retreated from the approaching enemies.

Dorothy watched in horror. Jasper may be the Nome King's son, but he wasn't like his father. She knew it in her heart.

"Run, Jasper!" She strained against the guards holding her. "Go get help!"

Jasper's body tensed. With this rain, he had nowhere to go.

The Nome King bellowed with laughter. "Yes! Run out into the storm!"

Dorothy realized the Nome King was right. There was no escape. She was going to watch Jasper die. The mere thought of it was enough to start her tears flowing.

Just then, a white horse charged through the main gate and into the courtyard, rearing back and smashing its hooves into the

Nomes, knocking them down. One of the buckets of oil spilled, splashing onto a fallen torch, igniting into a wall of flame. Several of the Nomes had been drenched by the oil and caught fire, running off into the rain to douse themselves.

"Chalk!" Jasper was overjoyed by the sight of his friend.

Dorothy laughed, choking back tears.

Chalk snorted and huffed as he took position next to Jasper. "Sorry, I'm late! Ended up a few miles from here."

The Nome King watched from afar, his temper flaring. "Don't just stand there, get him!" he bellowed to his Nomes.

"We're in some trouble, friend." Jasper readied his sword.

"As usual." Chalk stamped his hooves toward the Nomes, making them back up. "What's the plan?"

"Haven't a clue." Jasper tightened his grip on his sword. While Chalk held the Nomes at bay, Jasper took a moment to glance around and size up the situation. His gaze landed back at the main gate, on the oversized shields the two guards had been carrying. "That'll work. Follow my lead."

Chalk snorted and nodded.

Jasper sheathed his sword and faced the Nome King. "My Queen has spoken! I have my orders!" He then turned and ran for the main gate.

"STOP HIM!" the Nome King roared to his minions.

As the Nomes rushed toward Jasper, Chalk reared back and struck them down, then galloped after his companion.

Jasper reached the front entrance and snatched up one of the fallen guard's shields just as Chalk was racing by him. Jasper grabbed the saddle and swung up onto the stallion. "GO! GO!"

He bent forward holding the oversized shield over his body, protecting himself from the rain as he and Chalk rode out into the stormy night.

The Nome King's stony lips curled into a snarl. "After him! He won't get far!"

"You sound like you're trying to convince yourself." This time it was Dorothy's turn to sneer.

He looked down at her. She was smirking at him.

Dorothy could see the rage building up inside him, about to boil over into violence, then he caught himself and simmered down.

He grinned at her. "How I've missed your sharp tongue, child." He glanced at the guards holding her. "Bring her inside. We have much to discuss."

CHAPTER 15
THE PRISONER

The Royal Palace of Emerald City.

One of the most lavish, beautiful structures, not only in Emerald City, but in all of Oz. It is from here that the Great and Powerful Wizard of Oz once ruled. And before him, the eighty eight Kings and Queens of old.

Built by the finest architects and artisans, its beauty is well known throughout the land. Inside, the throne room greets visitors with a spectacular high arched ceiling composed entirely of giant flat emeralds that when sunlight passes through, casts a warm green glow down onto the polished green marbled floor, creating a wonderful dreamlike atmosphere.

With the dark sky above, there was no such glow. The room was cold and stark. The throne itself, made of smooth, gleaming gold with emeralds lining it, sat in the back of the room, covered in dirt. Residue from the Nome King.

They passed rounded doorways that led off to various rooms. Each entrance was trimmed with elegant gold that flowed along the jade walls in extravagant swirls and swoops, framing portraits of the royal heritage of Kings and Queens that once resided here, as well as paintings of the outlandish and colorful landscapes of Oz. A gallery of exquisite art.

Even after years of neglect, the palace's beauty showed through the dust and dirt.

All of this magnificent decor was lost on the Nome King.

He saw none of it as he strode through the hall with Dorothy at his side, escorted by the two guards.

Dorothy, however, still felt a thrill run through her at the sight of it. This had been her home during her brief year as Queen. She had been all of thirteen years old.

"Are you going to tell me where you've hidden the Ozma?" the Nome King asked, without bothering to look at her.

"Not a chance." She had since stopped struggling and was conserving her energy to withstand whatever lay ahead.

When he glanced down at her, his eyes didn't show anger, but instead something far more disturbing—delight. "I thought you'd feel that way."

They entered the ballroom. Or what was left of it. There was rubble and debris everywhere. Shattered emerald chandeliers lay in pieces next to torn bits of scarlet red banners and curtains. The marbled floor was fractured with jagged, broken edges jutting up, overlapping itself.

To Dorothy, it resembled the aftermath of an earthquake.

The Nome King led them to a hole in the floor, where the marble had fallen inward, creating a sloping path down underground.

Dorothy was escorted into a dimly lit chamber several feet below the ballroom. Even though there were two burning torches on the walls, it took a moment for her eyes to adjust to the low light. As the details became clear, she was able to see that they were in a large room carved out of the rock beneath the palace. It was rough and uneven—and dismal.

But that wasn't what grabbed Dorothy's attention. What drew her gaze was a swirling globe hovering over a wide, circular pool of water. The pool took up half the chamber. The globe itself, measuring around seven feet high, looked like it too was made of water.

As her vision continued to adjust, she was able see through the globe's thin layer of rippling water and make out a hunched shadowy form inside, standing on a round floating platform.

The figure wore a black robe with a hood over its head.

The Nome King spoke to the figure with a certain amount of amusement. "I've brought you a familiar face."

The dark figure turned toward them, straightening a fraction.

"Ahhh. Finally caught you, have we, my pretty?" The creaking voice was that of an old woman, laced with hate and malevolence.

Fear wrapped itself around Dorothy's heart, squeezing it, sending an icy chill along her spine. She knew that voice. That awful hideous voice.

The cloaked figure pulled back the hood, revealing long, ratty coarse black hair and a hook-nosed, wart covered face that happened to be a dark unpleasant shade of green.

Dorothy recoiled in horror. There was no mistaking it.

It was the Wicked Witch of the West!

The Witch glared at Dorothy with one angry eye. The other

was clear and glassy, with neither an iris nor a pupil—it was artificial—she had lost that eye long ago in a battle with one of her sister witches.

Dorothy shook her head, unable to comprehend what was clearly in front of her. "NO! You're dead! I saw you die!"

"Yes, yes. So I did, so I did," the Witch chuckled, then her eyes blazed, locking onto the slippers in the Nome King's hands.

The Nome King caught this and smiled, leaning toward Dorothy. "By the time I found her, there wasn't much left. But it was enough."

"H-how?" Dorothy sputtered.

The Nome King was reveling in his show of power. "That small trace of her, that tiny remnant of her, still burned with enough hatred for you that it was easy to reconstruct her.

"But why?" It didn't make sense. The Witch was dangerous to everyone, including the Nome King. Why would he bring her back?

"I knew she'd be able to hunt you down," he said, as if it were obvious.

And there was the answer. It *was* obvious. Dorothy knew the Witch hated her and would stop at nothing to exact revenge. With the Witch on her tail, hiding back home had only delayed the inevitable.

The Nome King walked up to the rock wall and nonchalantly waved his hand. A section of stone groaned and snapped, grinding against itself, magically sliding apart, revealing a cache. Deep inside, were the Witch's pointed black hat and battered broom.

The Witch watched him with narrowed eyes as he placed the slippers next to her belongings, then sealed the rock once more with another gesture of the hand.

He nodded to the guards holding Dorothy and they proceeded to lock her in shackles, chaining her to a wall facing the Witch.

The chains anchored her arms up above her head. The thick metal was heavy and cold against Dorothy's skin. She shivered slightly, causing the chains to clink and rattle.

"Since you insist on not cooperating, I'm going to have to extract the information from you." The Nome King's crooked lips sneered. "It's probably going to hurt."

"Oh, I can assure you it will." The Witch chimed in, cackling.

Dorothy was absolutely terrified. She hadn't seen the Witch since her first adventure in Oz a lifetime ago and all of the old fears were stirring up inside her. The Witch had given her nightmares for years after Dorothy had defeated her. Now she was back, angrier than before. Dorothy was almost shaking.

The Witch plucked out her glassy eye, leaving a floppy empty socket, and placed both hands on the orb. She pulled her hands apart and the eye grew between them to the size of a bowling ball. It was a crystal ball suspended in the air.

She held her bony hand over her crystal sphere like a hawk's talon. Bright purple mist swirled within it. The Witch watched Dorothy out of the corner of her eye as she dragged her sharp, jagged fingernails across the glass surface.

It felt like the Witch's nails were cutting directly into the skin on Dorothy's back. She squeezed her eyes shut, screaming in agony.

Cackling gleefully, the Witch dragged her nails across the crystal once more, this time at a different angle.

The pain moved to Dorothy's face. Her eyes popped open and she gasped, drawing in shuddering breaths. It was excruciating. Like knives slicing into her flesh, though no actual cuts formed.

Again and again, the Witch tortured her from afar. The hag's expression contorting into a smug grin of satisfaction as Dorothy screamed and cried out.

The Nome King held up a hand for the Witch to cease.

Dorothy slumped against the wall, her legs trembling, barely able to hold her up. The pain was subsiding and she breathed hard, trying to regain her strength.

The Nome King bent down, his face close to hers. He spoke softly into her ear. "Tell me where it is and I'll stop her."

She looked up at him, exhausted, but determined. She blew a sweaty strand of hair off her face. "No."

The Witch was smiling ear to ear, exposing her crooked, yellow teeth. "Are you hoping one of your friends will come to your aid? Is that it? Let me show you what's to become of you."

Even through the globe of water that imprisoned the Witch, Dorothy could see the pleasure the old crone was getting from this moment.

The Witch slid her spider-like fingers over the crystal ball in a circular motion. The purple mist inside, followed suit, spinning faster and faster. She snatched her hand away and pointed to the back of the cavern.

A sound came from the shadows in that same spot. A soft thud. Like a bag of sand hitting stone. Wisps of violet smoke curled and spiraled out into the torchlight.

A raspy, scratchy whisper came from the shadows. "You've summoned me?"

"Yes," crooned the Witch, "come out into the light."

A tall, lanky shape stepped out of the darkness, dressed in raggedy clothes with straw stuffing poking out of every rip and tear. A wide-brimmed straw hat cast his stitched canvas face in shadow.

"Scarecrow!" Dorothy couldn't hide her shock.

The Scarecrow saw Dorothy, but didn't respond in any way.

The Witch thrust a finger at Dorothy. "Teach this girl not to disobey the King."

The Scarecrow nodded once. "As you wish," he said, his voice sounding like a chilled breeze cutting through fields of wheat.

"Scarecrow! It's me! Dorothy!" Dorothy strained against her chains. This wasn't happening. Not the Scarecrow. Not her dear friend.

He raised his arms outward like wings, his long fingers spreading apart.

A sound echoed from somewhere above in the palace. A sound Dorothy had heard before.

The cawing of crows. Lots and lots of crows.

She sank against the rock wall, realizing what that meant. The Scarecrow was commanding the crows. Her trusted friend had helped the Witch to hunt her down.

"Please," Dorothy pleaded one last time, choking with emotion.

The Scarecrow stood motionless, arms still outspread, as dozens of the black noisy birds poured into the chamber, shrieking and squawking around him.

With one sudden movement, he swung both hands toward Dorothy, commanding his army to rain down on her in a black cloud of feathers, beaks and talons.

With her hands in chains, she buried her face in the crook of her arm, trying to protect herself from the onslaught.

Her screams were drowned out by the nightmarish screeching of the winged beasts.

CHAPTER 16
RACING THE RAIN

Outside, the rain was coming down in heavy sheets, sweeping across the decaying lands of Oz.

Chalk's blistering pace had carried Jasper far from Emerald City, away from the clumsy Nomes that had tried to give chase.

"We've lost them!" Chalk huffed, between breaths. It hadn't taken him long either. He was swift and knew the lay of the land.

Jasper wasn't faring as well. He was hunched low on Chalk, holding the shield above him with a weakening arm. The shield wasn't big enough. Parts of his face were literally sagging and sliding as the raindrops continued to find their way to him.

"Chalk… I'm washing way," Jasper managed to say, his voice coming out slurred since his lips were drifting toward his chin.

"We're almost there! Hold on!" Chalk shouted.

They were so close! Chalk wouldn't let Jasper down. The two of them had been in tougher scrapes before. This was nothing. He had to get Jasper out of the rain. That was all there was to it. Chalk pushed himself, somehow achieving an even faster gait.

Jasper gripped his friend's mane, trying desperately to stay conscious. He didn't have much time left. Too much water was getting to him.

His eyelids were slipping down past his eyes, blocking most of his vision, but he was able to see part of the countryside blurring by.

His mind drifted and he wondered if Chalk might be the fastest horse in Oz. If not, then he was definitely in the top two.

Jasper chuckled. *Good old Chalk,* he thought. Best friend he ever had. *He'll get me back to camp.* He had all the faith in the world in his four-legged friend.

It was Jasper's last thought before everything started to go black.

CHAPTER 17
THE OZMA EXPOSED

Ice cold water splashed across Dorothy's face, bringing her back to the waking world with a start.

She shook her head, disoriented. A pulsing headache pounded away, making it hard to think straight. She hung limply by her chains, breathing hard. Her wrists were hurting from where the metal shackles were digging in. She rose to her feet, flexing her fingers, getting the circulation back.

Blood was dripping from cuts and scratches on her hands and face. Her jacket and slacks were riddled with rips as well. Her jacket had shielded her from much of the attack and she was grateful for it.

A Nome guard stood nearby, using his helmet like a bucket, readying another throw of water in case she blacked out again.

The Witch and Nome King were both watching her.

Studying her.

The Nome King was seated in a blocky, stone throne he had formed out of the ground itself. He was stroking his grey beard and staring at her with humorless eyes.

They had been at this for countless hours. Maybe days.

Dorothy was borderline delirious, having lost all track of time. Her throat was hoarse from screaming and her mouth was dry. She hadn't had any food or water for however long they had been at this. She was starving and her lips were cracked.

The cold water dripping down her face was refreshing and she licked her lips, catching what she could. The water tasted sweet. She wanted more.

All she had to do was tell them where the Ozma was.

But that wasn't going to happen. She had kept silent and would continue to keep silent, no matter the pain they inflicted. She'd never tell them. Never. She'd die before betraying her friends.

All of the crows were gone, except for one perched on the Scarecrow's shoulder. Its head twitched this way and that, tilting it back and forth, observing everyone and everything.

Seeing that Dorothy was once again conscious, the Witch hunched back over her crystal ball with a fierce intensity.

The Nome King patiently watched the Witch, waiting. At times like this, standing perfectly still, with his grey chiseled features, he really could be mistaken for a stone statue.

Creepy, Dorothy thought. He was like an insect, waiting with absolute stillness for some unsuspecting victim to wander into his clutches. He had waited twelve years to capture her, after all. She shuddered. She hated insects and to equate the Nome King to one, just made it harder for her to be strong.

"I see something," the Witch said, her eyes riveted to her

crystal ball. Both hands hovered over it greedily. The purple mist within threw an eerie glow onto her wretched face.

The Nome King came to life, eagerly slinking closer to the pool.

Dorothy's head shot up, worried. She could feel the throbbing in her skull. Instead of trying to get her to give up the information willingly, the Witch was probing her thoughts directly. Dorothy squeezed her eyes shut, trying to block the Witch and cast her out.

The purple mist was swirling at a phenomenal rate inside the crystal. A white light in its center widened outward.

The Witch's long fingers twitched in anticipation.

A fuzzy image formed in the crystal. A hazy blob that slowly coalesced into the shape of a man standing amongst vines and trees. He was metallic and composed of hard angles. It was difficult to see the details, but it was what the man was holding that made his identity immediately apparent to the Witch.

In his hand was a mighty axe.

The Witch's crusty lips curled up into a sinister, gargoyle-like grin. "The Tin Woodsman."

"NO!" Dorothy cried out, desperate to hold onto her secret.

"She's given it to *him* to protect." The Witch continued to focus on the crystal sphere. A predator intent on its prey. She brought her face closer to the polished surface, searching its contents.

"Where is he?" the Nome King demanded, not bothering to hide his excitement.

Dorothy shot the Witch a murderous look. With jaw clenched and hands balled into quivering fists, she put everything she had into keeping the Witch out of her head.

The Witch finally broke contact with her magical crystal and looked over at Dorothy, chuckling.

"The Wild Isle," she said with triumphant satisfaction.

"Nooooooo!" Dorothy burst into tears, losing all strength. She sagged against the cold wall. She hadn't known the Witch would be able to invade her thoughts. To steal the secret out from under her. Dorothy had failed.

The Nome King didn't waste a moment. He called out to his guards. "Gather a team! We leave at once!"

The two guards nodded and rushed out of the room.

The Nome King moved to the back of the cavern and extended both hands.

Almost immediately, the room began to rumble and quake. Bits of loose rock dropped from above, some plinking against the stone floor, others plunking into the pool.

Dorothy could see the strain on his face. The sheer amount of power he was using. His hands were shaking.

He flung his arms wide and the ground in front of him ripped open with an ear-splitting crack. He had created another sloped tunnel leading further below into the underground. His domain.

For a moment the Nome King looked unsteady, rocking from side to side, then he quickly regained his composure, glancing menacingly at the Witch and Dorothy.

Dorothy was too tired to say anything flippant, but it was obvious that the King's power was weakening.

A team of thirty-five Nome guards rushed into the room, armed and ready. Behind them, two mechanical men made of scuffed and dented, riveted copper stomped and clomped into the cavern.

One of the mechanized men was a tall, imposing figure and had circular saw blades for hands. His face was lean, set in a frown. His strong jaw jutted forward with attitude. The shape of his head resembled a football helmet.

The other was shorter and rounder and had massive conical drills for hands. He looked heavier, more solid. His legs were thicker and had wide feet to maintain stability while drilling. He had a cro-magnon brow and his expression was cocky. Ready to pick a fight.

They were construction workers. Dorothy remembered seeing them back when she was younger. Ripsaw and Drillbit were their names, if she recalled correctly. Or maybe their nicknames. She had never actually talked to either one of them. It didn't matter. They were big and tough. And now they worked for the Nome King.

"Our destination is the Wild Isle! Make haste!" the Nome King commanded.

Ripsaw and Drillbit thumped down into the tunnel, followed by the rest of the Nomes and then the Scarecrow.

The crow on the Scarecrow's shoulder took flight, perching on a shard of rock jutting out from a wall.

"I'll let you two get reacquainted." The Nome King winked at Dorothy, chuckling as he disappeared down into the tunnel, leaving her alone in the cavern with the Witch.

The two women stared at each other in heavy silence. The only sound was that of the Witch's watery cell rippling around her in the shape of a perfect sphere. It sounded like a babbling brook.

The silence was broken by the Witch's laughter which started out low, then grew into a full cackle.

"You're not going to get out of this one, my pretty," the Witch teased.

"You're his prisoner too. Do you think he's going to let you live once he's found it? We're both dead," Dorothy said, locking eyes with her. The fear inside was giving way to anger.

"It would seem so, wouldn't it?" The Witch glanced at the one remaining crow and with a twitch of a finger, signaled for it to come over.

The crow leaped off its perch and dove through the watery barrier into the Witch's cell.

She snatched it out of the air, bringing it to her lips.

Dorothy watched as the Witch whispered to the crow, then released it. The bird flew out of the cell and up into the Royal Hall, splattering Dorothy with droplets of water as it flapped by.

"The King is weak. He's dying with the land," the Witch continued, with much more boldness now that they were alone. "Besides… I've been dead before." She shot Dorothy a searing look with her single eye and smirked.

"I hope it hurt," Dorothy said bluntly.

The Witch's grin faded into a grim line. With a quick slice, she scraped her nails across the crystal ball.

Pain lanced through Dorothy's face again. She didn't scream. She was feeling stronger now and able to endure it.

"Do you have any idea what it feels like? To melt away? To have your insides liquefy?" the Witch snarled.

Dorothy grinned. "You should have heard them celebrate." The Munchkins had thrown a huge party for Dorothy after they were told about the Witch's great defeat. While dancing merrily about they had broken out into spontaneous song. Dorothy sang it now, teasing her enemy. "The Witch is dead! The Witch is dead!"

"Stop that!" the Witch growled.

"Sleep tight tonight in bed! Because the Wicked Witch is *DEAD!*"

"STOP!" The Witch brought her hand down onto the crystal with a loud slap. The mists inside whirled about, changing colors.

First yellow, then a bright reddish-orange.

Sweat began to bead on Dorothy's brow. The air around her was heating up to an uncomfortable degree.

"Wicked! You turned them against me with that word!"

"That's what they called you!" Dorothy snapped back.

"They called me the Witch of the West! Just as there was the Witch of the East, North and South!" The Witch's face was twisted with disgust. "It was you with your smug, bratty ways that named me the 'Wicked' Witch and named Glinda the 'Good' Witch."

"It was the truth!" Dorothy gasped, her skin flushing from the heat. The Witch was cooking her alive!

"Oh, make no mistake. You were always a perceptive child." The Witch grinned. "I *AM* wicked. After the Nome King finds your Tin friend, I'm going to let you watch as I destroy him and everyone you've ever cared for!" Her dark eye flared with unholy rage. "Then I'll pluck out your eyes and feed you to the crows! And this time, my pretty—"

She spat that last part out with such venom that Dorothy winced.

The Witch continued, "—your friends won't be around to save you."

CHAPTER 18
THE KNIGHTS OF OZ

Thunder cracked and boomed, sending animals burrowing deeper into their holes, hoping for a brighter day. Pummeling rain continued to fall from the storm laced night sky.

The sound of rumbling thunder didn't fade though. Instead, it seemed to grow. Soon, the ground was shaking and the reason became clear.

It wasn't thunder.

It was hooves.

A team of horses raced over the plains, pounding the ground, carrying their riders.

The lead horse was brilliant white. It was Chalk, snorting and breathing hard, galloping ahead of the others.

Sitting astride him was an imposing sight.

An emerald Knight of Oz.

He was dressed entirely in stylized green armor with gold trimming. His helmet, which completely shielded his head and face, was shaped to resemble an eagle's beak.

As he rode through the downpour, the raindrops struck the metal armor, creating a militaristic musical rhythm.

Riding beside the Knight, on a brown stallion, was a fierce looking warrior. Though his form was human in shape, there was no mistaking his feline heritage. His muscular body was covered in tan fur with a darker, shaggy, lion's mane framing his ferocious face. A patch covered his right eye.

To the other side of the Knight, rode a mechanical man on a mechanical horse. Both made of riveted copper.

The metal man was a stocky, powerful soldier, with a distinctive face design that gave him the appearance of having a thick handlebar mustache. The very top of his head resembled a soldier's helmet from the first World War. The kind that looked like an upside down plate. It had an extended rim all the way around that tilted forward, adding a sense of doggedness to him.

Riding beside the copper soldier was a striking warrior woman composed of bark and greenery. Both she and her horse were living plants. Her long cascading hair was actually ivy and leaves that rustled about her shoulders. Her horse's mane was made of the same. In her left hand, she carried a mace and her stern demeanor showed that she knew how to use it.

Beside her were seven more riders. Some in partial armor, wielding swords and shields. They were all slightly shorter, averaging a little over four feet high.

Munchkins.

The local citizenry of Emerald City. At least they were, until the Nome King had driven them out.

The emerald Knight unsheathed his gleaming sword and

held it forward, leading the charge toward their destination:

Emerald City.

CHAPTER 19
ESCAPE FROM EMERALD CITY

A horn sounded in the distance, drawing the attention of Dorothy and the Witch. Soon, the shouts of battle could be heard along with the clashing of swords.

The two of them looked at each other.

Dorothy couldn't help but to smile. "You were saying?"

The Witch's single eye narrowed and her lips shook with rage. She could barely keep control of herself. "You wretched little girl!" she hissed between clenched teeth.

"I'm not a child anymore." Dorothy stood straight, taking on a regal presence. Confidence coursed through her. She wasn't afraid anymore. "I am Queen of Oz. And this will be the last time that you or the Nome King will threaten this land."

"So be it. The last battle for Oz." The Witch's tone was icy.

No sooner had she spoken, when a Nome guard flew down

into the room, smashed against a wall, then crumpled to the ground.

Dorothy heard metallic feet stomping down the slope toward her. First she saw a pair of copper legs, then the familiar stout body that waddled side to side a little like a penguin, and finally the unique handlebar mustache design on his face.

Dorothy's face lit up. "Tik Tok!"

His stiff features somehow formed into a beaming picture of joy at the sight of her. "Miss Dor-o-thy!"

His halting, robotic voice was deep, reverberating inside his hollow chest. It was also strong, full of compassion and bravery. A soft, mechanical whirring and clicking accompanied his words.

Happy to see her old friend, tears streamed down Dorothy's cheeks. She had always felt safe when he was around. He was, after all, the One Man Army of Oz. A truer friend she had never known.

He rushed to her aid, hesitating only momentarily as he spied the Witch in her watery prison. He gave the hag a sour expression, then in quick succession, he gripped each of Dorothy's chains and snapped them apart with a powerful tug.

The shackles remained on her wrists and would have to be dealt with at a later time.

Dorothy wrapped her arms around him, ignoring how cold his metal frame was. "I'm sorry I took so long."

Tik Tok patted her on the back. "It could-n't be helped. No re-grets, no re-grets. You're here now and that's all that mat-ters."

Another pair of metallic footsteps was coming down the slope. The emerald Knight charged into the room, sword in hand, ready for a fight. He focused immediately on Dorothy, then noticed the Witch who scowled in his direction.

The sight of the emerald Knight standing so heroically left

Dorothy a bit wide-eyed. He stepped to her side and removed his helmet. Dorothy's eyes grew even wider. Underneath was Jasper.

His jaw tightened seeing her cuts and bruises. "Are you alright?"

She nodded. Starry eyed, a lopsided grin spread across her face. "You came back for me."

"I had my orders," he said with a devilish smile and a wink.

"Sweet words poison my ears and sicken my soul," the Witch groaned with disgust.

Jasper gave her a piercing stare. "I thought you were dead, Maghamil."

"Did you miss me?" she said sarcastically, arching a brow.

"I joined in the celebrations," he replied.

The Witch's expression darkened.

Once again, Dorothy was perplexed by the exchange, but before she could ask, the feline soldier strode into the room carrying a sword.

"LION!" Dorothy was shocked and elated to see another of her old friends. Then she noticed the patch over his eye and the grim weariness that clung around him like a stormy cloud.

He glanced at her, then fixated on the Witch. A growl rose from his furry chest. "I should have known you were part of this." His words rolled out with a snarl and flash of fangs.

The Witch eyed them all bitterly. Her body stiffened with apprehension at seeing so many of her enemies in one room.

With a ferocious growl, the Lion launched himself at her.

The Witch instantly placed a hand on her crystal ball and raised the other toward the Lion.

An invisible force struck him, knocking him back. He regained his footing and snarled again, this time throwing his sword at her.

With one hand still on her crystal, the Witch swung her other out, swatting the air inside her cell.

The invisible force struck the sword aside, flinging it straight at Dorothy!

Jasper barely managed to bring his own sword up to deflect the flying blade, sending it clanging against the cavern's wall. He turned to the Lion. "General! Stop, before the Queen is injured!"

Dorothy rushed up to the Lion, pressing her hands into the wet fur on his chest. She traced the scars around his patch-covered eye. "Oh Lion. What happened to you?"

His haggard face softened slightly, looking down at her.

The Witch cackled in the background. "Be careful what you wish for. It was foolish courage that claimed his eye."

"Shut up!" Dorothy was letting the Witch get to her.

The Lion lifted Dorothy's chin with a thick claw. "It's the truth. I rushed into battles without thinking. There was a price for my bravery."

"Thorns, my pretty. With a rose come the thorns," the Witch said, taunting her.

Dorothy turned toward her, shaking with anger. "I said, SHUT UP!"

The Witch broke into a maniacal cackle.

That was it. Dorothy couldn't take it anymore. She snatched up the fallen Nome's helmet and scooped it into the pool, filling it with water. She lifted it, giving the Witch a deadly stare as she prepared to throw it at her.

The Witch flicked her wrist and the invisible force knocked the helmet out of Dorothy's hands, spilling its contents harmlessly onto the floor. "You had your chance once before. You won't get another," the Witch said, laughing under her breath.

Dorothy was still shaking with anger. Jasper held her back,

calming her.

Tik Tok glanced up the slope into the ballroom. Angry shouts and metal striking metal continued to echo from above. "Gen-e-ral, we should de-part. The sounds of bat-tle will soon draw the Nome King."

The Lion nodded, his attitude shifting back to that of a soldier.

Dorothy stopped him. "He's already gone. He knows where the Ozma is. We have to get it before him!"

The Lion's square jaw clenched, making his whiskers quiver. "Where is it?"

"The Wild Isle." Dorothy watched all of the Knights glance at each other with hesitant eyes. She knew how remote and dangerous the island was. Home to some of the most frightening creatures of Oz. It was the main reason she had asked the Tin Man to hide the Ozma there.

"You can transport us with your slippers," Jasper said, then looked down and saw that she was just in her white socks. "Where are they?"

She slapped the stone wall, feeling how hard it was. "He put them in here. Deep inside the rock."

Jasper felt the cool, solid surface. "We'll never get through that. We'll have to travel without them."

The Lion looked down into the gaping, newly formed hole in the floor. "He's tunneling underground?"

Dorothy nodded. "Yeah."

"Why didn't he use the slippers himself?" Jasper asked.

Dorothy shook her head. "He's tried that before. His own magic interferes with them. He never knows where he's going to end up."

"Then we can overtake him by land if we hurry." The Lion

picked up his sword and headed up the slope into the ballroom.

Tik Tok stomped out after him.

Jasper took Dorothy's hand, about to escort her up the slope.

"Your journey will be perilous," the Witch teased.

Dorothy stopped and looked back at the Witch.

The Witch pursed her lips, shaking her head. "It would be a shame for you to die before I get my hands around your neck, my pretty."

"Don't worry. I'm coming back for you." Dorothy turned and walked out with Jasper at her side. They could hear the Witch burst into wild laughter behind them.

Making their way through the Royal Hall was easy. Most of the Nomes had been slain and merely had to be stepped over. Black sand and dust was everywhere. The courtyard was the same.

Once outside, Jasper donned his helmet again to protect him from the rain.

They freed an extra horse from the guard's stable for Dorothy and soon they were outside the city, riding into the night.

The rain felt good. Cold, but good. Dorothy closed her eyes, letting it wash away the sweat and blood.

Wash away the remnants of her previous life.

It was refreshing, rejuvenating her tired body. When she opened her eyes again, they were clear and focused.

She leaned forward, spurring her horse onward ahead of the group.

CHAPTER 20
THE SIGHTING

The following day, the sun hid behind a wall of smoky clouds, leaving Oz in a dreary, somber state.

Chilled winds blew from one direction, then another, changing every hour, so that there was no way to keep warm. At least the rain had ceased.

Dorothy and her troop had ridden nonstop for most of the day since escaping Emerald City. They had crossed the once golden fields of Shimmer Plains, now a blackened blight on the landscape. Then through the shrunken and shriveled fruit trees of Flavorful Forest and over the desolate rolling hills of Tumbletown. All of these places mere shadows of their former selves. Ghostly and deserted, a grim reminder of how much was at stake.

It was quiet. No animals stirred, preferring to hide or to migrate to the farther reaches of Oz. The only sound was the suction of hooves in drying mud and the clunking of stones being kicked aside.

No one had really spoken the entire day, other than to deliberate which routes they should take. Except for Jasper, who occasionally checked on how Dorothy was doing. Those little moments made her smile and brightened her mood.

So it was a surprise when the Lion swung around toward the rest of the group and snapped sharply at them, "Take cover!"

The Lion jumped from his steed and crept up behind a massive boulder, holding onto his horse's reins.

Dorothy and the others did the same. She leaned over the Lion's shoulder to spy what had gotten him so tense.

It was a mountain range known as the Fearsome Four. Four unconnected sky high mountains that were treacherous to cross and inhabited by Lurkers—terrible frog-like goblins that lived inside a network of caves and were extremely territorial.

The mountains were definitely something Dorothy intended on avoiding, but they were far enough away that she found it strange that the Lion should be so cautious. She wondered if he had lost his courage again.

Then she saw it.

It was hard *not* to see actually.

Walking around the base of the mountains was a gigantic, hundred-foot high mechanical man, patrolling the area. Geysers of steam shot out from pipes in its back in sporadic bursts.

"An Iron Giant?" Dorothy asked, incredulous.

The Lion nodded. "The Nome King brought over a dozen or so. They police the lands, looking for any rebels."

Ready to pound them into dust, thought Dorothy. She had encountered one before. They carried massive hammers that they were more than willing to use.

The Nome King had commissioned the first giant as a sentinel to his own fortress back in the day. The Iron Giants were literally that—giants made of iron. Non-thinking behemoths constructed by Smith & Tinker, a factory in the Land of Ev, a country in the outer lands, across the Deadly Desert. Near the Nome King's dominion.

Smith & Tinker were also responsible for Tik Tok. One of the few positives to come out of that mysterious factory. They had built him and given him as a gift to the Wizard as a peace offering during a troubled time, long before Dorothy had ever set foot in Oz.

That first giant had nearly killed Dorothy and her friends. Luck and some magic had been on their side. They had no magic now and it would be almost impossible to survive another encounter without it.

The rest of the Knights had edged around them and had seen the danger. The Munchkins whispered amongst themselves in awe.

They watched the Giant rip up handfuls of trees, scattering scores of frightened birds into the air. It lifted the trees up above its head and dropped them into its open mouth, devouring them like tasty treats.

There was a loud gasp. Dorothy glanced over to see Willow Bitterbark, the plant woman, recoiling in horror. Dorothy realized those trees could be her relatives. "Are they your kind?"

Willow shook her head, her wooden face contorting into hard lines of anger. "No. But the death of any tree is a tragedy."

"Why does it eat trees?" asked a portly Munchkin named Pok, who was visibly disgusted at the thought of such a bland diet. His rounded belly was proof that he knew a thing or two about food and trees weren't on the menu.

"Burns them for fuel. It's steam powered," answered Dorothy.

"Mag-nif-i-cent de-sign," Tik Tok said with admiration.

Dorothy and Jasper both looked at him.

Jasper put a hand on Tik Tok's round shoulder and leaned in. "Take a good look, friend, because I don't want to get any closer."

Tik Tok nodded. "A pi-ty that they weren't giv-en a clock-work brain."

Dorothy silently agreed. If the Iron Giants had just half of Tik Tok's personality, the world would be a better place. And if they were as loyal as Tik Tok... well, Oz would never have to worry about being invaded again.

They waited, watching it pass by the mountains, then away from them in a westerly direction. Deep reverberations were felt in the ground from each of its colossal footsteps.

With so many of the giants roaming around Oz, Dorothy knew she and her Knights would have to stay alert. The farther away the metal giant went, the more the Knights relaxed.

The group was so focused on one potential threat that they failed to hear the approach of another.

The large shadow fell over them, followed by a great rush of air.

Before anyone could react, the Munchkin named Pok was snatched first.

Then Dorothy.

CHAPTER 21
THE FLIGHT OF THE GROON

The world had dropped away from Dorothy's feet, as did her stomach. She found herself flailing her arms and legs, trying instinctively to find something solid to stand upon.

Far below, she glimpsed Jasper and the others looking up at her in shock. They were growing smaller and smaller. Jasper jumped onto Chalk and chased after her. The rest of the Knights instantly followed suit.

Casting a glance to her right, she spotted Pok gripped firmly in the claws of a huge bird creature.

Well, it was feathered and had wings, but that was where the similarity ended. Its long neck led to a monstrous, bulbous shaped jaw full of crooked sharp teeth. Its beady black eyes squinted ahead, its lids protecting against the winds. A featherless rat-like tail dangled behind it. Its feathers were bright red with yellow stripes, giving it a predatory look and its wingspan was over twenty feet!

It was a groon.

Dorothy looked up and saw that she was in the clutches of an almost identical monster, the only difference being that hers was a darker shade of red.

She'd never seen a groon in person, but had heard about them. They normally kept to themselves near the peaks of the Fearsome Four mountains.

Which is where they were currently heading.

Why are they so far from their home? Dorothy wondered. Maybe food was scarce now and they had to fly farther out to hunt. Or maybe the Iron Giant had disturbed them. Either way, it was bad. She was helpless.

Pok was heavier and fighting mad. His groon was having a hard time carrying him. Dorothy caught a glint of light and saw that Pok had pulled out a dagger, with which he proceeded to stab at the creature.

The groon howled and wavered in its flight, trying to drop him, but he held on, slicing and poking at it. The creature swooped down low, trying to scrape him off its leg. That was Pok's intent, and he let go, rolling across the dirt, free of the creature. The wounded groon shot upward, retreating as fast as it could.

Dorothy watched the Knights ride toward Pok, helping him up. Jasper and the Lion didn't stop, continuing to chase after her. They were almost underneath her.

I'm too high up, she thought, *they can't help me.* Her groon had climbed skyward and it was a good fifty foot drop now to the ground. She had no blade of any kind to follow Pok's example. She was stuck.

Dorothy had stopped struggling while watching Pok's brief battle and had just let herself dangle under the creature, buffeted by the winds. She had the uneasy feeling of sliding down, away from the monster. She was slipping out of her jacket! The groon's claws were clamped tightly onto her jacket and nothing else.

Acting quickly, before she lost her nerve, she maneuvered one arm out and grabbed onto the creature's leathery leg, making sure she had a firm grip.

It let out a yelp of surprise and snuck a glance underneath itself, giving her a suspicious glare.

Dorothy yanked her other arm out of her jacket and threw that hand up towards its side, grabbing a handful of feathers.

The monster squawked, jumping a couple of feet higher in alarm. After it settled again, Dorothy let go of its leg to grab another section of feathers, pulling herself up toward its back. It felt her movement and started to tilt side to side, trying to shake her off.

Holding on for dear life, her feet swung out into open space, giving her a cold sweat. She managed to hook an arm around the base of its right wing and leverage herself up, her socked feet scrambling against its body.

The groon shrieked in a panic and rolled, diving down toward the ground.

The movement gave Dorothy a split second to save herself. She wrapped both arms around the beasts neck and clamped her feet under its wings. Her stomach didn't just drop this time, it parachuted out of her body. The ground was spiraling toward her. She screamed and shut her eyes.

Then there was a surge of gravity. It pulled on every part of her. The feeling left her queasy. She felt herself rising… rising. She opened her eyes to see that the creature had changed course at the last minute, wrenching itself back up into the air. It hurled itself to the side, in a series of rolls. Dorothy hugged the groon's neck so tight, her arms were beginning to cramp.

She had to get control of this thing if she wanted to survive. When it finally stopped spinning and stabilized itself, she seized its long, pointed ears, twisting them slightly to let it know she was in charge.

The groon screamed and bucked, which only made Dorothy twist its delicate ears harder. The creature learned quickly. Sudden movements caused more pain. With minor yanks and squeezes, Dorothy gained control, making it descend toward the ground. It was coming in a little fast and with a quick tug from her, it flapped its wings to slow itself.

"Good girl," Dorothy said, giving it a pat on the head.

It honked appreciatively.

She grinned triumphantly as it touched down for a gentle, if awkward, landing.

She slid off, grateful to feel the ground under her feet again. She gave the groon a slap on the rear. "Off you go!"

It made a chastened sound, like a bark and chomp combined, then flapped up and away, stirring up a cloud of dust.

Too late, she realized her jacket was still hanging from its claws. She watched it rise higher and higher as the groon flew back home. She sighed. That was her favorite jacket and she was really going to miss it.

Jasper and the Knights arrived only seconds later, skidding to a stop, creating a bigger dust cloud. Jasper didn't even wait for Chalk to stop before hopping to the ground and rushing up to her aid.

She was fine and said so. "What about you, Pok? It looked like you had a rough landing."

Pok rubbed his left elbow and grinned. "Just a scrape, M'Lady. Didn't think to ride the blasted beast. Silly me."

They all laughed. With the danger gone, it all seemed comical in hindsight.

Jasper crossed his arms. "So this is how it's going to be?"

"How what is?" Dorothy asked.

"A lot of you showing off in the face of danger?" Jasper said, smirking.

"Basically, yeah." Dorothy laughed, her nose wrinkling slightly. "It's kind of what I do here."

* * *

Several hours later, the Knights had made good time after the groon attack, heading northeast into a wasteland of rock and canyons.

They had to slow their pace as they traversed the dried mud and loose shale. Chalk had told them their horses needed the break anyway. They had ridden them pretty hard chasing after Dorothy and Pok.

Their sluggish march was making them all impatient.

Dorothy knew that they were in a race for the fate of Oz itself, but killing themselves wouldn't help. They and their horses were going to have to rest along the way. It was a fact they had to accept. She just hoped that the Nome King's weakened condition was slowing him down too.

Lost in their own thoughts, the group rode through a patch of dead trees, oblivious to two crows perched high on a twisted branch. The dingy birds watched the troop pass underneath, cocking their heads, keeping their sharp eyes on them.

As the Knights made their way down a steep ravine, the

Lion was the only one who heard the crows leave. After the groons, he was alert to the sound of flapping wings. He looked back and saw the two crows departing from the dead trees, heading off in the opposite direction.

It made the hairs on the back of his spine straighten. His lip rolled up over his fangs, making his whiskers quiver in irritation.

It was a bad omen.

CHAPTER 22
FAMILY SECRETS

The campfires crackled under the night sky.

The storms had mercifully moved on. A blessing since there was no cover to be had.

Dorothy and her Knights were camped out in the open, near the remains of a meadow, huddled around their two fires.

It was a dry night, but still cold. Icy winds whistled across the plains, making Dorothy's bones ache. Without her jacket, she was freezing. She held out her hands toward the fire, basking in its soothing warmth.

They knew they were taking a chance with the campfires. That they might draw attention, but the group would freeze otherwise. And the Iron Giants shouldn't be a problem, since they tended not to be active in the dark, due to poor night vision.

Tik Tok and Willow Bitterbark stood at the edges of the

camp, keeping watch. Tik Tok had no need for warmth and Willow, with her wooden limbs, had a deep respect for fire, knowing what it could do to her kind.

Willow had been appalled to find out that their mission was to locate the Tin Woodsman. She considered him to be a murderer of trees. Which, Dorothy thought, she had a point. It had been a touchy situation, but Willow knew they were fighting for the land of Oz itself, so she was willing to put aside her personal bias. Dorothy was relieved as the group needed whatever help they could get.

Grouped around the other fire, were the seven Munchkins, chattering amongst themselves, laughing occasionally and singing lively little tunes which brought a smile to Dorothy's face.

Most of the Munchkins were unfamiliar to her, simply citizens of Emerald City who took up the fight after the Nome King decimated the city's royal guards. During their journey, there hadn't been much conversation, but she had learned their names.

There were the twin brothers, Wik and Mik, both with a splash of blonde hair and freckles. They were very close and the most athletic of the bunch. They both always seemed to be on the verge of laughing at a private joke between them.

Hup was the jokester, always ready with a sarcastic quip or playful prank. He was the most handsome of them, with shaggy red hair and a twinkle in his hazel eyes.

Kob had curly dark hair and piercing blue eyes. He was the quietest of the group. He was also the most serious, or what passed for most serious amongst Munchkins, since they were known for being quite joyful.

Pok was a sweetheart. He loved food and food loved him. He had a round belly that didn't seem to slow him down, surprisingly enough, as she had seen during his fight with the groon.

From what she could gather, they had all been part of a club or guild. She also noticed that they all had a tendency to suck on lollipops, of which they seemed to have quite a stash packed away in their saddlebags.

And then there was Boq and Bom, who were father and son. She knew Boq from the old days. Once the wealthiest Munchkin, now grey of hair and living hand to mouth like the rest of them.

He had been one of the first Munchkins to welcome her on her initial visit. Well into his elder years, he was obviously still in fighting shape.

Bom, who was only a child the last time she had seen him, was now a young man, probably nineteen, she guessed. Curly auburn hair stuck out from under his farmer's cap. His friendly face a mirror image of his dad.

Except for Boq, they were all much too young to be going to battle. It broke her heart to hear them joking and having fun, knowing that where they were going, there was a chance some of them wouldn't be coming back.

"Here." Jasper draped his green military jacket around her shoulders.

Dorothy pulled it tight. "Thanks."

Jasper sat down next to her, thankfully taking her mind away from the distressing thoughts.

He set his helmet and gauntlets on the ground beside him and handed her some bread and cured meat.

"Your Highness," he said with a mischievous grin.

"Enough of that. Call me Dorothy." She took the food and nibbled on it, while stretching her legs out in front of her. She still wasn't wearing shoes and her white socks were now a light brown, caked with mud and grime. One hung pathetically low around her ankle.

"My socks have seen better days," she said, wiggling her toes.

He laughed. "You want my boots? They'd be a little big."

"I'll be alright." She looked over at him, studying his ruggedly handsome face. A thought was nagging her, pulling at the corner of her mind. "Jasper?"

He caught her staring at him. His grin widened. "Yes?"

"What you said to the Nome King back there…"

Jasper's smile vanished and he quickly held a finger over his lips, signaling for her to be quiet. He glanced around to see if anyone was listening, then leaned close to her and whispered, "No one knows. Well, except Chalk. And now you."

Dorothy drew closer, talking in a hushed voice. "Then it's true? He's really your—" She left the word unsaid.

Jasper's face hardened. He nodded.

She couldn't believe it. "And how do you know the Witch?"

He took a bite of meat and chewed. For a moment, it seemed like he wasn't going to answer, then—"He created her before me. I guess you could say she's my sister."

Dorothy was dumbfounded. This man beside her—this very *attractive* man—was related to two of her worst enemies. She stared down at the ground in front of her in shock.

"You can see why I don't want anyone to know," he said earnestly. "With a heritage like that, no one would trust me."

She looked back at him, sizing him up. She could see how tense he was for having told her. His penetrating eyes were searching hers for solace. His jaw muscles clenched and released repeatedly. A random thought surfaced in her mind, wondering if he even had muscles. He was made of clay after all. He was made of dirt. Not human.

Then again, the Tin Man, Tik Tok and the Lion weren't human either and she considered them family. She loved them without reservation.

He was right though. He would be deemed a spy if anyone found out. Who could trust someone like that? Dorothy looked into his bright, pained eyes. Saw how he looked at her. How brave and honest he was. She knew there was at least one person he could rely on. "*I* trust you."

Jasper's features relaxed, relieved of the secret burden he'd been carrying with him all these years. That he'd been hiding from her. The pain started to ease away. "That's all that matters then."

They both stared at the fire in silence. It crackled and sent glowing ash drifting up into the night sky.

Though the storms were gone, the clouds remained. A constant oppressive blanket that kept the land engulfed in a suffocating haze of gloom. At night however, at least this night, there were a few holes in that blanket and she could see the stars were out.

The stars didn't resemble any that Dorothy had ever seen back home. They were closer. And more brilliant. Maybe they weren't even stars at all, but fairies or some other wonderful Ozite resident living above the clouds. In Oz, nothing was ever what it seemed.

She felt closer than ever to Jasper. Bonded. They were sharing secrets. Now it was her turn.

"I'm not sure I can do this," she said softly, almost under her breath. "Saving Oz, I mean. Everyone's counting on me…"

Jasper shook his head and pointed at her. "Now see. That's where *I* trust *you*. You're stronger than you know. Look at how you handled that groon."

His smile was contagious. It sparked a small explosion of

fuzzy warmth in Dorothy's chest that quickly spread throughout her body making her feel slightly drunk.

The flickering firelight reflected off his green armor, making it seem alive. Magical. It was hard not to stare at him. "I have to say… that armor looks good on you. Makes you look dashing."

"I know."

"You jerk." She slapped him on the arm and the shackles, still on her wrists, clanged against his armor. Tik Tok had broken the chains off, but the shackles remained intact. Her hand bounced off the metal. "Ow! See if I say anything nice about you again." She shook her hand, trying to alleviate the pain.

He laughed. "Here, let me take care of that." He produced a slim dagger, hidden about his waist, and held out his hand.

Dorothy placed her hand in his palm. It was warm for a man made of clay. She watched him carefully slip the tip of the dagger into the shackle's keyhole and expertly twitch the blade back and forth, followed by a half circle spin and then—click! The metal bolt popped off, freeing her hand.

He gently massaged her wrist, getting circulation back into the area. "You know, M'Lady—" he hesitated, then used her name, "Dorothy…"

She laughed at his awkwardness.

Jasper gave a wry smile and continued, "—assaulting a Knight of Oz is grounds for arrest."

"Oh?"

"Lucky for you, I know the Queen. I can put in a good word on your behalf." He arched an eyebrow, taking on an air of cocky self-importance.

"Wow, pretty impressive," she said, feigning surprise. "So, you and the Queen… are you *just* friends?"

Jasper paused, caught off guard, then continued massaging

her hand. "I wouldn't presume to guess what goes on in the Queen's heart."

She clasped his hand. "You strike me as a pretty good guesser."

He froze. Their eyes locked. With that stare, questions were silently asked and permissions given. Ever so slowly, they both started to lean in for a kiss—

Just then, the Lion approached, shattering the moment. He sat down off to the side, across from them.

Dorothy and Jasper pulled away from each other, covering their actions.

Jasper took her other wrist and made a show of struggling to get the last shackle off.

She felt her face become hot, not because she was embarrassed, but because of what had almost just happened. This was a new experience for her. Her emotions were running wild and she was having a hard time regaining control of them.

Was this love? She'd never been in love before. Never had a boyfriend. All of her adult life—including her teen years—had been lived in a state of limbo. Walking around in zombie mode. She had missed out on puppy loves, crushes and first kisses. Now her feelings were crashing against themselves, yearning to be let out.

The shackle finally popped free and fell to the ground with a thunk.

She rubbed her wrist. "Thank you, Jasper." She meant it in more ways than one.

He slipped the dagger back into its sheath, then held it out to her, handle first. "Take it. In case another groon kidnaps you."

She smiled and took it, placing it on her lap, resting both hands on it.

Jasper glanced fleetingly at the Lion.

The Lion seemed unaware of them, lost in thought, staring at his food with his one good eye.

Jasper threw another dead branch onto the fire. It popped and hissed angrily, the flames eagerly consuming the fresh fuel.

Dorothy found herself focusing on the Lion.

He was so sad. So alone. It was a far cry from the lively Lion she used to know. He had been cowardly, true, but full of spirit. Now he was a solemn warrior, bereft of joy. She was drawn toward the worn leather patch covering his right eye.

"It was the Scarecrow," the Lion growled.

She jumped, not thinking he had noticed her. "What?"

The Lion turned to her. "You're wondering how I lost my eye. It was the Scarecrow and his birds."

CHAPTER 23
CHILDHOOD'S END

"Why?" The question came out of Dorothy's mouth in a shaken whisper.

"I don't have an answer. I walked into the Scarecrow's trap, not suspecting he had switched sides." The Lion tapped his head with a thick claw. "I do know that with his new brain, he was becoming obsessed with learning as much as he could. Maybe the Nome King used that to sway him."

She shook her head, refusing to believe it. "No, they did something to him. He would never intentionally harm us."

"As the Witch said—be careful what you wish for. There were drawbacks to our gifts," he glanced at her. "Mine cost me my eye. Maybe the Scarecrow's cost him his loyalty. Yours cost you your home."

"And poor Tin Man has been alone all these years, cut off

from the people that he loves," Dorothy said softly, almost to herself, realizing the truth in the Lion's words. She shook her head, trying to make sense of it all. "Everything is so different now."

The Lion ripped off a piece of cured meat. "You saw the world through the eyes of a child," he said, while chewing.

She glanced back over at him, surprised. "Weird. The Wizard said almost the exact same thing."

"You found him?" The Lion perked up, his lone amber eye swinging around to look at her.

"He's not in any danger. We can go back for him after we find the Ozma. He's so old and frail, he would've only been a liability." Look at that, she thought, she was starting to sound like a Queen again.

The Lion nodded, contemplating the new information. Strategizing. Truly looking like the General that he was.

Dorothy remembered something. "When I left, I gave you the order to evacuate the Munchkins—"

The corners of the Lion's mouth curved upward. "They're safely hidden in the south." He paused, then added, "Along with Toto."

Dorothy couldn't contain her excitement. "Toto? But how is he still—?"

"Time works differently here, you know that." There was a twinkle in the Lion's eye. "He's old, but still very much alive."

Tears started to burn in her eyes. Dorothy wiped them away, before they fully formed, otherwise she'd crack. *Toto*. Her trusty canine companion who had accompanied her on so many of her escapades. How she would love to see him again.

When she looked back up at the Lion, there was a glimmer of amusement in his expression and soon he was chuckling.

"What's so funny?" She couldn't help herself and started to giggle. It was a relief to see her old friend finally lighten up.

He shook his head, his silky mane fluffing out side to side. "I was thinking of what a terror you were as a child."

"A terror! Thanks a lot!"

"You have no idea the trouble we had trying to protect you on your adventures," he said, with a big broad grin. His fangs glistened, but there was no animosity in it, only affection.

"I didn't think I was so bad." She leaned forward, elbows on her knees, laughing.

"You were brash and confident. Hard to restrain."

Jasper was laughing along with them. "I can see that."

"I'm sorry." Dorothy gave the Lion a sincere look of apology. In that moment, it was as if no time had passed. They had shared so many experiences together. They were the closest of friends and trusted each other with their lives.

The Lion gazed at Dorothy with a fondness that made her heart swell. "You've grown into a strong woman, Dorothy. You were a *good* Queen when you were young. Now—I think you will be an *excellent* one."

Jasper nodded in agreement.

"I con-cur." This from Tik Tok, who was never far from Dorothy or his General. He had sidled up without them hearing his heavy footsteps.

Tears welled up in her eyes again. She wiped them away with the sides of her hand. "Thank you. I've missed you all so much."

Jasper placed his hand on her back, moving it in small gentle circles, giving her strength.

She took a deep breath, regaining her composure. "We better get some rest so we can get an early start."

"I will stand watch while you sleep, Miss Dor-o-thy," declared Tik Tok, his short powerful body somehow appearing taller and larger than life. It was the way he held himself. So noble and proud.

"Do you need me to wind you? You should be low on power by now." Dorothy just noticed that she hadn't seen anyone wind him up during their travels. That was his one weakness. Always at the mercy of his gears slowly running down.

Tik Tok thrust a copper finger into the air. "Ah! Al-ways room for im-prove-ments, Miss Dor-o-thy! The Oz en-gin-eers have solved that prob-lem," His mustache almost seemed to wiggle back and forth with excitement. "Thought, ac-tion, and speech are now com-bined and fur-ther-more, I am self wound now!"

She clapped her hands together. "That's wonderful, Tok! I'm so happy for you!"

He thumped his chest, so that a deep reverberating echo rang out. "Rest eas-y while I'm on du-ty. You need not wor-ry a-bout me an-y lon-ger."

Dorothy watched him stomp away to the camp's perimeter, where he took up position. His body motionless, but his head swiveling back and forth, scanning the area. Tik Tok was one of a kind and she loved him for it.

"Some things are still the way I remember them," she said wistfully.

The Lion grunted in agreement. "If there's one thing in Oz you can count on, it's him. Loyalty to the land was built into his gears."

Dorothy continued to watch Tik Tok.

So much had changed. The Lion's gift of courage had left him scarred, both physically and emotionally. The Scarecrow had switched sides, thirsty to fill his new brain with knowledge. The Witch was back and wanted revenge. Even the land itself had become grey and dreary.

Tik Tok was the only thing that *hadn't* changed and she was grateful for that small favor.

Looking at him now, she mourned the loss of a very happy and very innocent childhood.

CHAPTER 24
THE SCARECROW'S MISSION

The two spies flew through the night, soaring high above the land of Oz.

Their wings were tired from their journey, yet they pushed themselves, knowing by instinct that their goal was near.

It rose up on the horizon, a beacon signaling the end of their strenuous flight. The city of Emeralds.

Soon they were weaving between the jade towers, closing in on the Royal Palace. They folded their wings and dove straight down, extending them again at the last possible second to glide into the building's arched entrance.

They streaked through the halls like black arrows, whipping around corners, then into the ballroom and down into the cavern, where a surprised Witch watched them with interest as they disappeared into the underground tunnel.

* * *

Deep inside the tunnel, the Nomes worked furiously, digging further and further for their master.

They had but a fraction of the Nome King's power, enough to soften sections of rock and dirt, to carve away and apply to the sides of the tunnel walls, reinforcing them. They labored diligently and silently, with only the occasional grunt of effort.

Both Ripsaw and Drillbit did their part to cut through the strata.

Behind the frontline, the Nome King patiently watched his minions toil away.

The Scarecrow stood nearby, hunched a bit, with glazed eyes, simply waiting for the King's next command.

Alarmed squawks echoed from back down the passage.

The Scarecrow turned his canvas head to see two crows rushing toward him. He lifted his arm for them to perch.

Upon landing, the birds launched into a series of excited squawks.

The Scarecrow listened intently.

"Silence those birds before I rip off their beaks!" the Nome King snapped in irritation.

The Scarecrow held up a hand to the crows, quieting them. "They bring news."

"What is it?" The Nome King was becoming more annoyed. He knew the Ozma was within his grasp and everything else was just a distraction.

"The girl has escaped, my Lord."

That got the Nome King's attention. He whirled around to give the Scarecrow a piercing stare.

The Scarecrow continued, unfazed by the Nome King's reaction. "The Lion and his Knights are with her. They appear to be heading toward the Wild Isle as well."

"Doom and damnation!" the Nome King bellowed in frustration, punching a hole in the rock wall. He took a deep breath, exhaling in one long rumbling sigh as he mulled over the news. "She's too dangerous. She can't be allowed to interfere anymore." He turned back to the Scarecrow. "Do you understand?"

The straw man nodded once. "Yes."

"Then go," The Nome King said, "Seek her out and destroy her."

"As you wish, my Lord," the Scarecrow said, bowing slightly.

The Nome King concentrated, drawing his power into his clenched fist. He threw it up into the air, opening his hand.

The rock above them exploded outward in a series of bursts, creating a narrow fissure to the surface. Murky daylight glinted near the top.

The Scarecrow climbed up into the fissure, moving like a spider with his long limbs stretching out, seeking purchase. It was barely wide enough to let his slender form fit inside.

Up he went, past exposed tangled roots, past the Wombo Worms wiggling back into their square holes, and past aggressive Blister Beetles that snapped at his sleeves.

Creeping from the crack in the ground, the Scarecrow stood tall, surveying his surroundings. The winds rustled his straw and made the brim of his hat flap.

He was in the middle of nowhere. A stark flatland of dead grass.

She was out there somewhere. And he had his orders.

CHAPTER 25
THE MYSTERIOUS MORNING

On the very next morning, it wasn't the pleasant chirping of the songbirds that pulled Dorothy from her deeply satisfying slumber, nor was it the scent of the dazzleday flowers (her favorite!) that filled the air.

No, it was the delightfully warm sensation of the sun on her skin that finally did it.

Dorothy rubbed her sleepy eyes and sat up. She was greeted with a world bursting with color. It was all so bright and bold that she had to squint, allowing her eyes to adjust.

The first thing that struck her was the startlingly beautiful blue sky above.

After two days of being trapped under the impenetrable cloud cover, it was finally gone and in its place was a clear sky that was almost too pretty to look at. A few puffy brilliant clouds were scattered about and an absolutely gorgeous sun beamed down on her.

She inhaled deeply, sucking in a lungful of fresh summer air. Mingled with the flowery smell, it was intoxicating. She looked around and saw that she was sitting in a luscious field of vibrant green grass that was so soft, she had to fight the urge to lie back down and go to sleep again.

Trees swayed in the light breeze, making a pleasant rustling sound. The sounds of summer.

Pockets of dazzledays surrounded the area, their bright orange, spiral-shaped petals spinning like pinwheels, showcasing their eye-popping bright blue interiors.

There were also pockets of tinglebells. Red flowers shaped like upside-down bells, trimmed with green. Their stems were white with red striping, like a candy cane. They even had a peppermint aroma. They got their name because if one touched the stem, it would give out a tingling shock of static electricity.

Dorothy stood up and stretched her arms out, thrilled to see Oz back to the way she remembered it.

Walking over to a patch of flowers, she picked a dazzleday and held it under her nose, taking in its wonderfully spicy smell. Like vanilla and cinnamon with a hint of strawberry. Maybe a little nutmeg too.

A thought crossed her mind. Where had the others gone? She twirled the flower in her hands as she looked around. She didn't see any sign of them. No imprints in the grass where they may have slept. No gear sitting nearby. Come to think of it, no sign of their campfires either. Curious.

Another aromatic pleasure wafted her way. It was the smell of yumberries. *No, better yet,* she thought, *that's yumberry pie.* Her stomach growled. The name said it all. *Yummy. Best pie I've ever had.* She licked her lips, craving a taste.

The lingering scent led her through the trees, where she emerged into another grassy field near a stream. A little white and yellow cottage stood by the water with puffs of smoke rising from its chimney. It was a charming residence and very inviting.

Dorothy strolled up to the cottage and peered through the windows, wondering who it belonged to.

Inside, she saw Hup, Kob and Pok! It looked like all of her friends were inside. They were sitting around a table having a feast!

Excited, she tried the doorknob. It was unlocked.

She opened it and was met with the sounds of conversation, laughter and the tinking of silverware on plates.

All of the Knights were seated at a square wooden table that had abundant food and drink all along it. There was the yumberry pie, with plenty of slices left. And several roast buzzbirds with mashed magogo on the side. There were also steaming soups and pitchers of various drinks. It all smelled so delicious.

"There you are!" Jasper saw her and waved her over. He pulled up a chair for her and she sat down.

"I was wondering where you all went," Dorothy said, raising her voice to be heard over the raucous laughter of the Knights.

She plated a piece of the pie and took a bite. It melted in her mouth, sending her taste-buds into a state of euphoria. Warm yumberry inside a crumbly cinnamon crust. She closed her eyes savoring it.

The pie was perfect. So sweet with just the right amount of tanginess. The flavor was hard to describe to someone who's never had it. There was a bit of an apple pie flavor with some boysenberry and banana mixed in.

Jasper leaned in close, so she could hear him. "We woke up early and decided to let you rest. We went exploring and found this cottage, so we made ourselves at home."

His voice pulled Dorothy out of her pie induced haze. She nodded, completely understanding why they didn't come back for her. Who would want to leave? "It's okay. Couldn't be helped."

"Miss Dor-o-thy..." There was no mistaking that voice. It was Tik Tok. It sounded like it came from somewhere across the room.

Dorothy looked up, but couldn't see him. She stood and even stretched onto her tiptoes to see over everyone. She still couldn't find him. "Tik Tok?"

There was no answer.

She shrugged and sat back down, taking another bite.

Jasper poured her some pongo juice and pointed at the roast buzzbird. "You have to try that, it's amazing."

Boq agreed. "It's the best I've ever tasted and believe me, I've had my share." He patted his stomach, smiling cheerily.

Pok nodded emphatically, taking another bite. "The best."

That was enough for Dorothy. She grabbed a knife and carved off a slice. It was even better than the pie, which Dorothy thought was impossible to top. Chicken, turkey, and duck had nothing on buzzbirds.

"Miss Dor-o-thy..." It was Tik Tok again.

She glanced around the table, then turned to Jasper. "Did you hear that?

Jasper gave her a quizzical look. "What?"

"Did you hear Tik Tok say my name?" she asked.

Jasper shook his head. "No. I didn't hear anything."

Hup, Mik and Wik were playing a game of balancing their mugs of pongo juice on their foreheads. Each of them, heads tilted back, were trying not to giggle. Wik cheated by purposely nudging his brother, causing Mik's drink to topple over, spilling its blue contents all down his shirt. All three of them burst into hysterical laughter.

It was contagious and Jasper joined in the laughing fit. He slammed his hands on the table, gasping for breath. Seeing Jasper completely lose it, gave Dorothy uncontrollable giggles. Soon everyone at the table was nearly falling to the floor from laughing so hard.

"Miss Dor-o-thy… please an-swer me." Tik Tok again. Louder now.

Dorothy wiped the tears from her eyes and settled down. Tik Tok's tone sounded serious. The rest of the room was still in a fit of giggles. She scanned the area. There were no other doorways. No other rooms. This was it. Her brows knit together. "Where are the horses?"

Jasper stifled a laugh and shrugged. "Probably out grazing."

Dorothy shook her head, leaning back. "I didn't see them."

He took a drink. "I'm not worried."

"What about Chalk?" she asked, knowing how close they were.

"I'm sure he's fine." Jasper pointed to another delectable pie. "Try this. You'll love it."

She stood up. "No. I've had enough."

"Try it." He started to plate it, but Dorothy was already up and moving for the door.

"I'm going for a walk," she said, and stepped outside.

Shutting the door behind her, she was able to cut off the loud festivities of the Knights, letting her head clear. She was positive she had heard Tik Tok. Where was he? Why wasn't he with the rest of them? If he would just show himself, then she wouldn't have to worry and they could all relax and enjoy themselves. Maybe build a few more cottages here, since this area was so serene and lovely.

Dorothy smiled at the idea. She and Jasper could stay here forever and raise a family. A boy and a girl. Her grin grew wider, picturing that image. A nagging tug in her brain, kept giving her the feeling that she was supposed to be *doing* something.

Looking for something.

And she was sensing it was important.

"Miss Dor-o-thy… Fo-cus on my voice."

Dorothy perked up. Tik Tok's voice was clearer now that she was alone and could concentrate on it. It seemed to be coming from the open field to her right.

There! Far in the distance, she could see a dark figure standing in the high grass.

She ran toward it, an urgency compelling her to not waste time walking.

Maybe he had run down. He had said that he was self-wound now, but maybe he was wrong. She was feeling a sense of dread that it was more serious than that though.

As she neared the figure, she could see it was definitely Tik Tok. He was standing completely still like a statue. She slowed as she got closer.

"Tik Tok?" she asked cautiously.

"Miss Dor-o-thy! I knew you would hear me!" When he spoke, his mouth and mustache didn't move. It was almost as if his voice wasn't coming from his body, but from inside her own head.

"Why are you out here all alone? Have your actions run down?" Dorothy set her hand on his back. He was warm from standing in the sun.

"You must wake up!" he exclaimed.

"I am awake. What are you talking about?" She wondered if his thinking actions had run down too. There were a few times that had happened and he had started speaking nonsense and gibberish.

"Wher-ev-er you are, it is not real."

"What?" She glanced at her surroundings. It all looked real to her.

"We are in dan-ger, Miss Dor-o-thy. You must wake if you are to live!" Tik Tok sounded alarmed.

"I don't understand," she said, genuinely confused.

"There is no time, Miss Dor-o-thy! You must trust me and wake your-self! Quick-ly!"

Dorothy had never heard him so tense. It rattled and unnerved her. In all the time she had known him, he had never steered her wrong. If Tik Tok said she had to wake up, then that was what she had to do.

She stood straight and gave her arm a hard pinch.

She winced and the world around her flickered for an instant. It was so fast, it barely registered with her eyes. But it had happened.

Pinching wasn't going to be strong enough. She slapped her own cheek.

Another brief flash of darkness filled with bizarre shapes and strange smells.

A chill ran down her spine and along her arms, giving her goosebumps. The brilliant sun above did nothing to warm her this time. The glimpse had filled her with dread. It had also refreshed her mind, like a splash of cold water.

She remembered they were after the Ozma. To stop the Nome King.

Something had happened after they had camped for the night. Something had stopped them and she was afraid to find out the truth. But her friends were counting on her and she wasn't going to let them down.

Once more, she readied herself, then slapped her own face so hard, her ears rang.

The illusionary world dropped away and what she saw made her recoil in horror.

CHAPTER 26
THE LAIR OF THE WISPIDS

They were ghastly.

Their long limbs, covered in short spiky hairs (as was the rest of their horrid body!) folded and extended as they traveled, moving with a smooth jerkiness that made Dorothy's skin crawl.

Their dark purple—almost black—torsos were vaguely humanoid, but the rest of them were all spider.

Spiders that stood five feet tall.

They had six spindly arms (or legs) that ended in unsettlingly small hands, each with their own set of three spindly fingers and a thumb. Some of the hideous monsters walked on two legs, using the other two pairs as arms, while others crawled about on all six.

Inhuman faces twitched about, consisting of four black globes for eyes and a too wide, human-like mouth, from which a disturbing clicking came.

Below their torso, hung a shiny bulbous bottom, that gave Dorothy the shakes.

She had always had an aversion to insects and spiders. The mere thought of one touching her would make her shiver. Now she was trapped in a cavern filled with spider-like creatures that were worse than any nightmare she could ever dream up.

The cavern itself was drowning in shadow. Portions of the cave walls gave off a blue-white glow—some form of moss—that was enough for her to see by.

Webbed walkways were everywhere criss-crossing at every angle. The webbing attached to the cave walls, where tunnel openings went off in all directions, including above, below, and diagonally. It was dizzying. There was no up or down.

That incessant clicking echoed up and down the tunnels and all around her. It made the hairs on Dorothy's neck stand on end.

None of the spider-things were nearby, they were all busy elsewhere, skittering and climbing and jumping.

She looked (down?) at herself and saw that she was wrapped in webbing, attached to a mass of the stuff. Judging by the direction her hair was falling and by the way her head was throbbing, she deduced that she was hanging almost upside down.

Bom and Kob were immediately to her left, cocooned as well. Beside them was the Lion, Boq, Willow, Wik and Mik. They were all unconscious.

To her right was Hup, Tik Tok, Jasper and Pok. They were also unconscious. All except Tik Tok, who was staring directly at her.

"Miss Dor-o-thy. Good to have you back," Tik Tok said in a low voice.

"What's going on?" she asked in a whisper.

"We are in trou-ble," he said as if it was obvious.

That's an understatement. "I can see that. How did this happen? Where are we?"

"I am sor-ry. I was so bu-sy watch-ing the per-im-eter for in-tru-ders, I fa-iled to no-tice that we had cho-sen to camp right on top of one of their tun-nel doors. They came up un-der-neath us and kid-napped you all with their dream spells. Of course their ma-gic would not work on me, so they used force. I put up a fight, but their web-bing is stron-ger than steel.

"Do you know what they are?" Dorothy asked.

"Wis-pids. Vile crea-tures. While their vic-tims slumber, they pre-pare them for feed-ing."

The blood drained from Dorothy's face. "Feeding? They're going to eat us?"

"Well, in this case, their chil-dren are." He motioned with his head, toward a clump of opaque, glistening orbs (above?) him.

Eggs. Dozens and dozens of eggs.

Dorothy and the Knights were going to be baby food for the hatchlings.

She spastically tried to move her arms and legs, ready to break through the webbing with herculean strength, but it was far too strong. It stretched a bit, but it really was like steel. She shot Tik Tok a panicked look. "We have to get out of here!"

"Yes. I know," he agreed.

"You can't break free?" She was on the verge of hysteria.

"I have al-rea-dy tried. That is why I woke you. You might be ab-le to think of an al-tern-a-tive to brute strength."

An alternative? How am I supposed to think in a nest of these monsters? She took a deep breath. *Get ahold of yourself, girl! Calm down, calm down. Think. Think. Think.*

Strength wasn't an option. She had no magic to rely upon. What did she know about spiders? She knew that webs back home tended to have miraculous tensile strength, yet could be easily cut. Maybe that was the case here. Sadly, there was no way to get to the dagger on her belt. The dagger that Jasper had given her.

The thought made her look over at him longingly. She wished he was awake to help. He could think outside the box. Like how he disguised himself at the airport. Her thoughts narrowed in on that memory and she stared hard at him. He was made of clay! He could get out of his bindings!

"Jasper's the only one of us that can get out," she whispered to Tik Tok. "We have to wake him."

"I have tried. You were the on-ly one that re-spon-ded to my voice."

Dorothy had responded to Tik Tok's voice because of how much she loved and trusted him. Jasper would respond the same way to her voice. She knew he would. But he was too far away. She would have to talk louder and that would draw attention, endangering them all.

Think. Think. Think. It was getting harder to concentrate. The sleep spell was still affecting her, wanting her to stop fighting it and succumb to dreamland.

That was it!

"I'm going back into the dream to get Jasper," she said with confidence.

"I do not think that's a wise choice, Miss Dor-o-thy," he said with concern.

"We don't have any other option, Tik Tok. As soon as you see that I'm asleep, talk to me again. Tell me to find Jasper and wake him. I don't want to get lost in there."

"You can count on me," he said resolutely.

She gave him an affectionate look. "I know I can."

She closed her eyes and let the pull of the sleep spell lull her back into dreamland.

CHAPTER 27
WAKING JASPER

Dorothy yawned and sat up in the bed of grass.

The flowers and birds welcomed her with cheerful color and sound. The sun bathed her in comforting warmth.

She wondered where she was and how she had gotten there. Not that it mattered. It was such a gorgeous day, why worry?

"Miss Dor-o-thy," Tik Tok's deep, staccato voice echoed down from above, "Wake Jas-per."

A rush of memory poured into the forefront of her mind. *This is a dream. Find Jasper. Wake him. Right!*

"Thank you!" she called out to Tik Tok, knowing he couldn't hear her, but it made her feel connected.

Dashing through the trees, she once again found the happy little cottage by the stream.

She was at the door in an instant. Inside, the sounds of

infectious laughter surrounded her and the smells of the feast nearly knocked her over. It was hard to resist sitting down and joining in. She could feel her thoughts becoming murky.

"There you are!" Jasper saw her and motioned for her to sit next to him, as he had done before.

He looked so happy. And handsome. She started to sit down. Wanted to spend time with him.

It was happening again. She had to be careful not to become complacent. It was so easy to just let go and not care.

She stood back up. "Jasper, I need to talk to you."

"What's wrong?" He glanced at her, taking a bite of pie.

"Come outside. I need to talk with you alone."

"Just tell me here. You're among friends," he said around a mouthful of food.

This wasn't going to work. The spell's influence was too strong. He wasn't going to willingly leave this cottage. She'd have to pull rank on him. "Jasper, as Queen of Oz, I order you to step outside with me. Now!"

The Munchkins were too busy telling each other stories to notice that Dorothy had raised her voice.

The Lion, however, did glance at her, in-between bites of his buzzbird drumstick.

Jasper took a drink, then with an irritated look, he nodded once and rose to his feet. "Yes, M'Lady."

The Lion set down his food and watched them go.

As soon as Jasper saw the blue sky and lush colors outside, his annoyed attitude vanished. "What a beautiful day! Why was I even indoors?" He gave her a sideways glance and held out his elbow. "Care for a walk?"

Her arm slipped around his without even thinking. "Alright." She leaned her head against his shoulder, as they strolled out among the flowers.

Willow was sitting at the bank of the river, dangling her feet-roots into the water, soaking up the sunlight, giving her plant body the nutrients it needed. She waved at them.

Dorothy and Jasper waved back. *No, no no!* Dorothy caught herself and lifted her head, focusing.

"Do you remember how we got here?" she asked pointedly.

He shrugged. "Not really. But why don't you just relax and enjoy yourself?"

"We're trying to stop your father, Jasper. He's after the Ozma."

The mention of his father made him stop. Then he slowly shook his head, his expression showing that his thoughts were conflicting. "We already did that. Didn't we?"

"No. We still have to save Oz. And right now, we are prisoners of Wispids. None of this," she gestured to the world around them, "is real. It's a dream."

"Wispids. I've heard of them." His gaze drifted over the picturesque scene around them, lingering on a flower's petal here, a flying bird there, the texture of the tree bark.

Dorothy watched his mood change as he studied the world, taking in the details. She could see she was losing him. The illusion was too convincing.

Sure enough, he glanced back at her with a big grin. "You almost had me." He laughed. "Come on, let's get back to the cottage, I could go for a piece of popcake."

"Jasper! Listen to me!" She grabbed the front of his shirt with both hands. "You said that as a Knight of Oz, you would defend me with your life. Did you really mean that?"

"Of course!"

"Then I'm telling you—none of this exists! It's a dream! And you have to wake up, right now, because we are going to die soon in the real world. I'm asking you, Jasper, if you care anything for me," she choked back tears, "then save me."

That did it.

His whole demeanor changed. A calm came over him, his expression becoming deadly serious. He took each of her hands, gently lowering them from his collar.

"Slap me as hard as you can," he said.

Dorothy leaned forward and gave him a kiss. It wasn't long, but it was sweet and put aside any doubt the other may have had.

When they separated, he gave her a small smile and nodded. "Do it."

She slapped him so hard her hand stung.

Instantly, Jasper blinked out of existence.

There was a stillness afterward as Dorothy pondered her next move.

"I'm next." A deep voice said from somewhere to her left.

Dorothy jumped and turned to see the Lion leaning against a nearby tree. "You scared me!"

He walked over to her, "I saw you both leave. Forgive me for following."

"You overheard?"

He nodded. "I suspected something was wrong. The smells are off." He looked down at her, his face long and weary. "I haven't known happiness in a long time. I can tell when its real or not."

"Oh, Lion, I'm sorry it's been so hard for you." Dorothy put her hand against the side of his face, her thumb ruffling his fur.

He brought his hand up and touched hers. "Wake me."

She had a better idea. "No, not yet. You have to wake the others. They respect you, but they're also afraid of you."

A fraction of a grin played at the side of his mouth. "I'm sure I can find a way to get their attention."

Stepping away from him, she readied her hand for another slap to her own cheek. "See you on the other side."

The Lion bowed slightly. "I will join you shortly."

CHAPTER 28
THE ALARM

With an abrupt jerk, Dorothy woke.

She looked over at Jasper and saw that he was awake. Tik Tok was already filling him in. He looked at her and nodded, giving her a private smile.

"Miss Dor-o-thy said that you were the on-ly one that could get out of this, al-though I can't say I un-der-stand how."

"Watch and learn," Jasper whispered back, "Watch and learn."

Jasper began to lose shape, oozing out of the webbing in a blob like form. His empty clothes came out with him. Once clear of the cocoon, his clay body reformed, filling out his clothes, as he clung to the web.

"Im-press-ive, Mis-ter Jas-per. You've quite the tal-ent."

Jasper patted Tik Tok on the shoulder. "If you don't mind,

I'd appreciate it if you'd keep this a secret between us."

"If you say so, Mis-ter Jas-per."

"Thanks." Jasper reached back inside the cocoon that had held him and retrieved his sword. He unsheathed it and sliced through the webbing holding Tik Tok.

The mechanical man rolled out and immediately latched onto the web to stop his fall. The webbing sagged under his weight slightly, but held firm.

Jasper crawled over to Dorothy and with a quick slash, she rolled out into his arms.

She gave him a sly grin. "My hero."

"We're not out of this yet," he whispered, setting her down against the web. "How are we supposed to wake the others? We can't carry them."

"The Lion's taking care of that. Get on the far end and be ready." Dorothy said, pointing.

Jasper scrambled along the web, keeping his movements slow and smooth so as not to attract attention. The wispids were keeping busy on the outer sections of the web, which was just fine with Jasper. He hunched down between Wik and Mik.

Dorothy pulled out her dagger and waited for the first Munchkin to move.

It was Boq who jolted awake.

Jasper was closer to him and quickly moved in, clamping his hand over the Munchkin's mouth. "Keep quiet," Jasper hissed at him.

Boq looked around with startled eyes as he nodded vigorously. His expression was one of terror.

Dorothy wondered what the Lion had said or done to get him to wake up.

Jasper's sword swished across the silky strands, cutting

them away. Boq steadied himself and whipped out his own sword defensively.

Pok snapped awake next. Dorothy slid over and held her hand over his mouth. "Shhh." Pok nodded.

While she sliced him free, the others started snapping awake, one by one, in startled jerks. First, Mik, then Wik, Bom, Kob and Hup. Then Willow, who woke with a startled gasp and panicked eyes. She quickly recovered, then scowled at the still sleeping Lion.

Judging by Willow's reaction, Dorothy suspected the Lion had resorted to fire to wake her.

Each one that they freed, helped cut away the next, until finally, there was only the Lion left.

When he woke, it wasn't with a snap or jerk. He merely lifted his head and slowly opened his one good eye, casting it about to survey their situation. Dorothy quickly cut him loose.

"That tunnel up there is the highest one. Should be the closest to the surface. Move slowly," the Lion said in a low growl.

He led the way, crawling up the webbing. The rest of the group followed silently.

Dorothy hated the feeling of the webbing. It gave slightly under her weight and felt tacky. Enough of a stickiness to be unpleasant without actually trapping her like a fly. The image made her shudder.

Fortunately, it seemed like the wispids weren't paying attention to them. It was an enormous cavern, and they were skittering in the outer reaches doing who knows what.

Arrogant monsters, she thought, *thinking that no one could ever dare escape their lair. Either that or their senses weren't that sharp.*

Moving effortlessly from one web walkway to another, the Lion chose the least angled path for the group.

Unfortunately, the walkways were all at steep slants, made for creatures that could walk up walls. It was getting harder and harder for the others to keep up.

Boq, being the eldest of the group, was being pushed to his limits. He was fit for his age (seventy-one), but climbing up giant webs, while shaking off the effects of a dream spell, were definitely a young man's game.

He was grunting his way up, sweat glistening on his brow, when his foot slipped off the silky strands. With a short surprised yell, he fell backwards past his son, Bom, then past Wik, Mik and Kob.

Hup caught Boq's arm and swung him back onto the web.

It wasn't Boq's yell, so much as the impact of him hitting the web that alerted the wispids.

A vibration coursed along all of the strands of webbing, sending out an alarm to every wispid in the room. They felt the signal under their sensitive, frightening feet.

Silence hit the room hard like a shockwave, as all the creatures turned toward the Knights.

Dorothy and her group stood still on a thin stretch of webbing, fearful of what was going to happen next.

They didn't have to wait long.

CHAPTER 29
SWARMED!

In the eerie silence, the Knights held their breath, hoping upon hope that somehow the wispids would ignore them.

That hope died when an ungodly cry rang out.

It came from all the creatures at once. A nerve-jangling screech that turned into a chorus of clicking.

Then the wispids moved as one. An avalanche of the creatures raced toward their prey. More poured out of the tunnels, joining the growing swarm.

Knowing that being slow and quiet no longer mattered, the Knights all yelled and grunted, ascending as fast as they could, helping each other out when needed.

The wispids were fast—faster than their size should have allowed.

Quickly drawing their swords, the Knights hacked at the

first wave, slicing off long thin limbs that sprayed dark purple ichor when cut.

The wounded wispids tumbled down the sloped webbing, taking more of their kind with them.

In-between kills, the Knights inched their way up. They had to be vigilant, since an attack could come from any direction.

One wispid leaped across a gap and landed on the underside of the web, opposite Dorothy. She screamed and acting on reflex, plunged the dagger forward, stabbing the thing in the chest, splattering the purple goo on her arms and face.

It fell away, screaming, leaving the web bouncing from its initial jump. The motion almost flung Dorothy off, but she held tight, getting her footing again.

The Lion made his way onto a more level section and they all ran uphill, stabbing and cutting any attacking wispids along the way.

They reached another steeply angled series of strands and proceeded to clamber up it. The top of the cave was getting closer.

Another wispid leaped from afar, snagging Hup, taking him with it. It landed on a lower section of the web.

"Hup!" Kob was nearest when it happened. He spun and threw himself off the strand, after his friend. He landed on top of the wispid, stabbing it in the back of its head, then rolled it over to see if Hup had survived.

Hup sat up, happy to be alive. "Well, that wasn't fun." He slapped Kob on the shoulder, "Thanks to you, I might live another few minutes!"

Kob laughed, knowing this was probably true.

A group of wispids veered toward Kob and Hup seeing that they were separated from the group. Both Munchkins tightened their grips on their swords, preparing for an ugly one-sided battle.

Wik, Mik and Bom landed next to Hup, bouncing onto the springy strands.

"Thought you might need an extra hand!" announced Wik with a grin.

"Ah! Finally making yourself useful, then!" quipped Hup, as he took down a wispid with a quick swing. "Better late than never, I always say!"

Wik laughed as he speared another of the monsters.

"Slice the web! Cut them off!" barked Kob, seeing a solution to their dilemma.

They all swung their swords down severing the part of the walkway where the wispids were attacking from. It fell away from the Munchkins, sending dozens of the creatures plummeting to the hard rock below. Some of the creatures were able to save themselves, grabbing onto lower rungs of the web.

It gave the Munchkins a chance to find another series of strands and resume their climb upward.

Dorothy was relieved to see the others making their way up another path. She had been devastated to see them fall into a horde of the creatures and had feared that they wouldn't survive.

But they had. And she had seen Kob's plan of action. Had seen how well it had worked.

She looked up at the Lion, who was currently taking care of two wispids, clearing the way for her, Jasper, Tik Tok, Pok and Boq. "Lion! Start cutting the strands! Take away their bridges!"

He didn't respond and she wasn't sure he had heard her, but after the two wispids dropped past her in pieces, he hacked through nearby walkways, cutting off other means of approach.

Kob, Hup, Mik, Wik and Bom progressed steadily on their own path, also shearing off any walkways that they came upon, narrowing the wispids access to them, making it easier to maintain a defense.

Losing many of the higher support strands was having an effect on the web's overall structure.

Several of the threaded walkways snapped of their own accord, due to the weight of the ball of webbing in the center where the eggs were stored. The ball shifted, dropping several feet, straining the remaining strands.

Dorothy saw that their own walkway was being stretched to its limit. If it snapped in the wrong spot, or disconnected from the ceiling, then they were done for. She glanced down at her team. Boq and Pok were last in line. "Pok! Cut us loose! Everyone hold on tight!"

Pok nodded and hacked through the silky threads below him.

The effect was immediate. Their strand sprang loose like a slingshot, launching them all upward.

The dank air rushed by Dorothy's face. She hoped they wouldn't be crushed against the rock wall.

The loose end of the webbing went slack and they started to drop back down. Tik Tok's weight was really slingshotting them around and Dorothy worried that the web would snap loose.

They all had their arms wound around the webbing, securing themselves and were able to hold on during the whiplash inducing ride.

All except Jasper.

CHAPTER 30
TO THE SURFACE!

The threads in Jasper's hands snapped apart and he sailed away from the group, through the air, his arms windmilling.

"Jasper!" Dorothy almost lost her own grip at the sight of him falling away from her.

Jasper caught another walkway with one hand, barely making contact. He pulled himself up and looked over at Dorothy.

She was a good forty feet away and the strand Jasper was on wasn't going to connect anywhere near them. He saw that a walkway above angled almost perpendicular to Dorothy's. If he could get to it and cut it loose, it looked like he might be able to swing back across and rejoin the group.

He scrambled up the webbing and as he got closer, he saw that the walkway he wanted was farther away from him than he thought. The space between was at least twenty feet. He needed more height. Up he went, until a wall halted any further progress. It would have to do. He turned and leaned out, bending his legs, coiling his muscles, then leaped off!

The space closed in an instant with the walkway rushing toward him. Jasper latched onto it with room to spare and swung himself up. A wispid suddenly dropped down on him, clicking its tiny, razor sharp mandibles at his face.

The weight of the creature prevented him from drawing his sword and he couldn't resort to clay form, otherwise he'd ooze through the webbing under his back. He'd have to use brute strength.

He punched the thing in the eye, making it flinch. In that moment, he brought his legs up and kicked it off with everything he had. It toppled over backwards into the empty air, all six of its legs clawing frantically for something to hold onto.

Wasting no time, Jasper cut loose the strands he was on. His weight carried him across the cavern in a great arc, like a trapeze artist. Leaning out as far as he could, he grabbed the loose end of the web that Dorothy and the others were using and transferred himself to it.

"Who's showing off now?" she called down to him, laughing, relieved to have him back.

He made his way up to her. "That?" he gasped between breaths, "That was nothing. When I start showing off, I'll let you know," he said with a smile.

She giggled and continued after the Lion.

The Lion reached the tunnel first, clearing it of three wispids with three precise slashes of his sword. He cast each of the dead creatures out into the void, while Dorothy and the rest climbed inside.

Peering over the edge, Dorothy felt a little bit of vertigo. The bottom was so far away, it was shrouded in darkness. A black pit she knew was swarming with the hideous monsters.

A mass of wispids was streaming up the web and along the walls toward them.

Over to her right, Hup and his group of Munchkins were scaling another series of strands, edging closer to her.

"Hurry! They're right behind you!" Dorothy called down to the splintered group.

"You two, watch the tunnel," the Lion ordered, jabbing a clawed finger at Jasper and Tik Tok.

Both Knights nodded and guarded the dark passage ahead, while the Lion clung to the web, leaning down to lend a helping hand to Hup and the rest of the Munchkins. He took each of their hands one by one and lifted them up into the tunnel's opening. Mik was the last one, and once he was safe, the Lion cut the strands they had used.

The wispids screamed, falling away into the depths.

A series of snaps echoed in the cavern. The egg sack was too heavy and the remaining strands were breaking. The Lion and Dorothy watched the loose egg sack swing low and crash into a wall with a wet smack.

Another shrill scream rose from the surviving wispids over their loss.

"Time to go!" Dorothy shoved the Munchkins forward into the tunnel.

Needing no further incentive, they all ran headlong through the irregular, winding passage, Jasper and Tik Tok in the lead and the Lion guarding the rear.

There wasn't much of the glowing moss in here. Dorothy felt the darkness swallowing her up. She could just make out the shapes of her friends around her and that was all. The sounds of clinking armor and ragged breathing guided her.

They ran and ran.

Luck was on their side and they encountered no enemies ahead. Behind them was another matter altogether. She could hear the hundreds of spindly legs hitting the tunnel walls, chasing after them. Could hear the angry clicking.

If she tripped...*don't think about it! Just run!* she scolded herself, *RUN*!

There was a solid thump from up front and Dorothy was suddenly blinded by bright light.

Her eyes quickly readjusted and she saw that Tik Tok had barreled through the tunnel's camouflaged door and burst out into the open. The surface!

A second later, she and the others stumbled out too, squinting in the gloomy daylight.

Dorothy never thought she'd be so happy to see those grey skies again.

Judging by their surroundings, they weren't too far from where they had camped. The hills and terrain all looked familiar.

Their horses were nowhere to be seen.

The Knights turned with swords ready at the scuttling sound behind them.

The wispids poured forth from the tunnel entrance. The creatures came to a stop, forming into a constantly twitching mob. All around the Knights, in the hillsides, trapdoors swung open and more of the things skittered out completely surrounding them.

Dorothy and the Knights kept their backs to each other, forming a circle, looking at the gathering monsters, taking in the enormity of the threat they faced.

There were too many. Hundreds and hundreds of wispids.

No matter how hard they fought, there was no way they could hold off this many.

They were done for.

"Where's Chalk and our horses?" Dorothy said in a stressed whisper.

"I don't know," Jasper replied. He sounded distant, overwhelmed by the abominable army. "But we sure could use the help." He put his finger and thumb to his lips and let out a piercing whistle that echoed through the hills and across the dried meadow, perturbing the wispids, setting them into an agitated frenzy. "Maybe he'll hear us."

The wispids lurched forward as one, closing in on the Knights' defensive circle. Just as sword and fang were about to meet, the creatures all froze, legs quivering.

Then, much to the Knights' surprise, their enemies backed down, slinking away.

Without warning, the creatures scattered toward their tunnels, disappearing down them like water into a drain. In a matter of seconds, there wasn't a wispid in sight.

The Knights were still in battle stances, swords up in attack positions. They slowly relaxed, wide-eyed and perplexed.

"They had us," Bom said in a hushed, breathless voice.

Dorothy turned to the Lion, in shock. "What happened?"

The ground shook.

"You feel that?" The Lion asked in a low tone.

They heard a whinny and turned to see Chalk and the rest of their horses come tearing around a hill at full speed.

Dorothy laughed. "Chalk! You saved us!"

Jasper could see the fear on Chalk's face. "No. Something's after them. Something bad."

"RUN!" Chalk screamed as he galloped toward them.

The ground quaked as the Iron Giant came into view, its thunderous feet pounding down in pursuit.

CHAPTER 31
THE IRON GIANT

A colossal shadow fell over the area as the hundred foot tall metal man lumbered toward them.

Its iron limbs let out long creaks and groans, while hissing steam shot from its back. It sounded like a monstrous runaway train was behind them.

The hammer-like club it held in its right hand, came down, hitting the ground with an earth-rattling shake, missing the horses by a good sixty feet.

The team of horses reached Dorothy and her group. Each Knight ran alongside, grabbing hold and leaped onto their ride.

Panic made Dorothy a skilled equestrian and she found herself swinging up onto her galloping horse like she'd been at it for years.

The Giant's shadow loomed over them, stretching out far

ahead. As fast as the horses were, that shadow didn't seem to be receding.

Dorothy could feel the stallion's labored breathing under her legs. Its chest was heaving. They couldn't keep this pace for long. She scanned the landscape, looking for options.

They were cutting through the bottom border of Gilliken Country where the color purple seeped into most of the rocks and flora. The odd color scheme had always strained her eyes.

Northward, she spotted a field of violet stalks the size of redwood trees. The trunks of the stalks resembled asparagus, but with sprouted leaves like a cornstalk.

"The stalks!" She pointed toward the field and yelled to be heard over the Iron Giant's massive footsteps and the pounding hooves of their horses, "Head for the stalks!"

Dorothy hoped that the Giant might lose sight of them once they entered the field.

Responding with a curt nod, the Knights nudged their mounts in that direction.

The ground shook again. Another strike of the Giant's hammer. Dorothy could feel the gust of air hit her back from the impact. *Too close, too close.*

The horses were really pushing themselves and they reached the field in a matter of minutes. They shot between the stalks. The towering plants shrouded them in welcoming shadows.

The Knights split along different paths, weaving between the violet spires, never slowing down.

From behind, great cracks and snaps signaled that the Iron Giant had entered the field.

Dorothy glanced back and saw the Giant swinging his club in wide arcs, knocking over stalks by the dozen. They were barely slowing him down. In fact, the broken stalks were now another danger, as she saw one fly overhead and crash into the stalks ahead of them, blocking their path!

The Knights pulled on their reins, bringing their horses to a near stop, changing directions, and scattering to the sides.

Dorothy saw there was a gap under the fallen trunk and she was already going too fast to stop. She threw herself down onto her horse, flattening herself. Her horse raced under the stalk with less than an inch to spare.

She sat back up, adrenaline pumping through her. Everyone had split up to avoid the blockade. She caught glimpses of some of the others in-between stalks.

More stalks were being ripped apart by the Giant's wild swings and the violet trunks were crashing to the ground randomly all around her.

Dorothy had already swerved away from disaster several times and no longer knew what direction she was riding. Her friends were faring the same. She'd spot Hup cross her path one way, then Pok going the opposite. They were all turned around.

The Giant's heavy foot stomped down off to her left. Close enough to jolt her bones. She yanked her reins, pulling her horse to the right.

Dorothy glanced up and immediately wished she hadn't.

The Iron Giant had focused its attention on her—its expressionless eyes tracking her. She saw the hammer dropping right for her!

She yanked the reins again, bringing the horse to an abrupt halt.

The hammer overshot, smashing into the ground directly in front of her, the concussive shockwave making Dorothy's teeth hurt.

In a panic, her horse reared back on its hind legs.

The action threw Dorothy high into the air. She landed on her back, knocking the wind out of her.

Rolling onto her stomach, wincing with pain, she saw her ride taking off without her. She couldn't blame it. It probably didn't even realize she had fallen off.

Nearby, the Giant's hammer lifted up from the dirt with a crunching, sucking sound, leaving a ragged crater behind.

Above her, she saw the Giant step back and raise the hammer for another strike.

It gazed down at her with cold, empty eyes.

CHAPTER 32
THE PERILOUS PLAN

"Dorothy!"

At the sound of her name being called, Dorothy whipped around to see Jasper and Chalk charging toward her. He was leaning low in the saddle, his hand out.

Behind him was Tik Tok on his mechanical horse.

She jumped to her feet and grasped Jasper's hand as he rode by. He swung her up to sit behind him. She wrapped her arms around his chest.

They dashed between the Giant's feet as the giant hammer boomed down into the ground behind them.

They gained precious time as the titan lifted its weapon and twisted and turned, trying to follow them.

She looked to her copper friend riding beside them. "Tik Tok! How can we stop it?"

"You can't," Tik Tok replied matter-of-factly.

"There must be some way!" she shouted.

"I sup-pose if his steam-works ran out of fuel..." he thought out loud.

There was little chance of that happening, Dorothy knew. Not after the way she saw the Giant throwing all those trees down its gullet. Dorothy thought of Willow, wondering if her tree-like companion was okay.

"...Or if his gears mal-func-tioned," Tik Tok finished.

That caught Dorothy's attention.

Maybe there was a way she could get inside the Giant. Sabotage it from the inside. Because there was no way to damage it from the outside.

She studied Tik Tok. The factory that produced the Giant, also made Tik Tok. There had to be similarities. She didn't want to attempt entering the Giant's mouth. That was where it had tossed down the trees for fuel. It probably led to a shredder of some sort and then on to a furnace. Her eyes glided over Tik Tok, looking for openings. The only other entrance were his earholes.

Dorothy tilted her head back and took a good look at the Giant following them. His head swiveled toward her. She glimpsed earholes, the same as Tik Tok. She had to get up there.

At that moment she spotted the Lion zipping by in the distance, avoiding a falling stalk.

Dorothy pointed ahead and leaned in to Jasper's ear. "Catch up to the Lion!"

Jasper headed after his General, riding hard to close the gap between them.

"Lion!" she screamed to him. He looked over his shoulder at her. "I'm coming over!"

"What? Are you crazy?" Jasper said, glancing back at her.

"Yeah, I think I am. Bring us as close as you can get."

Chalk did most of the work to keep pace, while the Lion slowed down and brought his steed to ride right beside them.

Dorothy brought her feet up under her, squatting precariously, then jumped over to the Lion's horse, landing firmly behind him, her fingers gripping his fur. "Lion, we need to get inside the Giant!" she shouted, "The only way in is through his ear! We have to climb one of the stalks!"

"What?!" Jasper exclaimed, in shock.

The Lion simply nodded, unfazed by the crazy plan. He knew Dorothy well enough to trust her. He started to peel away from Jasper and Tik Tok.

"It's the only way!" she called back to Jasper as she and the Lion tore off between the purple pillars, "Distract him until we're ready, then draw him toward us!"

Jasper was speechless.

Dorothy looked back at Jasper, watching him grow smaller in the distance. She felt bad leaving him behind, but he would have tried to stop her had she told him what she was planning. Besides, only the Lion could get them to where they needed to be.

"Hold on tight!" the Lion said over his shoulder to Dorothy.

She threw her arms around his torso, up near his neck, clutching thick handfuls of his soft mane and wrapped her legs around his waist.

The Lion brought his feet up onto the saddle into a crouching position, then leaped onto a passing stalk. His claws sank into the violet trunk. The surface was dense, yet easy to cut. The Lion bounded easily up the shaft.

Dorothy held on, watching the ground drop away under them. She was amazed at how swiftly the Lion could climb. She didn't seem to be slowing him down at all.

Soon, they reached the top and were able to get a sense of scale of what they were facing.

The field of stalks spread out all around them. There were great swathes of emptiness, where the Iron Giant had laid waste to the towering plants in his pursuit of the Knights.

Dorothy could see her companions far, far below, weaving in-between the massive plants, scattered and disoriented.

The Giant itself, stood taller than the stalks, its head bent low, scouring the field, looking for its prey.

Being this close, its creaking metal joints sounded like a building's steel girders bending, getting ready to collapse. An ominous sound that was enhanced by the sporadic release of steam jetting from spouts on its upper back.

Dorothy watched it raise its hammer and bring it down again. The stalk she was on shook and swayed.

Down below, she saw that Jasper and Chalk had barely missed being squashed under the hammer's blunt end. They were running circles around it, getting the Giant's attention. As soon as it started to lift its hammer, Jasper charged toward the stalk that Dorothy and the Lion were on.

The Giant followed Jasper, its torso swiveling, its massive feet stomping after him. It moved through the field, brushing the heavy stalks aside like they were blades of grass, sending them crashing to the ground.

Dorothy could feel the Lion's muscles tense under her. The Giant was coming right for them, still fixated on Jasper below.

They jumped just as the Giant's broad, curved chest hit their stalk, snapping it in two.

The Lion landed on the Giant's left shoulder and quickly began to slide off, his claws scrabbling for a handhold. The iron surface offered no purchase. He slid down over the front of the shoulder with Dorothy hanging from his back.

Feeling the Lion's dismay, Dorothy let out a small cry and clenched handfuls of his mane.

The Lion caught hold of a strip of iron that ran along the edge of the Giant's shoulder joint. He held tight to it with both hands. His legs dangled below, searching for a foothold to leverage himself up. There were none.

The Lion's fingers were slipping with each of the Giant's movements and at this high of an altitude, the winds were strong, seemingly wanting to pry them off.

"Dorothy, this isn't looking good…" the Lion growled.

"Just hang on, we'll figure something out!" she shouted, wishing she was as confident as she sounded.

"Better make it fast!" he yelled back.

Dorothy looked around, scouring the smooth metal near them. There had to be something! Anything! She looked down and immediately wanted to throw up. She was so high up. If she fell…*don't think about it!*

It was at that moment she saw Jasper looking up at her.

She instantly regretted leaving his side. Poor Jasper. She knew he could see that she was in danger and he was helpless to do anything about it.

No matter how hard she wished, Jasper wasn't going to be able to save her this time.

CHAPTER 33
RIDING THE GIANT

Jasper and Chalk were outracing the Giant, giving the metal monster a good workout, when Jasper glanced back to make sure that Dorothy had landed safely.

The sight of Dorothy and the Lion hanging precariously from the Giant made Jasper's insides knot up. Watching the Lion thrash about and almost slide off was more than Jasper could bear.

"She's insane!" Jasper announced. "Absolutely insane."

"But you're going to follow her," said Chalk, in between gasping breaths. The chase was pushing him to his limit.

"Of course," Jasper replied as if there was any doubt. He unhooked a coil of rope from his saddlebag. It was a grappling hook. "The next time his hammer comes down, head right towards it! I'm going to hitch a ride!"

Chalk laughed. "And you say *she's* insane!"

They timed it, slowing down, allowing the Giant to think it had them, then bolted away at the last second as the hammer struck. A dangerous game of chicken that Jasper and Chalk barely survived.

It was so close, Chalk's legs turned to jelly, nearly crippling him. A hard spray of dirt and gravel hit their backs, feeling like a thousand needles.

Chalk spun around, kicking up hunks of dirt and charged back toward the hammer which was still buried deep in the ground.

Swinging his grappling hook in a wide circle like a lasso, Jasper launched it at the Giant's weapon where it connected just beneath the hammer's head. As Chalk rode past the weapon, Jasper was yanked out of the saddle.

Jasper swung toward the hammer, his boots slapping the rough iron surface. He quickly scaled the face of the hammerhead and retrieved his grappling hook, then crouched down, ready for the next part. Timing was crucial.

The hammer lifted up into the air, dropping great chunks of mud after it. Jasper saw the world shrink away at a speed that was unnerving. He wasn't afraid of heights, but the view he now had of the world left him a little unsteady.

The hammer continued to rise, higher and higher, moving into its striking position.

Now!

Jasper let go and slid down the length of the handle until he landed on the top of the Giant's thumb joint. From there he sprang across its hand, then sprinted along the massive forearm, leaping over thick ridges where enormous rivets held the iron plates together.

The arm continued to rise. The forearm was tilting now, so

that Jasper was running downhill toward the inside of its elbow. He leaped down to the upper arm, landing firmly on the Giant's bicep, then charged across toward the shoulder.

He knew that Chalk was down there somewhere, acting as a decoy, baiting the Giant.

The hammer was over the Giant's head now and continuing back, readying itself for a powerful swing. The Giant's forearm was now well above Jasper and the upper arm was following it.

It was lifting too fast.

The surface tilted crazily underneath Jasper and he began to slide toward the shoulder. At the last moment, he kicked off from the arm, using his momentum to rocket himself onto the Giant's shoulder. He skidded over the weathered surface, catching himself before sailing off its back.

Getting to his feet, Jasper moved behind the Giant's neck, heading to the left side of its body, where he knew Dorothy and the Lion were dangling.

The Giant bent forward slightly, its hammer plunging down.

There was a thunderous boom as it hit the ground below. The tremendous sound traveled up through the Giant's body, resonating like a gong.

It made it difficult to hang on, but Jasper ignored it and shimmied around its neck to the other side. He threw his grappling hook up to the Giant's ear, securing it, then ventured out onto its left shoulder, holding onto the rope with one hand.

He leaned out over the edge and was relieved to see the Lion still clinging to the ridge with Dorothy wrapped around his back.

The expression on Dorothy's face was about the best thing Jasper had ever seen. It was sheer joy because he was there. She was beaming at the sight of him.

Jasper wore a crooked grin as he tossed the line down to the Lion, who snatched it and began to climb steadily up. When they got near enough, Jasper took Dorothy's arm and lifted her up to join him. He held out his hand to the Lion.

"Thanks." The Lion said gruffly, letting Jasper help pull him up.

The Giant lurched back, beginning to lift its hammer again.

The group rushed over to the Giant's neck to steady themselves and to have something to cling to.

"I saw how you got up here," Dorothy said accusingly, shaking her head, giving him a sideways look. "You can't tell me you weren't showing off that time."

She smiled when she said it, her freckled nose scrunching on one side. Her ponytail and loose hair blowing freely in the winds.

It was an image that burned itself into Jasper's mind. He recovered before she noticed his dazed look. "Nope," he said with a nonchalant shrug, "Had I known you were watching, I'd have put more effort into it."

She laughed.

"Alright you two, we've still got work to do," the Lion said, wedging himself between them, giving them each a scolding glance. He climbed the line up to the ear and slipped into the opening.

Dorothy and Jasper gave each other a guilty stare.

She pointed at him. "You're in *trou-ble*."

"I think he was talking to *you*." Jasper lowered his hands, interlocking his fingers, so that she could step into them. He boosted her up.

She climbed into the earhole. "Sorry, but I'm the Queen. I *can't* get in trouble." She flashed him a huge smile before she disappeared inside.

She's magnificent, Jasper thought as he pulled himself up and followed her into the Giant.

CHAPTER 34
THE INSIDERS

The Giant's ear canal was a brass tube that tapered as it curved upward. It was shiny and smooth and Dorothy was having trouble moving through it. She kicked off her socks to gain traction. As the tube shrank around her, she had to lay flat and shimmy through the rest of it.

When she emerged from the interior opening, the Lion was there to greet her. Jasper popped out after her.

They were inside the Giant's head.

To Dorothy's surprise, it was quite empty inside—well, there was *some* machinery—the back of its eyes were connected to thick jointed pistons that jerked, rotated and hissed as the Giant looked around outside. She had expected more though. Then again, she knew that the Iron Giants had never been given any clockwork brains like Tik Tok.

Laying nearby were pieces of some sort of instrument that used to be attached to the ear tube to receive outside sounds. The Lion had destroyed it to gain entrance into its head. He was in the process of sabotaging the same instrument on its right ear tube. Dorothy doubted making the Giant deaf would help, but it couldn't hurt. Seeing how big the pistons were for its eyes, though, left little hope of blinding it.

Dorothy, Jasper and the Lion stood on a platform, welded to the back of the cranium. Directly below them was the inside of the Giant's mouth, which led to its gullet—a gigantic pipe that was a great black pit. A place where whole trees vanished, ground up, and then fed to the fire.

"Over here." The Lion waved them over.

He had found a closed hatch with a wheeled handle. He turned the wheel and the hatch loosened. It squeaked as he opened it.

The first thing they noticed was the tremendous noise that rose up from inside the opening. The next thing they noticed was a series of rungs that ran down beside the throat pipe into the Giant's body.

They descended the ladder and entered the Giant's chest. It was an enormous chamber with huge gears everywhere they looked, slowly turning, all interlocking, a miracle of engineering. Some were horizontal and some vertical, all at least one foot thick.

The noise was overwhelming, rebounding off of the iron walls. The squeaking of joints, the hiss of pistons, the clicking and knocking of gears shifting into different positions. Speeding up or slowing down, depending on what action the Giant was performing.

At the moment, there was only a side-to-side swaying as it walked. Each footstep shuddering its way up through the Giant's body, shaking the metal under the group's feet.

The enormous gullet pipe continued on past them into the Giant's stomach—a heavily constructed round furnace that took up most of the abdominal area of the mechanical monstrosity.

A series of pipes snaked out from the furnace to a multitude of mechanisms making up the Giant's internal system. Four of the pipes ran up the rear wall where they connected to the spouts on its back. The ones that Dorothy had seen venting steam earlier.

Dorothy was already sweating. The sweltering moist heat was amplified by the metal walls. The smells didn't help either. Oil and grease hung in the air and left a metallic aftertaste in her mouth.

She followed the Lion down onto a narrow catwalk that ran along the side. She ducked under the moving cogs that threatened to take her head off at any moment. The metal catwalk was warm under her bare feet, almost to the point of being uncomfortable.

Down they went onto another series of ladders, onto a shorter catwalk. They saw more of the same. Large rotating gears waiting to crush anyone foolish enough to come close.

"Maybe we can jam one of those gears," the Lion said, watching the complex mechanisms revolve around him.

"With what?" Dorothy didn't see anything handy that they could make use of. She jumped, hearing a sharp jarring sound. It was Jasper kicking the railing. He repeatedly hit it with the heel of his boot.

The railing was made of a smooth silvery-grey metal, probably steel, welded together in short segments to follow the curve of the walls. At each juncture was a rounded joint. The struts running from the floor grating to the railing didn't appear to be that solid.

With each of Jasper's kicks, the railing bent further out.

The Lion motioned for Jasper to step aside while he took over. He gripped the railing and gritted his sharp teeth, pulling as hard as he could. His muscles flexed to the point of bursting until finally a three foot piece of metal relented and broke off in his hands.

"Sure, after I loosened it for you," Jasper said, smirking.

"I didn't want to wait the two hours for you to do it." The Lion shot him a gruff smile and handed him the piece of railing. He then pulled loose another segment and crouched, tensing his leg muscles. "Stand back."

He vaulted forward over the railing across a big gap out onto a slow moving gear that was six feet across in diameter. He landed easily, still clutching the railing rod and positioned himself near the edge of the cog. As the gear turned, its teeth engaged with another of its kind, keeping things functioning like clockwork.

The Lion jammed the metal rod between their teeth, where these cogs met.

The gears didn't even hiccup. They snapped the rod in two, shooting the fragments out into the distance.

Dorothy could hear the pieces cling and clang their way down to the bottom. "We need something stronger."

The Lion shook his head. "All of this is too big. I don't think we can stop it."

"There has to be something we can do to it," Dorothy said with desperation. They were doomed otherwise.

There was a sudden wrenching motion and the room tilted forward at a terrifying angle. At the same time, dozens of the gears whirred with a burst of speed.

One of those gears was the one on which the Lion stood. He was thrown off and smacked into the face of a vertical cog, his shoulder taking the brunt of the impact.

He then fell down between a series of spinning gears, narrowly missing being ground into pulp. A rod struck his side and he bounced away, grunting in pain, landing on a huge slow moving cog in the lower levels where he immediately started to slide toward the edge. He was losing consciousness and his hand limply reached out for a handhold.

In the initial jolt, Dorothy and Jasper were thrown over the railing, but they both had managed to hang on to it.

"Hold on!" Jasper said to Dorothy as he struggled to climb back onto the slanted catwalk.

"Hurry! I'm slipping!" Her sweaty fingers were sliding off of the smooth metal railing.

BOOM.

The loud sound echoed outside and shook the interior of the Giant. It was enough to make Dorothy lose her grip.

She fell from the catwalk just as Jasper reached for her.

CHAPTER 35
MECHANICAL MAYHEM

Dorothy fell away, fingers stretched out toward Jasper, missing him by mere inches.

Down she went, terrified, seeing the whirling gears move in and out, coming dangerously close.

She seized onto a rod, but it too was spinning and she lost her grip. It slowed her fall though, so when she landed on a nearby cog, it didn't hurt as much. Unfortunately, because of the tilt, she too started to slide toward the edge.

The room lurched back into an upright position. The gears slowed and a number of them reversed direction.

The change in angle stopped both Dorothy and the Lion from falling off their respective cogs.

Dorothy laid there a minute catching her breath. She worked out what had happened. The Giant had obviously swung its hammer again (the speeding up of gears) and leaned forward to do it (the tilting of the room). Now it had leaned back up and was raising the hammer (the reversing of gears).

"Are you alright?" Jasper called down to her.

She looked up at him. He was a good thirty feet above, glimpsed between revolving gears. "Yeah. Just a little bruised up."

"Stay there. I'll find a way down," he shouted.

"Okay." Dorothy wasn't going anywhere. She was too tired and too achy to move. At least until she realized she hadn't heard anything from the Lion.

She crawled over to the edge and searched the area for him. She spied his prone form laying on a cog halfway across the room on a lower level. The way the gears were laid out, she could get to him.

She hopped onto another cog that was interlocking with hers and ran across it. The next cog was one level below and on a rotating mechanism. It was only in jumping distance for a brief moment. She would only have a few seconds to make the leap and run across to the next. Holding her breath, she waited and saw her chance—she jumped down and raced over it, then leaped onto the next gear.

"What are you doing?" Jasper's voice echoed from behind.

Dorothy looked back and saw Jasper standing where she had originally fallen. He was agitated. *Oops,* she thought.

"The Lion's over here. I'm trying to get to him." She pointed down at the Lion.

Jasper traced her path with ease, jumping nimbly between gears and was soon at her side. "The General was right."

"About what?" she asked.

"You really are a royal pain to watch over." Jasper said with a smile.

She grinned. "You knew the job was dangerous when you took it."

He shook his head. "I might have to resign after this."

She laughed. "C'mon, we're almost there."

They both hopscotched across three more gears and came to an impasse.

The Lion was just ahead, but too far for them to jump and there were no nearby cogs to bridge the gap.

Jasper uncoiled his grappling hook and threw it up to a rod above the gap. He put his arm around Dorothy. "Ready?"

"Yeah," she nodded.

He stepped off the cog and swung across the chasm using one hand, clutching Dorothy with the other. They both landed gently on the same cog as the Lion.

Dorothy rushed to his side, while Jasper whipped the grappling hook's line, unsnagging it from its perch and quickly reeled it in.

The Lion lay still. Dorothy put a hand on his furry chest and felt it rising and lowering with each breath. He was alive but out cold. She slapped his face several times, starting softly, then hit him harder. "Lion! Wake up!"

His eyes fluttered open, focusing on her. "Are we still where I think we are?"

"Afraid so," she said.

He sighed, rolling up into a sitting position. He rested an arm on one bent knee, surveying the maze of machinery. His gaze stopped on the pipes leading away from the furnace. He looked up at Jasper and saw that he still had the other steel rod tucked into his belt, next to his sword sheath. "Give me that."

Jasper handed the piece of railing to the Lion. "What are you thinking?"

"I'm going to hammer away at those pipes down there and see if I can put a crimp in them. Maybe the steam's pressure will build and damage him. You two stay here." The Lion jumped off, making his way down, hopping from cog to cog. This area was thick with gears and he made it to the bottom in short time.

Dorothy started to follow, but Jasper held her back.

"It'll be easier for him if he doesn't have to worry about you," Jasper said.

Reluctantly, she agreed and watched the Lion take out his aggression on one of the pipes. He repeatedly swung the steel rod down with a vengeance. It was working. She could see a deep dent forming, blocking the flow of steam.

The Lion stepped back, breathing hard. Satisfied with the result, he set to work on another pipe.

She craned her head back, looking up to where they had entered through the Giant's neck. It was extremely far away now. "It's going to be a tough climb getting out of here,"

"I was already thinking that." Jasper said, following her line of sight.

Dorothy's gaze wandered, examining the complex machinery all around her. It was all constantly in motion. All connected in some way, each part integral to keeping the whole thing functioning. Her eyes followed the pattern down to a smaller group of gears, hidden in the shadows of the larger components. One in particular was only about twelve inches in radius.

"Wait a minute…" she said, looking closer at the small gear.

Dorothy leaned over the edge and called down to the Lion who was starting on a third pipe. "Lion! Throw me the railing!"

He stopped and gave her a quizzical look, then tossed the piece of steel up to her.

She snatched it out of the air, then skipped across a series of cogs to the smaller set of gears.

The smallest one that she had spotted was vertical and spinning fast. She held the steel rod like a baseball bat and smacked the gear with it. The vibration in the rod made her hands hurt. The small gear hadn't budged.

Jasper had joined her and held out his hand, offering to take the club. "Let me try."

"No, I've got it." She hit it again. Harder. It moved a fraction, but continued to spin. She ignored the pounding ache in her palms. This time she pulled back and swung with every ounce of strength she could muster.

The rod clanged solidly against the small cog, sending it flying off its shaft. The gear fell down to the bottom of the Giant's belly, where it landed with a small clunk.

At first, it didn't seem to have made a difference, then the surrounding gears started to slow. Without the missing cog to turn the rest, they were all coming to a stop.

Dorothy smiled, pleased with herself.

She and Jasper watched the domino effect of slowing gears, following it all the way up to the massive array of mechanisms above them.

Then they heard it.

The sound of rigid metal snapping. A loud, crisp popping sound that sent shivers through Dorothy. Her smile disappeared.

Gear shafts were breaking.

Certain gears were on rotating, orbiting frameworks and were now left hanging in awkward positions, their weight stressing the shafts they were on. Parts that were never meant to be static were now shattering under the strain.

Falling cogs crashed into others cogs, and soon huge pieces

of machinery started to collapse down around Dorothy, Jasper and the Lion.

Jasper grabbed Dorothy's hand and pulled her onto a nearby gear as a tree sized shaft slammed into the cog they had been standing on, upturning it, sending it twirling into a piston, knocking it loose.

Dorothy and Jasper jumped down to the furnace level next to the Lion. They braced themselves against the wall, trying to avoid the falling debris.

It was chaos!

Dorothy screamed at the deafening storm of metal that was raining down around them!

They were trapped!

CHAPTER 36
UP AND DOWN

There was no way out!

Massive mechanical parts crashed down, making Dorothy's insides shake from the colossal vibrations. The sounds of impact threatened to shatter her eardrums.

A squealing groan rang out as a toppling shaft fell toward them.

Dorothy gasped, seeing the looming column of steel coming at her. Jasper and the Lion threw themselves in front of her in a futile attempt to protect her.

The end of the shaft hit the wall instead, screeching and grinding, sending out a shower of sparks as it slid to one side. It tore into one of the pipes that ran up the inside of the Giant's back, splitting it in two, knocking the bottom half loose.

The bottom half of the ruptured pipe let out an angry hiss,

spewing scalding hot steam into the air. It was so close, it was instantly unbearable for Dorothy and her friends. They didn't have much time before they would be cooked by the furnace's loose exhaust.

Seeing the split pipe gave Dorothy an idea. The top half wasn't channeling steam anymore.

"If we can get inside the top half of that broken pipe, we can climb up it! We can get out through the vent in its back!" Dorothy shouted over the sounds of rending metal.

Jasper and the Lion looked up with wary faces. They nodded, knowing it was the only hope they had.

The Lion started swinging the steel rod at the base of the damaged pipe, crimping it to reduce the amount of steam pouring out. When he had gotten the scalding vapor down to a non-lethal level, they all climbed up the fallen debris and twisted catwalks, toward the top section of the broken pipe.

The Lion held out his hand to Jasper. "The metal's going to be too hot for you to climb. Give me the end of your line."

Jasper passed the end of his grappling rope to the Lion, who then wrapped it several times around his own furry waist, tying it into a knot.

The Lion gave Jasper the grappling hook end. "You hang on, I'll pull you up!" The Lion turned to Dorothy. "Get on!"

Dorothy jumped onto the Lion's back and he ducked into the interior of the severed pipe.

The pipe was an extremely tight fit, barely wide enough for the both of them. If they weren't in so much danger, the claustrophobic nature of it would have sent Dorothy into a panic. The fact that the pipe was still hot from the all of the steam that had been passing through didn't help matters.

Hooking his claws into the metal, the Lion started up,

ignoring the pain whenever his flesh brushed against the hot surface.

Up they went. The farther they climbed, the darker it got. Soon they were engulfed in a muggy, stifling, inky darkness.

Dorothy had to slow her breathing, taking in shallow breaths. If she took in too much of the hot air, it made her feel like she was cooking her lungs. It was a miserable, terrifying climb. She held on tight, clinging to the Lion's thick mane. She tried to stay still so as to not make the Lion's job harder.

Below, Jasper dangled under them, very aware of how hot it was. Not enough to bake his clay form, but enough to make him worry.

The Lion moved incredibly fast. Dorothy felt his muscles strain under her. She could hear him breathing hard. With all his fur, she realized he must be suffering from the heat worst of all.

Dorothy could also feel the Iron Giant swaying side to side. She could hear more of its internal workings grinding and snapping, coming apart, echoing through the metal pipe.

A bright light broke through the blackness from above, illuminating the inside of the tube. The pipe curved toward the light source at a lower angle so that all of them were able to stand on their own feet, however as soon as Dorothy's bare feet touched the hot metal, she hopped back onto the Lion. "Ow! Sorry! It's too hot!"

They had reached the vent opening on the back of the giant. There was a grate standing between them and the outside world. Tantalizing traces of cool air brushed across their faces.

The Lion kicked at the metal grate repeatedly. The grating bent more and more, until it finally gave way and popped off, spinning end over end out into the fresh air.

Looking out of the pipe's opening, they watched the grating

plummet down a hundred feet to the ground where it kicked up a small dust cloud.

The ground was pitching back and forth, tilting crazily as the Giant tried its best to stay upright. Judging by its shaky, jerky movements, the three of them had only minutes to spare before it collapsed.

As it lumbered about, they could see the towering violet stalks swish by.

"We'll have to jump for it!" the Lion shouted over the noise. He untied the rope and handed it back to Jasper.

At that moment, a frightening blast echoed from inside the belly of the Giant, sending it into a wild stagger. The furnace had exploded.

Dorothy screamed as the Lion lost his balance and they both tumbled over the side.

Jasper was thrown onto his back, unable to help.

The Lion fell a dozen feet before catching onto a ridge that ran horizontally along the Giant's back. He seized it with one hand and growled at the sharp pain that lanced through his arm.

The sharp stop ripped Dorothy off his back. Her fists still holding tufts of loose fur as she fell away.

"NO!" The Lion's lightning fast reflexes were still too slow to catch her.

Jasper, watching from above, reacted immediately. He dove off the edge of the vent, tucking his arms to his side to decrease wind resistance and fell like a rock. He shot past the Lion, his gaze locked onto Dorothy.

This is it. Dorothy thought. Then, impossibly, she saw Jasper coming for her. *My protector. My hero.*

She held out her hands to him. He was flying toward her. *No.* Not flying… *Falling.* He was going to die for her.

Jasper saw the panic in her eyes. He was closing in on her. He reached out… his left arm wrapped around her waist. A perfect fit. Like it was supposed to be there. Always.

"Hold on to me!" he yelled.

She wrapped her arms and legs around him, burying her head under his chin.

With a snap of his right hand, he threw the grappling hook out toward a passing stalk. The hook's sharp ends sank deep into the tough bark of the towering violet plant.

The rope unraveled quickly, becoming taut, jerking them to a stop and sending them into an uncontrolled swing. Their momentum carried them around and around the stalk, the rope winding tighter and tighter. As they slammed into the side of the enormous plant, Jasper used his legs to take the brunt of the impact, cushioning the blow.

The two of them hung there, breathing hard.

Dorothy looked around in disbelief. They were only fifteen feet away from the ground. It had been a close call. "I can't believe we made it," she said breathlessly.

"Now see, *that* was showing off," Jasper said, grinning.

"Very impressive." She laughed and traced a finger down the length of his chin. The thrill of being alive was surging through her and being so close to him was bringing up all of her emotions again. "Thank you for saving me. Again." She smiled, leaning in to kiss him—

"We're not safe yet!" the Lion's deep voice urgently called down from above.

They both looked up to see the Lion jumping down from stalk to stalk in a mad dash.

Behind him, the Iron Giant was teetering backward. It was finally going to fall. And they were in its path!

Jasper and Dorothy separated and slid down the stalk. They hit the ground running. The Lion jumped down, joining them.

They raced between the stalks. A gargantuan shadow fell over them. Groaning metal and the sharp cracks of breaking stalks sounded from far above them. None of the group bothered to look up. They knew what was coming.

With a tremendous, earth shaking impact, the Iron Giant crashed down right behind them. It struck with such force that the ground under Dorothy, Jasper and the Lion literally lifted up and threw them a good twenty feet. Their breath was knocked from them as they hit the ground, tumbling, rolling and sliding. A shower of dirt and rock rained down on them for a brief instant then all was quiet.

At least until the Giant's right hand crashed down near them, still clutching its gargantuan hammer. That last impact was a little too close for comfort and made Dorothy's bones ache.

They sat there amongst the purple grass and dirt, surrounded by fallen stalks and a motionless metal giant.

There was still a small amount of hissing and creaking coming from inside the giant, but otherwise it was astoundingly quiet.

The three of them looked at each other, knowing that they had been lucky to survive.

The Lion brushed a clump of dirt off his arm and gave Dorothy a wry smile. "Welcome back to Oz."

Dorothy burst into laughter. After all the danger she had just experienced, it was a relief to relax and laugh. She couldn't stop and soon Jasper and the Lion were laughing with her.

They were still laughing when the rest of the Knights found them.

CHAPTER 37
THE VALLEY OF WHISPERS

An enormous, impassable mountain range loomed before the Knights of Oz. It stretched from horizon to horizon in multiple shades of purple.

It was a little after noon. Though they couldn't see the sun, they could feel it. They were beseiged by a muggy heat that threatened to suffocate them. The strong winds didn't help, since they were only channeling the hot air.

All morning long Dorothy and her companions had crossed increasingly precarious terrain. More than once, the loose, shifting shale and crumbling rock caused horse hooves to slip over the ledges of sheer drops. Navigating these precipices slowed them to a crawl.

And now this. A wall of stone.

Still, in comparison to the previous day's adventures, there were few complaints. It had been a relatively uneventful morning.

They sat astride their horses, facing the only option available to them—a deep valley cutting through the mountains.

The valley walls rose up into towering cliffs, jagged and ominous. The cliffs turned inward as if they were tidal waves frozen in time.

"The Valley of Whispers," the Lion said grimly.

As soon as the name was spoken aloud, the horses became skittish, snorting and bucking nervously. The Knights had to yank on their reins to steady their animals. Even Chalk shook his mane anxiously.

Boq licked his cracked lips and rubbed the white stubble on his chin repeatedly. "I've heard stories about this place. Rumors of death."

The other six Munchkins were equally apprehensive, their eyes darting back and forth amongst themselves. Even Willow's expression was fearful. They had all heard the stories.

Dorothy was very aware of their discomfort and looked at the Lion. "Is there any other route?"

He shook his weary head. "Not without adding weeks of travel. If we intend to reach the Wild Isle first, we have to go through this valley."

"Then it's decided." Dorothy turned to the group. "I know some of you have families and I won't ask you to risk your lives. I'll understand if you wish to stay behind."

Willow was first to answer. "I have no family. I fight for the land. You can count on my assistance."

The Munchkins glanced at each other, their faces hardening with resolution. A silent mutual agreement was made. They looked back at Dorothy and bowed.

Boq spoke for the group, "We follow our Queen."

Dorothy nodded, her eyes brimming with tears. She knew that would be their answer. They were loyal to Queen and land, and could never be swayed. But deep inside, she was afraid for them all.

"I'm honored." She faced the Lion. "Lead the way."

The Lion grimaced, taking on the burden of keeping them all alive. He looked each of them in the eye, as he growled out the order. "We ride quietly and slowly. No one makes a sound until we're through. Understood?"

They all nodded.

"Wait," Hup said, pulling out a lollipop. He popped it into his mouth.

There was a murmur of activity as the other Munchkins did the same.

Hup nodded at the Lion. "Now we're ready."

Down the hill and into the valley they went, following the Lion. They moved cautiously. The sounds of the horses' footsteps echoing faintly along the mammoth interior.

The valley was composed of dull purple stone, with bleached shades of thistle, heliotrope and magenta making up the strata running the length of its walls.

The group scanned the cliffs, searching for any hazards or potential threats. None of them had ever been in the Valley of Whispers or knew anyone that lived to tell the tale. They just knew it was deadly. The reason why, however, was completely unknown, so they were alert for anything.

Every now and then, small rocks and pebbles would cascade down the walls, startling them. Sweat began to trickle down their faces and not just because the air was hot and thick. The stress of making no sound and maintaining a constant vigilance was starting to take its toll.

It was so quiet they could hear every breath they took. A cough or clearing of the throat drew scolding stares.

Tik Tok's mechanical horse was moving as slow as possible, but in the deafening silence, its heavy copper hooves seemed to magnify into explosive cannon shots. Dorothy and the others winced with each of its strides.

After a grueling, excruciatingly slow thirty minutes, they reached the Valley's midpoint. Had they been moving at normal speed, it would have taken less than five.

More and more debris fell down as they progressed.

Thunder rumbled in the distance.

Inwardly, Dorothy groaned. Rain would only slow them down further. She glanced at Jasper and saw that he had heard it too. He wasn't wearing his helmet or gauntlets and would have to stop to put them on. It wasn't a quiet process. The armor would clank and clink against itself. Hopefully they would clear the valley before any rain started to fall.

More gravel rolled down from the cliffs.

Thunder rumbled again, louder this time.

Dorothy saw Jasper tense up. The storm must be moving fast toward them.

The Lion squinted, peering up at the sky. The clouds were gray, but they weren't storm clouds. His ears twitched, listening intently to every sound. He twisted around in his saddle, one way, then the other, scanning the cliffs. His feline ears were flicking and rotating, trying to hone in on the source of the sound.

The others followed suit, wondering what they were looking for.

Gradually, the Lion's troubled gaze dropped down to the valley floor.

The ground trembled violently.

They all realized it wasn't thunder that was making the sound—it was the valley itself! They could feel the vibrations through their horses.

"A quake?" Dorothy asked in a hushed tone, even though she suspected something far worse.

The Lion looked back at the others, his wide face filled with dread. "The walls are closing in."

CHAPTER 38
THE WALL THAT WASN'T THERE

"RIDE!" the Lion growled, slapping the backside of Dorothy's horse sending it into a wild gallop. He charged after her, with Jasper and the others following right behind.

The ground shook and shuddered underneath them. Larger fragments of rock began to tumble down around them.

The Knights rode as fast as they could, pushing their rides to the breaking point.

Booming nerve-rattling roars reverberated inside the valley, drowning out the sounds of their escape. Boulders fell, smashing into the ground near them, spurring the frightened horses into a panic-ridden sprint.

They saw it now—the sides were indeed closing in! The cliffs moving toward each other like a colossal venus flytrap seizing its prey. The noise was overwhelming, burying every other sound.

Not being able to hear anything but the destruction around her, Dorothy's head swam, making it all seem like a dream. It was like being underwater. Deep sounds echoing off walls. Hearing her own strained rapid breathing. Everything happening too fast and too slow at the same time.

The massive walls of the valley moaned and cracked, sliding closer and closer, forcing the group to ride single file.

Dorothy took the lead, with the Lion right behind her. Jasper followed, then Boq and Bom, Willow, Tik Tok, Wik, Pok, Hup, Mik and Kob.

Under the enormous pressure, weak points in the walls shot geysers of crushed rock into the air, showering them with sharp pebbles.

Between the purple walls of death, a sliver of violet grass and open sky grew in the distance. The valley's exit.

It was so close! A beacon of salvation, if they could only make it. Dorothy focused on that image, ignoring the valley's crushing maw that was only a few feet away on either side of her. She was almost out. Almost…

Dorothy shot out of the valley, skidding across the slick grass, finally bringing her tired horse to a halt. Her mount was huffing and flecks of foamy saliva dripped from its mouth. She looked back and saw the Lion and his ride coming to a stop behind her.

Jasper and Chalk came flying out.

The valley walls were closing fast!

Boq and Bom barreled out into the open with Willow and Tik Tok hot on their heels.

Wik's horse almost stumbled from exhaustion as it spent its last burst of energy to clear the opening.

Pok and Hup raced out just as the valley walls crashed together.

Mik and Kob didn't make it. The thunderous, ear-splitting crash silenced the two Knights in mid-scream.

The ground bucked and rolled from the impact, knocking Hup off his horse, then leveled off, leaving them standing in an eerie stillness.

Wik jumped off his horse and ran to the sealed opening, slamming his fists against the hard rock. "Mik!" He tried to pry the valley walls open, bloodying his fingers in the process.

Hup approached him and placed a firm hand on Wik's shoulder, causing Wik to break down into sobs. Wik leaned his forehead against the stone and wept for his lost twin.

Dorothy was weeping too. Already her fears were coming to pass. She was leading them into death. She slid off her horse and went over to Mik, holding his shoulders. "I'm sorry. You all should have stayed behind," she said, voice breaking.

Jasper came up next to her, putting an arm around her, holding her close. "It wasn't your fault."

Pok shook his head. "It was our choice, M'Lady. It's our burden to bear."

"No—no one can die in Oz." Dorothy's shoulders trembled as she started to sob. "That's the rule."

The Lion hung his head low. "We told you that to comfort a lost little girl. We were only trying to protect you."

Wik turned around and wiped at his red eyes. "They're right, M'Lady. It's our choice and our burden. There is no blame toward you. We do this for Oz."

Dorothy sniffed, wiping her own tears away as she stood straighter and nodded. "For Oz."

Wik placed a hand against the stone, where the valley walls

met. "Goodbye my brother," he said, stopping, holding back a torrent of tears, sucking down choking sobs. Then when he had gotten control, he continued. "And Kob, my good friend. May you both have a safe journey in the next life."

They all lowered their heads to honor their fallen companions.

In silence, they mounted their horses and continued on. Their heartache was palpable, hanging heavy over them, but their mission gave them a purpose. A reason not to fall into despair.

* * *

Eventually the field of purple grass gave way to a steep slope that ran down to a raging river far below. The air was noticeably cooler here. Near the bottom of the slope, the area was dotted with oversized purple mushrooms.

The Knights stopped at the edge.

Dorothy stared down at the water, a twinkle in her eye. It had been a long time since she had seen it.

It was the Rainbow River.

A body of water that ran along the borders of the four countries of Oz—Munchkin, Gilliken, Winkie, and Quadling. She had never crossed it here at this spot, but many other times in many other places.

It was a literal rainbow of colors with vibrant stripes of red, orange, yellow, green, blue, and violet, all surging forward in a frothing race toward a waterfall which spat the water out into a deep canyon. It did this with such tremendous force that they could feel the vibrations under their feet.

A thick layer of multi-colored mist rose up, hiding the bottom of the canyon, making it seem that much more foreboding.

The Valley of Whispers had marked the end of Gilliken Country. The other side of the river was the eastern Winkie Country. Yellow was the dominant color there, but unlike the harsh purples of the northern lands of Gilliken, normal colors were allowed to flourish, making it easier on the eyes.

"We'll have to go the rest of the way on foot," the Lion said as he dismounted. He stood by the edge, staring down the length of the slope.

Jasper leaned forward and patted Chalk's muscled neck. "What do you think, buddy?"

Chalk shook his equine head, sending his ivory mane rippling side to side. "I think he's right. I'd break all four of my legs."

Dorothy slid off her horse and joined the Lion. She could tell he was troubled. "What's wrong?"

"It's too quiet," he replied, without taking his one good eye off the path ahead.

"I'm more worried about the river," Jasper said, walking up to them with Chalk by his side.

With a start, Dorothy realized that was going to be a problem. Jasper and water didn't mix. Then she saw the solution. "Looks like there's a bridge down there."

Spanning the river was a narrow, rickety mess of rotting wood planks held together with frayed old rope.

Jasper leaned forward and squinted. He scrunched up one side of his face and ran a hand through his disheveled hair. "I don't know if I'd call that a bridge."

Chalk tilted his head, giving the structure a good once over. "That doesn't look like it would hold a child, let alone a grown man."

"Only one way to find out," the Lion growled.

The rest of the Knights dismounted and made preparations, taking only their weapons and a light supply of food and water before sending their horses off to graze. Jasper removed his armor to lighten his load. No need to risk adding unnecessary weight to that bridge.

The Lion stepped down onto the slope. His clawed foot sank slightly into the soft purple grass. It was firm enough to support them.

Dorothy stepped down onto the soft ground. It felt good. A little like wet sand at the beach.

As Jasper was about to join her, Chalk sidled up to him and thumped him with his broad shoulder.

"Good luck," Chalk said, with brotherly concern.

"Yeah. We'll need it." Jasper slapped his friend on the side, then stepped off the edge.

They all carefully inched their way down the slope, step by step. Twice, Pok lost his footing and rolled a few feet before catching himself. Each time, he stood up sheepishly dusting himself off. Had Mik and Kob's death not been so fresh on her mind, Dorothy would have laughed.

As it was, certain areas were so steep, they all had to jog to keep from falling forward themselves.

That was why it hurt so much when they all smacked into the wall that wasn't there.

CHAPTER 39
THE GROMP

Dorothy picked herself up off the ground, getting back on her feet. She had hit it hard, seeing stars.

She rubbed her forehead. It pulsed in pain. When she lowered her hand, she saw a smear of blood on her fingertips. Not a lot. Minor scrape. Her right arm ached too. At first contact with the barrier, she had managed to bring her arm up to protect herself.

Around her, the rest of the Knights were gathering themselves up, shaking off the pain.

Ahead, there appeared to be an unobstructed path to the river, yet something had stopped them.

"It's a wall," Bom said, running his hands across the solid air.

Dorothy extended her hand and felt it. Cold and hard.

And invisible.

They all could feel it. The Knights began slapping it and hitting it.

Willow cracked her mace against it with no effect, other than making her hand hurt. "Whatever it is, we're not getting through it."

Tik Tok punched it with an extraordinary amount of force. His fist bounced off. "Sol-id con-struct-tion."

Jasper had his hand on the unseen barrier, sensing the wall's qualities. "Made of stone. Thick too."

"See how far it extends," the Lion said to his Knights.

The group spread out to the sides, searching for an end to it or at the very least, an opening.

"This blasted thing goes on forever!" said Boq, sounding quite irritated. "Give me a boost up, son." Boq said to Bom, who dutifully lifted his father up onto his shoulders.

Boq reached up and felt around, encountering only more of the transparent rock. "Still here. It never ends."

Dorothy heard a chirp and looked up to see a bright blue bird sail high over the invisible wall. Much higher than where Boq was testing. "Yes, it does! Look! We can go over it."

The Knights looked up to see the bird sail by.

They needed to climb it. Dorothy turned to Jasper, "Your grappling hook—

He shook his head. "Lost it back with the Iron Giant."

They all contemplated the blankness that blocked their way.

"Tik Tok, stand by the wall and I'll get on your shoulders," Hup said, guiding Tik Tok into position. Hup then climbed on top of him. "Okay, who's next?"

"I'll go," said the Lion, already climbing up. He stepped onto Hup's shoulders and extended his hand high above his head.

He grasped the edge of the wall and pulled himself up. The Lion stood in mid-air on top of the invisible wall. He glanced back down at the Knights. "If we do it this way, someone's going to be left behind. We need a rope to get everyone up."

"Let me try," Willow said, stepping up to scale the human ladder. She reached the top and stood next to the Lion.

He looked at her. "What have you got in mind?"

Willow grabbed a handful of her ivy hair and held the ends out for the Lion to see. They both watched as the vines started to grow at an accelerated rate, intertwining, twirling around each other to form a thick cable of living plant. It continued to grow, hanging down to her feet, then down over the side of the wall, until it reached the others at the bottom. The effort had drained her, using up many of her nutrients. She would have to rest later. In the meantime, she held up the section in her hands toward the Lion. "Cut it."

The Lion brought out his sword, hesitating. "That won't hurt you?"

"Of course it will. Cut it," she said, clenching her jaw.

With an expert's touch, the Lion severed the length of vines from her head with one swift slice.

Willow winced from the stinging pain. Sap dripped from the cut ends. She ignored it and wrapped the end around her hands, bracing herself. "Who's next?"

Up they went, two at a time. First Jasper and Dorothy. Jasper took Willow's vine, while Dorothy climbed up Tik Tok and Hup. Dorothy surprised herself, only needing a helping hand from the Lion at the top. When she stood up, she almost lost her balance, since it appeared to her own eyes that she was floating high above the ground. The effect was disconcerting.

After Hup made his way up the vine, there was only one

person left. Tik Tok. He was the last and he was the heaviest.

Tik Tok examined the vine in his metal hands. "I'm not sure this will hold my con-sid-er-a-ble weight, Gen-e-ral."

The Lion looked doubtful. "I'm not sure either."

"It will hold," Willow said, brusquely. She had been strong enough to support the vine for everyone else to climb up, but for Tik Tok, she was going to need the added muscle. "Just help me anchor it, so I don't get pulled down."

The Lion grabbed on to the vine and hunkered down, ready for the load.

Tik Tok began his climb.

The vine snapped taut and strained as he made his way up. Both Willow and the Lion leaned back, using all their muscle to hold him. The vine held and soon Tik Tok pulled himself up onto the wall.

The way down on the other side was much easier. Within minutes, they were all standing on the opposite side of the wall, looking ahead toward the bridge in the distance.

As soon as they stepped down, there was a noticeable change in the atmosphere. It was gloomier and chill winds blew through. A wispy fog blanketed the ground.

Dorothy hoped it was because they were closer to the river. That the waterfall mist was affecting the nearby area. Her instincts were telling her otherwise.

The group continued onward at a cautious pace.

The mushrooms growing on this side were abundant enough that the Knights couldn't walk in a straight line, they had to meander around them. The fungus caps were squat and low, but fairly large, at least three feet wide. They were a drab, dark shade of purple with big mulberry spots on top.

Dorothy didn't like the look of them. There was something

about them that was making her nervous.

"Trespassers!" The voice came from somewhere ahead, sounding like the croaking of a toad.

Startled, Dorothy jumped, sucking in a short breath. They all stopped, their eyes sweeping across the field. It didn't take them long to spot the source of that strange voice.

Sitting atop one of the giant mushrooms was a disturbing, ugly blob of a creature. They hadn't noticed it, since it was just another shade of mulberry, blending in with everything else.

It was only twelve inches high and was sitting like an infant with its short pudgy legs hanging down in front of it. Its body was comprised of bulging flesh. Its bulging head sat on a bulging neck, which sat on a bulging torso.

In fact, at first glance, Dorothy had thought it was a newborn baby, but it only took a second longer to see the gross differences.

The slightly more bulbous cranium. The slitted eyes. The lack of a nose. The wide toad-like mouth. Its hands ended in two narrowed fingers with a thumb, and its little feet only had two slug-like toes. It also had five short hairs sprouting from its head, spaced far enough apart to be easily countable.

A stubby, pointed tail as thick as its body, writhed behind it in slow serpentine movements.

Dorothy tried to hide the revulsion that swelled up inside her.

"Go back!" the hideous thing said with another croak.

At the Lion's signal, the rest of the Knights held back, while the Lion, Jasper and Dorothy edged closer to it.

"Hello. I'm sorry," Dorothy said as nicely as she could, "We don't mean to disturb you. I'm Dorothy. Who are you?"

Its head swiveled a fraction in its neck fat, watching them

approach. Its beady eyes squinting at them with a sour expression.

"Gromp!" it said, barking out its name aggressively.

As Dorothy got closer, she saw that the Gromp's body wasn't really flesh, but something firmer. Plant-like. Similar to a soft root. Dorothy didn't know if that fact made it less repulsive or more.

"Gromp? Is this *your* land?" Dorothy asked sweetly as if talking to a child.

"No!" the Gromp snapped back.

Dorothy winced at its abrupt response. "Whose is it?"

"The Witch Queen!" The Gromp shifted on its hind quarters, looking irritated by the extended conversation.

Witch Queen? Dorothy wondered. The Witch of the East (which is whose land they were entering) was killed when Dorothy's house had fallen on her (an accident!) during her first visit to Oz. The Witch of the West was a prisoner of the Nome King. That left Mombi and Glinda. The Witches of the North and South. Had one of them moved east to hide from the Nome King?

Jasper leaned in to Dorothy's ear. "He's a pretty small guy. I don't see how he could possibly stop us."

Dorothy nodded, but she knew things in Oz weren't always what they seemed. "Gromp? May we have permission to cross the river?"

"No! Go or die!" the Gromp croaked so loudly and so vehemently that it almost fell off its perch.

Well, that settled that, thought Dorothy. Though she didn't know if the Gromp was threatening them or warning them. Either way, the little thing wasn't going to help. She exchanged glances with Jasper and the Lion. She shrugged. They had tried.

"Okay Gromp, we're doing what you want, we're going away." Dorothy turned her back to the creature and motioned for the group to follow her.

Instead of retreating toward the invisible wall, she led her Knights around the Gromp, in the direction of the river.

"Trespassers!" the Gromp called out.

The Knights had to suppress laughter. The thought of that little creature trying to stop them was comical.

"Kill!" the Gromp screamed out, startling the Knights. "Kill! Kill! Kill!" it shouted again, never moving from its seat.

Several mushrooms started to quiver, then burst up from the ground, spraying dirt and grass, revealing themselves to be Mushroom Men!

Seven of them. Ten feet tall with thick imposing physiques. They had dark purple skin with mud and patches of pale mold covering them.

Under each spotted fungus cap, the Mushroom Men's gruesome faces frowned. Pale slits for eyes, with no hint of a pupil. Their eyes reminded Dorothy of soft boiled eggs. Their mouths, with no lips, were only a wrinkled grimace.

They held no weapon, but their three-fingered hands ended in long, sharp thorns that looked just as dangerous as any knife.

Dorothy froze. She wished now that she had tried harder to convince the Gromp. Deep inside, though, she knew that would have been futile. He was a guardian with only one duty. Keep people out. He was apparently good at his job.

There was a moment of stillness as the Knights stood facing these new enemies, hands on their sheathed weapons, readying themselves, then—

"Kill them!" the Gromp croaked out once more into the heavy silence.

The seven mushroom warriors charged the group.

CHAPTER 40
OVER THE RAINBOW

There was the sharp sound of blades unsheathing as the Knights drew their swords.

The Knights stepped forward and met their enemy head on.

Bom dodged the first attacker, slashing it as it lunged past him. The Mushroom Men's bodies were dense and hard to cut through, but that didn't stop Bom from trying. It took a couple of swings before he was able to slice off the Mushroom Man's hand.

There was no blood. The monsters were, after all, walking fungus. The wounded creature barely noticed its missing limb—if it noticed at all—and continued its assault.

With one mighty blow, Willow's mace removed a Mushroom Man's leg, sending the creature to the ground, where it continued to crawl after her.

The Lion lopped off a mushroomed head after several

strikes. The body clawed at the Lion, trying to find him without its eyes.

The other Knights were faring the same. They were able to wound and cripple the creatures, but it wasn't stopping the monsters from coming after them.

Dorothy, guarded closely by Jasper, Tik Tok, and the Lion, was the first to notice how deadly these opponents really were. "Watch out! They're regrowing!"

Sure enough, the Knights saw new limbs sprouting from the Mushroom Men's wounds. Even the decapitated warrior was gaining a new head.

Because the Mushroom Men wouldn't actually die, the Knights were in constant motion, evading their attacks. The Lion, Wik and Boq had already suffered deep cuts from the thorn claws. They couldn't help but to glance around at all the mushrooms in the area. There were hundreds. If all of these were hidden warriors…

Seven Mushroom Men were giving them trouble. Any more and this was a battle they couldn't possibly win.

As if to answer that thought, more Mushroom Men sprang from the ground, joining the fight.

"Head for the river!" the Lion commanded.

The Knights broke into a run.

It was a wild, reckless dash toward the water. Mushroom Men were bursting from the ground everywhere they looked.

There were so many enemies now, the Knights could no longer stay together. They separated, running for their lives, wasting no time engaging in combat. They simply ran.

The endless army gave chase, a mob of clawing relentless horror.

Dorothy was gasping, finding it hard to draw in breaths.

Jasper had her hand and was leading her to the river, fending off any fungal warrior that barred their way. He was so fast. His strides so long. She was stumbling. Tripping. Jasper didn't slow down. He couldn't. The monsters were right behind them.

It sounded like the Mushroom Men were right next to her. Moaning and growling, sounding like the very zombies that Dorothy had so often pictured her co-workers as. This was far worse.

She focused. She could keep up. She had to. Pushing herself, ignoring the sharp twangs in her leg muscles, she threw herself forward, running alongside Jasper.

The bridge was close. They were hurtling toward it. No stopping them.

Ahead, Hup and Wik crossed the bridge with little trouble. The structure would hold.

Dorothy reached the bridge first. It was thinner and more fragile up close. The river was wider than she thought too. Several feet below the bridge, the current was fast and rough. If one of them fell, they would be swept away in an instant with no hope of rescue.

Without stopping, she sprinted across. Boards creaked and cracked under her light footsteps, but she reached the other side safely.

She looked back and saw that Jasper had given her time to cross, by fending off three Mushroom Men that had been hounding them. He slashed away, keeping them from the bridge.

The Lion, Boq and Bom reached Jasper and helped to dispatch the creatures. They hacked at them, severing a few arms, then kicked the three Mushroom Men into the river where the strong current whisked them away.

"Go! Now!" the Lion ordered his Knights.

Boq and Bom raced over the bridge.

Jasper gritted his teeth and dashed out onto the weak-looking planks. The bridge protested, groaning and swaying under his weight, but held together. Halfway across, his boot suddenly plunged through a piece of rotting wood. He fell sideways toward the water—

"JASPER!" Dorothy reached out from shore, straining to help—a reflexive gesture—but he was too far away.

Jasper grabbed for the rope railing, caught it, and after a brief struggle, righted himself.

He shook off the terror that threatened to overwhelm him and rushed across the remainder of the bridge, joining Dorothy on solid ground. She threw her arms around him and he responded in kind, thrilled to be alive.

Willow, Tik Tok and Pok reached the Lion.

The army of Mushroom Men had followed.

Willow and Pok dashed across the bridge at the Lion's order.

"Leave, Gen-e-ral! I will hold them off!" Tik Tok said to the Lion.

The Lion hesitated, then nodded. He crossed the river, joining Dorothy on the other side.

Dorothy saw that Tik Tok wasn't crossing.

The wave of Mushroom Men were almost upon him.

Tik Tok waved a copper hand in her direction. "I'm a-fraid this bridge is lack-ing in pro-per strength! Rest as-sured, Miss Dor-o-thy, I'll not let an-y of these mon-sters pass!"

His deep voice sounded so distant over the noise of the river and the moans of the Mushroom Men. Dorothy shook her head, refusing to hear it. "TIK TOK! NO!!"

Tik Tok spun around to face the oncoming flood of horror. He leaned forward and planted his feet firmly into the dirt. Tik

Tok never carried a sword—his weapons were his fists—which he now swung like sledgehammers, decimating each mushroomed warrior that came near. His valiant effort took down the first two dozen, but the sheer volume surged forth, knocking him back onto the bridge. Wood cracked under his heavy form.

The Mushroom Men swarmed over him, flowing across the weakening wood and rope structure.

KA-RACK!!!

The sound was loud and sharp. The bridge buckled under the weight. Ropes snapped. Wood shattered into jagged shards. The structure literally disappeared under Tik Tok and the mass of Mushroom Men, sending them all into the river with a thunderous splash.

The turbulent current carried the monsters away with astonishing speed and flung them over the waterfall into the unknown.

Deprived of their goal, the surviving Mushroom Men gathered along the opposite shore, howling angrily.

Dorothy and the Knights were safe, but they had lost another of their group.

Tik Tok was gone.

Dorothy's throat closed up. Losing Tik Tok was almost too much for her. The loss hit her so hard, she couldn't even cry. She was going into shock.

A chorus of shrill screams yanked her out of her anguished thoughts. The sound was nerve-rattling.

It was coming from above.

Everyone's attention was drawn upward where they saw a black blot filling the sky.

Crows! Over a hundred of them, coming in fast, straight toward the Knights.

Dorothy squinted. The sun was still trapped by the ever present grey clouds, but there was still a glare. She held up a hand to block out some of the brightness. She could swear the crows were carrying something…

Yes, she was sure of it. Her eyes went wide, recognizing what it was.

The Scarecrow!

CHAPTER 41
FURIOUS FRIENDS

The Scarecrow's arms were outstretched, bird talons gripping him, carrying him through the air. As they neared, the large birds opened their claws, releasing him.

He dropped down, landing with a light plop—made of straw and canvas, he didn't weigh much.

Before any of them could react, the crows attacked. Razor-edged talons sliced through flesh. Beaks snipped and pecked.

The Lion dropped to one knee, throwing an arm up to cover his good eye. "Cover your eyes!"

The Knights followed suit, attempting to protect themselves. Even Willow. Though made of bark and leaf, she was still vulnerable, especially her eyes.

The rush of claws and wings caught Jasper off guard and he made the mistake of stepping back. He was near the river's edge and his foot slid off the dirt into empty space. Once more, he felt himself falling sidelong toward the river.

He dropped his sword and flailed his arms wildly, seeking a handhold. His fingers wrapped around something and his arm nearly jerked out of its socket as his fall came to an abrupt stop. He had grabbed onto the dangling remnants of the bridge still attached to the posts on shore. Jasper threw a glance down and saw the river surging by underneath him, splashing against his boots. Instant death should he fall.

Dorothy swung her free fist back and forth with force, managing to knock a few birds out of the air.

Having been assaulted by these birds several times now, she was more angry than scared. The winged terrors caused a lot of pain—*without question!*—but could be endured. The problem was that it left them blind and unable to fight back.

"Scarecrow! Stop!" she screamed.

The Scarecrow paid no attention to her pleas and pulled out a dagger that had been tucked under his belt. It was thin, with a long undulating snakelike blade. He raised it over Dorothy, who, with her eyes covered, was oblivious to the impending danger.

Yanking his feet up, Jasper desperately pulled his way back onto firm ground, where he saw the Scarecrow about to strike. Jasper snatched up his sword and rushed the Scarecrow, screaming in anger.

Surprised, the Scarecrow jumped back, barely having time to bring his dagger up to block Jasper's incoming sword. As the blades met, there was a clash of metal and a spray of sparks.

Jasper struck again and again, each time the Scarecrow parrying with his dagger. The Scarecrow's weapon was no match though and on the third strike, it went flying from his hand.

Scrambling backward, the Scarecrow hissed and pointed at

Jasper, commanding all of his crows to switch targets and attack him.

The crows clustered around Jasper, but he ignored them. One of the benefits of being made of clay was that he had no organs—such as eyes—that could be permanently harmed. All injuries, though painful, would heal quickly, reforming in seconds.

The crows cried out in frustration.

At the sight of Jasper walking toward him with his blade ready, the Scarecrow spooked, retreating.

Jasper continued to close the gap between them, unaffected by the straw man's feathered flock. Jasper smiled, leaning forward as he broke into a run.

The Scarecrow turned and dashed for the rocky mountainside, clambering up it like a monkey. He was almost out of reach when Jasper caught up.

Jasper grabbed the Scarecrow's right ankle and swung his sword, lopping off the leg. The leg fell away, spilling straw across the rocks and yellow dirt. Jasper dropped it and looked back up to see the Scarecrow still ascending, unhindered by his missing leg.

Jasper sheathed his sword and tried to follow. There weren't enough footholds and with each attempt, he would find himself sliding back to his starting point.

With their master distracted, the crows scattered into the air.

Feeling and hearing the birds' presence lifting away, the Knights cautiously uncovered their eyes.

Dorothy took in the situation at a glance. She saw Jasper striving to climb an unclimbable mountain. She saw the wounded Scarecrow escaping above them. She saw the dismembered leg on the ground with the straw around it. Even though the Scarecrow was now an enemy, the sight of the detached limb disturbed her.

A guttural growl beside her made her jump. The Lion was

baring his sharp teeth as his gaze locked onto the fleeing Scarecrow. Before she could blink, the Lion was gone, having launched himself up toward the mountain.

The Lion raced up the rocks, his claws finding purchase where there wasn't any. In contrast to his heavy form, he moved with incredible agility. He caught up to the Scarecrow in seconds and snagged his old friend's remaining leg.

The Scarecrow looked down and was horrified to see the Lion staring back up at him, eyes filled with uncontrolled rage.

The Lion jumped off the mountain, yanking the Scarecrow with him. They both tumbled through the air. The Lion sank his claws into the Scarecrow's chest, positioning the straw man to take the impact of the fall.

They hit the ground with a loud thud, sending plumes of yellow dust into the air.

"TRAITOR!" the Lion bellowed.

Wasting no time, the Lion ripped into the Scarecrow. There was the sound of cloth tearing. Straw flew in all directions. There was no chance of fighting back for the Scarecrow.

The others stood back, fearful of the Lion's ferocity.

Dorothy covered her mouth, but couldn't look away. It was primal and savage. And terrible. Her eyes welled with tears. Two of her dearest friends and one was tearing the other apart. She shook her head. *This was wrong. This shouldn't be happening.*

The Lion finally stopped. He was breathing hard.

Under the Scarecrow's tattered clothes, they could see that his canvas body was completely torn open. Most of his straw stuffing had been spilled. His face was split, one half sagging to one side. He could no longer talk. He twitched in pain.

The Lion held out a hand. "Fire stones." His voice was cold and final.

The Scarecrow's eyes widened in terror.

No one moved. Then Pok reached into a pouch on his belt and pulled out two flint stones, which he promptly handed to the Lion General.

The Lion held them over the straw stuffing in the Scarecrow's chest and banged the two stones together. They produced large sparks that quickly ignited the straw.

The Lion stepped back and watched the Scarecrow start to burn.

Dorothy rushed forward and kicked the yellow dirt onto the flames, snuffing them out before they did much damage.

The Lion shot her a furious look for interfering.

Dorothy's stern glare silenced him. "I won't allow you to do this. You've done enough." Dorothy wasn't asking. It was an order. From the Queen.

The Lion's lip curled over a fang as he held his anger in check. He nodded and stepped away.

Dorothy knelt down beside the Scarecrow and placed a hand on his forehead, gently stroking it. "What happened to you? What did they do to you?" Her voice was barely a whisper.

He looked up at her. His stare was unreadable.

Dorothy couldn't find any hint of the person she used to know. Of the friend that she loved. A tear rolled down her cheek.

"I'm so sorry, Scarecrow." Dorothy said, leaning down, kissing him on the forehead.

She sniffed back more tears and stood, looking at the others. "We leave him. Let's go."

"Wait for me, Miss!" The familiar low voice came from the river's edge.

They all turned to see Tik Tok climbing up onto shore. Water streamed down his copper body and leaked out of his joints.

"Tik Tok! You're alive!" Dorothy ran over, wrapping her arms around him, getting her clothes wet in the process, but she didn't care.

Tik Tok returned the hug, "It would take more than a bit of wa-ter to do me in, Miss Dor-o-thy! Slowed my pace is all."

She laughed. It felt so good to have her old friend back, she was momentarily overcome with sheer joy. Jasper and the others laughed too. Even the Lion managed to chuckle, in a growly way.

Soon, Tik Tok had managed to shake out all the river water and they were ready to continue their journey. As they walked into the nearby forest, Tik Tok noticed the Scarecrow laying in the dirt. "I say, is that—?"

"It is. Just keep walking." Dorothy said, nodding.

"He does-n't look well," Tik Tok said, eyeing the Scarecrow.

"There's nothing we can do." Dorothy guided him toward the trees.

"Dread-ful shame. He was such a jo-vi-al fel-low," Tik Tok said, shaking his head mournfully.

Dorothy leaned against her friend, resting her tired head against his cold, metal frame, feeling another wave of sadness wash over her. "Yes, he was."

CHAPTER 42
STRAW THOUGHTS

Numb

His body felt numb.

Empty.

It was hard to put thoughts together.

Can't move.

He turned his head, or maybe his head just fell to the side—it was difficult to tell anymore—and he spied a leg laying a few feet away from him.

Strange.

A leg all by itself with no owner in sight.

He realized with a start that it was his own limb he was staring at.

Oh yes, that's right.

It had been chopped off.

By the man with the sword.

For a moment, his thoughts wandered.

Why had the man been immune to his crows?

Was he not a man?

Perhaps he was made of something other than flesh?

Perhaps—

His canvas brows drew together with concentration as he brought his attention back to his current situation. There was a drive to know, a curiosity that was hard to control, but he willed his thoughts to focus on the problem at hand.

Repair.

The Scarecrow reached out and began to gather his spilled straw…

CHAPTER 43
THE MURKY MARSH

It was cold. It was wet. And it was foul.

Dorothy was disgusted with every footstep she took. Her feet squished deeply into the swampy grass, the slimy muck coming up to her ankles. She could feel things living in it, sliding against her flesh, sometimes catching between her toes. She shuddered, wishing she had some thick boots on to form a barrier between her and this horrible slop.

They were in the Murky Marsh. A dismal quagmire of twisted, leafless trees, old rotting logs and a dank, thick haze of white fog that made it almost impossible to navigate. The smells were pungent and putrid, full of decay, threatening to activate gag reflexes if one didn't breathe through their mouth.

Snakes, insects and other creepy, unidentifiable things slithered and crawled and jumped aside as the Knights made their way through. Occasional splashes and ker-plunks could be heard around them. Whatever was making the sounds was hidden by the soupy mist.

Dorothy almost preferred not to know. She focused on the simple task of walking. The cold mud would wrap around her bare feet, acting like glue, making each step a struggle. Her thighs and calves burned from the continuous effort. She fought to pull her foot out of the green-brown muck. It came out with a *plorp!*

The rest of the Knights were having the same trouble, stumbling as they went.

Tik Tok was having the most difficulty due to his weight. His metal legs sank into the slime almost up to his knees, causing him to fall behind. He more or less pushed his way through the thick gunk, rather than took steps.

Pok huffed and puffed, drawing in labored breaths. "My legs are going to fall off. Someone's going to have to carry me soon." he gasped.

Hup laughed. "That's a sight I'd like to see. Any volunteers?"

"I don't think any of us is brave enough to take on that task." Wik said quietly.

Laughter spread amongst the Knights. Wik had been fairly silent since the death of his brother. It was good to hear him crack a joke again. It eased some of the tension that had built around them.

"Cowards!" laughed Pok.

Dorothy saw how tired the group was. She was just as exhausted, but the thought of stopping—especially here—made her anxious. There was too much at stake. They had to get to the Wild Isle before the Nome King could get—

Her eyelids drooped and she suddenly found herself falling

forward into the brackish muck. The cold grimy water hit her face, revitalizing her. She looked around, startled.

"Careful," Jasper said, helping her to her feet.

A splash came from behind them as Hup collapsed into the swamp, followed a second later by Wik.

Pok grabbed Wik and lifted him back to his feet.

"What happened?" Wik blinked and looked both surprised and confused.

Hup on the other hand, was having a harder time recovering from the fall. Bom had gotten to him and stood him up, but Hup was limp and couldn't keep his eyes open. Bom slapped him once, with no result, then slapped him again, much harder this time. Hup jolted awake.

Boq shook his head, "We're too tired to go any further, M'Lady. Let us just sit and rest awhile." His eyes were heavy and he looked like he might be the next to fall.

Something wasn't right here. Dorothy could feel it. They weren't just tired. They looked like they were—

Her head whipped around, scanning the area. There were clusters of bright flowers growing near the base of all the trees. Yellow ones. Scarlet ones. Purple ones. Odd, that she hadn't noticed them before, since they were completely out of place in this sunless, black swamp. These beautiful flowers though, she knew all too well.

When she turned back to the others, the Lion had already met her gaze. He had seen them too.

"Poppies," they both said in unison.

"Oh no." Jasper spotted them now.

Dorothy pointed at the flowers. "Those are poppies! They'll put us under a sleep spell! Run or we'll never wake!"

They all bolted clumsily across the marsh, using the gnarled trees as leverage.

A tree branch snagged Dorothy's shirt, ripping it. She pulled and yanked, but couldn't free herself. She was having deja vu'. This had already happened to her. Back in New York. Or she had dreamed it had. It seemed so long ago now.

She stopped wrestling with the branch for a moment to notice that the tree's bark resembled a face.

Two large amber eyes opened up and stared down at her.

She gasped. It *was* a face! These were Terror Trees!

Another branch twisted down of its own accord and gripped her arm.

Wik found himself ensnarled in tree limbs.

A root lifted out of the mud and tripped Pok.

Branches and roots were grabbing, clawing, and catching the other Knights faster than they could react.

The trees cracked and popped as they uprooted themselves and closed in.

Willow broke several branches with her mace, but she too couldn't escape their clutches. "Traitors! How can you call yourself trees? You shame all tree-kindmmfff!"

The Terror Tree holding her, wrapped a branch across her mouth, not wanting to hear anymore.

Even Tik Tok's exceptional strength wasn't enough. One of the larger trees wrapped its thick branches around him, holding him tight.

Dorothy fought and kicked, but her arms and legs felt weighted, too heavy to lift. It was a desperate battle now to just keep her eyes open. The spell of the poppies was taking effect. She saw that the others were succumbing too. Only Tik Tok, continued to fight against his captor.

Just before surrendering to the sleep-spell, Dorothy heard a chorus of hissing, then saw several shadowy forms stepping out of the fog.

Lizardmen.

CHAPTER 44
CAPTURED!

Dorothy could feel her body swaying side to side.

The motion was making her queasy.

She tried to move and found she was incapacitated.

With great effort she managed to crack open her bleary eyes. What she saw made her head hurt and she clamped them shut again, letting her headache simmer down. She opened them once more and tried to make sense of what she was looking at.

The world was upside down. Literally.

No. Not the world. She, herself, was upside down. She was being carried.

Dorothy blinked, clearing her eyes. She saw that she was dangling from a wooden pole with her hands and feet tied to it like a dead deer. The ends of the pole were resting on green, scaly muscled shoulders.

She twisted her head about and saw that she was being carried by lizardmen.

Reptilian warriors with tall, narrow bodies layered in dull scales. Pointed fins ran along their spotted backs and down their snaking tails which whipped back and forth with smooth fluidity. Their rough textured skin was dark green along their backs, gradually fading into a lighter shade toward their front. In their fearsome webbed claws, they gripped primitive spears.

When Dorothy saw their faces, she had to suppress a shiver. A thin black slit of a pupil sat in their bulbous orange eyes, darting this way and that, examining everything with a chilling, emotionless stare. Sharp tiny teeth lined their pronounced snouts and a long pink ribbon of a tongue flicked out from between their thin lips every few seconds, smelling the world around them.

They were Sleeches. Dorothy had heard of them, but never encountered one before.

She tore her gaze away from the creatures, unable to look at them anymore. She caught sight of her friends, bound similarly, behind her. They were groggy, just now waking from the spell.

She glanced ahead and saw that they were crossing over a creaking wooden drawbridge toward a looming castle made of dark stone.

The castle was narrow at the base and wide at the top, defying gravity, which as Dorothy remembered, didn't always apply in Oz. As the structure grew outward, it spiraled upward, giving it a fanciful, almost whimsical feeling. It would have been inviting, if not for the colorless grey exterior covered in dingy ivy and black moss. The suffocating thick fog and bleak marsh that surrounded the castle added to the ominous atmosphere.

Her neck was aching from craning it all about, so she decided to just relax until she found out where they were taking her. Since her view was of the sky, she took note that it was now night. She and the Knights must have been unconscious for a couple of hours.

Dorothy watched a stone archway pass by overhead as they entered the castle, then a dim passage lit by flickering torchlight. Soon the passage opened up into a grand room with massive round pillars that stretched up to support the high ceiling.

The Sleeches stopped and unceremoniously dumped Dorothy and the others to the ground, cutting the ropes binding their feet. Nearby Sleeches quickly replaced them with heavy chains. Once that was done the lizardmen shackled the wrists of each one of the Knights, then cut away the remaining ropes, freeing them from the poles.

The reptilians stepped back, taking positions near the walls, their tails swishing and twitching.

A Terror Tree stomped into the room after them with Tik Tok trapped in its massive branches.

Standing in the middle of the room, Dorothy exchanged glances with Jasper and the others.

They were prisoners, that was clear, but of who or what?

CHAPTER 45
THE WITCH OF A WITCH

Dorothy and her companions faced a blood red, carpeted stairway that led up to an empty throne on a second level. A balcony ran along the wall on either side of the throne. The room was bathed in deep shadows, lit only by a few flickering torches, giving it a chilling atmosphere.

From a dark doorway on the second floor, there was movement. A young attractive woman appeared.

The woman wore a purple dress, cinched at the waist, that recalled the Victorian era with a high lace collar and puffed sleeves tapering out to her wrists. The color was so dark as to be almost black. Over her shoulders was draped a silky rich purple robe that shimmered in the torchlight. Bright yellow accents and trimmings adorned the edges of the outfit, leaving only her laced purple boots unaffected. Her smooth skin was ghostly pale, made all the more so by her short raven hair that encircled her face, ending just past her porcelain ears.

She sat on the throne, glaring down at Dorothy and her Knights with an icy stare. "This is my kingdom. I rule the Northern and Eastern lands. You have trespassed. Why?"

That would explain the purple and yellow color motif, thought Dorothy. *Gilliken and Winkie country combined.* Dorothy wondered what Mombi would say about this. Mombi governed the North. This woman was just another self-proclaimed ruler making a grab for power when no one was looking. Dorothy hid her disdain and took a step forward. "We were passing through. We mean you no disrespect."

The woman raised an eyebrow. "You travel with the Lion General and his Knights of Oz. A war party."

Dorothy hesitated, deciding whether she should tell the truth or not. Lying had never come naturally to her. She was someone who spoke her mind and dealt with the consequences. It had always seemed to work out for her in the end.

She licked her dry lips and stood taller, trying to present some semblance of authority. "We are on our way to the Wild Isle to stop the Nome King."

"Dorothy—" The Lion growled in a low tone and gave her a disapproving glance. He didn't want this woman knowing their business.

"Dorothy?" the pale woman exclaimed with sudden interest, sitting forward. "Dorothy the Traveler? The false Queen of Oz?"

"She is our *true* Queen!" barked Pok, furious at the remark.

Dorothy simply nodded. "I am she."

The pale woman threw her head back and laughed. Her mouth was wide, seeming to show all of her teeth at once, giving her smile a sinister appearance. "How sublime! An outworlder fancying herself ruler of Oz!"

Unlike her friends, Dorothy took no offense, but was curious as to who she was being interrogated by. "I've never met you. What have I done to anger you?"

The pale woman rose to her feet and slowly descended the stairs to stand in front of Dorothy. She was half a foot shorter than Dorothy, but that didn't make her any less threatening. If anything, it made her seem *more* dangerous. A predator, coiled and ready to strike.

Leaning in, the pale woman's large, piercing eyes locked onto Dorothy's. "You dropped a house on my *mother*."

Silence hit the room like a shockwave. Dorothy's ears pounded in the stillness. "I— I didn't know…"

"I am Fairuza, daughter of Harpiba, the Witch of the East. You killed my mother and stole her magic slippers." Fairuza's gaze dropped down to Dorothy's muddy bare feet. "Where are they?"

"I don't have them anymore. They're in the possession of the Nome King."

Fairuza's eyes drew into slits, studying Dorothy. "Hmm. Do I believe you?"

"It's the truth." Dorothy said simply.

"We'll see. We'll see." Fairuza said with a menacing sidelong look.

Fairuza's alabaster hand traced the necklace that she wore, arriving at the centerpiece hidden by the collar of her dress. She lifted the centerpiece, revealing it for all to see.

It was an absolutely stunning amethyst set in gold. Its multifaceted surface gleamed in the firelight, twinkling with various shades of purple.

The muscles in Dorothy's face tightened. She had seen this

necklace before. She knew its power.

Seeing Dorothy's spark of recognition, Fairuza grinned, savoring the moment. Her other hand slipped under her robe to her waistband and pulled out a wand with a brilliant white crystal at the tip that sparkled with magical energy.

Dorothy's breath caught in her throat.

Fairuza giggled, not bothering to hide her delight. "You recognize these, don't you?" She lifted the necklace. "Mombi's necklace. Source of magic for the Witch of the North." She lifted the wand, waving it in the air. "And Glinda's wand. Source of magic for the Witch of the South."

"How did you..." Dorothy couldn't finish the question, fearing the answer.

"They didn't willingly give them to me, I can assure you. No, they put up quite a fight, but in the end... *I* wanted them *more*.

"Glinda...?" was all Dorothy could manage to ask.

Fairuza's expression twisted into one of mock sadness. She shook her head mournfully. "Gone, I'm afraid." Her cheshire grin returned, somehow even wider than before. "So you see, one way or the other, I'm going to find out where those slippers are."

She snapped her fingers at the Sleeches. "Take these Knights away."

The reptilians grabbed the bound Knights and began to push them from the room.

Jasper looked at Dorothy, raising his chained hands. He was made of clay and could easily escape at any moment.

Dorothy gave him an almost imperceptible shake of her head.

He nodded and let the lizardmen shuffle him from the room.

Fairuza walked up to the Lion and twirled a strand of his

mane. He remained motionless, watching her with his single fierce eye. She tapped a slender finger on his sensitive nose, causing him to flinch slightly. His whiskers angled back and his fur bristled. A menacing growl rolled from his throat.

She giggled again. "Leave the Lion."

Fairuza then moved to Tik Tok, entwined in the Terror Tree's limbs. She knocked on his copper head. It clanged. "The one-man army of Oz. Your weakness is well known."

She peered behind him and saw his winding key. She plucked it out. "You won't be needing this."

"My wind-ing key!" Tik Tok shouted, sounding almost emotional.

With a flick of the wrist, Fairuza flung it across the room. It clinked against the corner walls and landed on the stone floor amongst dirt and shadow.

Tik Tok jerked and thrashed, but had no success at improving his current situation. "You're a heart-less one, I dare say!"

"Save your power, Tik Tok!" Dorothy said, knowing he was stubborn and wouldn't stop fighting unless he were told to.

Tik Tok immediately became still, ending his struggle with a grunt. "Quite right, quite right."

"Throw him into the spike pit," Fairuza ordered the Terror Tree.

"No!" Dorothy started to lunge toward Tik Tok to help him, but was stopped by the cool, scaly hands of the Sleeches. Their fingers feeling like snakes wrapping around her arms.

She watched helplessly as the Tree stomped away with her friend in its clutches.

Fairuza turned back to Dorothy and the Lion. "Now… about those slippers."

CHAPTER 46
THE PIT FALL

Tik Tok knew that Miss Dorothy was correct. Without his winding key, his action gears would soon run down. He had to conserve, if he was to be of any service.

The Terror Tree carrying him shambled out of the castle into an open courtyard overgrown by weeds. The ground was soft and moist, making it easy for the Tree's roots to sink into and propel each of its lumbering steps. Its top branches shook as it walked, rustling as if summer breezes were blowing by. No such winds existed in the Murky Marsh though. The air was thick and chilled, kept aloft by the creeping fog.

The Tree came to a stop near the opening of a large stone pit in the ground. The Tree leaned over the edge and opened its branches, letting Tik Tok drop into the dark pit.

As Tik Tok fell forward into the abyss, his copper arm shot

out, grabbing one of the Tree's main branches, pulling it in with him. "You're com-ing with me, you o-ver-grown stump!"

Terror Trees aren't able to speak, but this one managed to come close with a groan of surprise as it toppled over the side of the pit and joined Tik Tok.

They both tumbled into the darkness, spinning in free fall.

Tik Tok let go and waved his arms about, succeeding in digging his fingers into the wall's stone surface, leaving long depressions as he fell. This slowed his descent a fraction and he saw the Terror Tree plunge past him. Though made of metal, Tik Tok knew that a fall from this height would do him in, flattening him and breaking his gears. He had only seconds to act.

He pulled his left hand back and punched the wall, lodging his fist firmly in the stone, abruptly ending his fall. His forearm bent slightly with the sudden stop, but didn't snap off, much to his relief. The Oz engineers would have to straighten that arm out after all was said and done, but right now Miss Dorothy needed him.

A great crack echoed from below.

His head swiveled around to have a look down. The Terror Tree had hit the bottom and splintered apart on top of the many gnarled spikes jutting up from the pit's floor.

Tik Tok's copper eyebrows raised. "Oh my."

Dangling by his left arm, he looked back up at the pit's opening far above him. It was going to take awhile to climb back up. He shifted his bulky body, positioning his flat feet against the hard wall, and swung his free hand up to start his ascent.

His fingers gripped the stones, then unclenched and slid right back down. His right arm dropped to his side, immobile. His power was winding down.

"No. I won't fail you, Miss Dor-o-theeee….." His proud,

gruff staccato voice trailed off as his vocal gears ceased to spin. His head fell to one side.

Tik Tok hung motionless. Without power to his inner actionwerks, he was now little more than a statue made of copper.

CHAPTER 47
IMPRISONED

Down into the lower levels of the castle, along dimly lit stone corridors, the reptilian guards pushed and shoved the Knights of Oz toward their final destination—a dank, musty dungeon cell.

All of the Knight's weapons had been confiscated before they had entered the lower levels, so there was no chance of revolt against their captors.

The barred door was swung open and Jasper and his brothers-in-arms were thrown in, their chained ankles causing them to spill over each other.

The door clanged shut behind them, the sound reverberating inside the confined walls.

Molds ranging from black to brown to yellow were fighting for dominance along the damp rock walls, filling the air with their stench. Drops of brown water fell from random spots on the ceiling in sporadic, yet rhythmic sploshes. Depending on the size of the drop, they either plinked or plopped.

Somewhere nearby, the squeaking of a starving rodent could be heard.

The Knights pulled themselves into a sitting position, backs against walls, exhausted and angry. None of them spoke, but conversations were being had with glances and expressions.

Shifting his attention to the Sleeches, Jasper saw that the guards were heading back down the corridor. One of the burlier ones stayed behind, spear in hand, standing watch opposite their cell.

Willow shook her head, her ivy hair swishing back and forth. "It seems all of Oz is against us."

"What do we do now?" Pok whispered, wearing a miserable frown.

No one had an answer, but Jasper was already working on a plan.

CHAPTER 48
THE LION'S PREY

Fairuza slowly paced in front of Dorothy and the Lion, her suspicious, piercing eyes boring a hole into Dorothy. "What you say could be true. On the other hand, you could be sending me straight into the Nome King's clutches."

"I swear to you. I give you my word." Dorothy was drained. She had spent the last twenty minutes answering Fairuza's questions truthfully, trying to appeal to reason.

The Witch's daughter stopped and turned. "Your word has never been worth much here."

Holding Mombi's necklace, Fairuza gestured toward the Lion, her finger etching mystic symbols in the air. She began uttering strange and unfamiliar words under her breath.

"What are you doing?" Dorothy could feel the air becoming charged with magical energy. "Stop it! I told you what you want!"

Fairuza finished and flashed a sinister grin at Dorothy as she began to retreat up the stairs. "Fear is very good at bringing out the truth." The pale woman waved a dismissive hand at the Lion.

The chains unlatched on both Dorothy and the Lion, dropping to the ground with a clatter. He was free. He turned toward Dorothy and growled, baring his sharp fangs. His one good eye was hostile, showing no signs of recognition.

Dorothy backed away.

"Let's try again. If I think you're lying, I'll let him eat you," Fairuza announced with glee, taking position on her throne to watch the show.

Dorothy's chest tightened as the Lion advanced toward her, his growl increasing in intensity.

CHAPTER 49
JASPER'S JAILBREAK

The Sleech stared at Jasper. Its lizard lips stretching and curling into a serpentine sneer. "You talk too much, sssoftskin," he hissed, his tongue darting in and out.

Jasper leaned against the door's thick iron bars and tried again. "Do you understand that *all* of Oz is in danger?" He had been trying to appeal to the Sleech, but the creature wasn't having it, which was to be expected.

"I don't care about Ozzz," hissed the guard, "The Witch treats usss well and will protect ussss."

The rest of the Knights were watching the exchange, wondering why Jasper was even trying. These beasts obviously didn't rank very high in intelligence.

"So there's nothing I can say to change your mind and free us?" Jasper asked with an earnest raising of the eyebrows.

"I'd rather cook you up in a nice sssstew." The Sleech licked his lips and laughed, which sounded like someone choking on a piece of food lodged in their throat.

"I guess that's a no, then." Jasper sighed, giving him a friendly shrug then suddenly turned to clay and fell through the bars, plopping onto the floor outside with a loud slap. He had collapsed into a puddle of flesh colored mud, his empty clothes resting on top in a crumpled heap.

The Knights sprang to their feet in astonishment.

The lizardman spat in surprise, hunching, holding his spear out defensively. The Sleech hissed at the puddle and edged closer to it, prodding and poking it with his spearpoint.

Jasper's hands erupted out of the clay glop and gripped the weapon.

The reptilian staggered back, still holding onto his spear. It tried to yank it out of the puddle's eerie disembodied hands, but instead, the puddle shot upward, oozing back into the form of Jasper, his clothes sliding along, expanding and filling.

The two opponents faced each other, each gripping the spear, playing a form of tug-of-war. Instead of pulling the spear toward him, Jasper used his weight to leverage the lizardman toward the prison cell.

"Hold him!" Jasper shouted at his companions.

The Knights rushed the bars, their arms shooting through to grab the Sleech as he came into range. They held the reptilian tight against the bars, locking their elbows around its arms.

With the Sleech restrained, Jasper pulled the spear free from its claws and swung it like a baseball bat, whacking it across the face. The spear's pole snapped in two from the impact. The guard went limp, head lolling forward.

The Knights dropped him to the floor.

Hup looked up at Jasper, his boyish face full of curiosity. "What are you?"

Jasper looked through the bars at Hup and the others. They all wore the same expressions—*why hadn't he told them what he was?*

He met their questioning stares head on. "I'm a Knight of Oz. Same as you."

He knelt down and searched the lizardman's pouches for the prison key. His hands came up empty. "He doesn't have the key."

Boq, the eldest and wisest of the group, reached out and grabbed Jasper's arm. "Go son! Go save the Queen!"

Jasper nodded, grasping Boq's arm firmly. "I'll be back for you!"

With that, Jasper rushed out of the room to find Dorothy.

CHAPTER 50
THE GHASTLY GAME

"I've told you everything!" Dorothy screamed.

She threw herself behind a pillar, barely avoiding a swipe of the Lion's claws. They gauged out chunks of stone instead, leaving four long ragged indentations. She darted away running for the other end of the room. The Lion bounded after her, slavering.

Hearing him right behind her, Dorothy dove to the side at the last minute, letting the Lion ram into a pillar. He hit it headfirst. There was an unpleasant thunk of stone and bone meeting. The impact cracked the pillar and the Lion rolled away, clutching his forehead.

This gave Dorothy time to sprint across the room toward the safety of another pillar. Or so she thought.

The Lion recovered quicker than expected and attacked

again. Dorothy rolled to the side, missing his sharp claws by a hair's width. She felt several rips open up on the back of her jacket.

On the grime-covered stone floor, out of breath and out in the open, she looked up at the Lion towering over her. She wouldn't be able to avoid him this time.

"I believe you." Fairuza said.

"Finally!" Dorothy gasped.

The Lion backed away.

Dorothy allowed herself to relax. All of her muscles had been tensed to the breaking point from trying to stay out of reach of her old friend. She ached all over.

Fairuza produced an ornate dagger from a thigh sheath and twirled it expertly in her slender hand.

Dorothy froze at the sight of the blade. Her muscles tensed right back up.

The pale Witch threw it down at Dorothy, where it stuck blade first into the ground near her.

Dorothy glanced at the knife, then up at Fairuza.

The Witch's mischievous grin was back in place. "You're free to go. All you have to do is kill your Lion friend."

"No." Dorothy said without hesitation.

"It's either him or you," the Witch cautioned with a sickening smile.

The Lion stepped forward, snarling ferociously.

Dorothy snatched the dagger and ran for cover as the Lion leaped for her.

Fairuza's laugh echoed throughout the room, delighting in the spectacle.

CHAPTER 51
THE WINDING KEY

On the other side of the chamber, hidden in shadow, lay Tik Tok's winding key. Tossed aside by Fairuza and forgotten.

tik

A subtle yet distinct sound came from the unassuming key.

-tik tik

Unnoticed by everyone, parts of it began to slowly spin and unlock.

-tik tik tik

Pieces unfolded outward.

-tik tik tik tik tik tik

Two arms.

Then two legs.

Then a round head popped up from the top and swiveled around. The winding key itself was a miniature mechanical man!

It rolled into a crouched position ready for action. It generated a constant, almost inaudible, ticking sound.

-tik tik tik tik tik tik tik tik tik tik tik tik tik tik tik tik.

This was Tik.

The Oz engineers' solution to Tok's ever present problem of winding down at the most inopportune times. Tik could not only keep Tok wound, but should the two be separated, Tik was designed to instinctively locate and reunite with his other half.

Across the room, Tik witnessed the Lion General lunging for Queen Dorothy. Queen Dorothy screamed out in pain. The Lion General's claws had left red slashes on her back, but she had evaded him by weaving between a series of columns.

Tik's tiny mechanical brows came together in a determined slant. He hopped nimbly to his little copper feet and dashed around the corner, sprinting down a torchlit corridor. His light steps barely made a sound against the ground.

The castle was vast and if it wasn't for Tik's compassometer —his main component, which constantly pointed him at Tok's current location—Tik would have quickly lost his way. And time was of the essence, Tok had to be found before Tik's own gears wound down. He darted through an archway and had to quickly throw himself against a wall.

One of the lizardmen was on guard here.

Tik carefully crept behind him, hugging the wall, staying out of sight.

The Sleech's head jerked to the side, moving as lizards do, with quick birdlike movements. He sniffed the air, jerking his snout up, then down, his tongue whipping out.

Tik froze.

After another tense second, the guard resumed his position, disregarding the strange scent of copper in the area.

Tik continued to sneak along, then rounded a corner and hurried down another underlit corridor.

A closed oak door was coming up. There was a wide gap at the bottom with light streaming through. Tik dove to the floor and rolled underneath. Once on the other side though, he stopped in his tracks.

Another Sleech. This one stood in front of Tik, a massive mountain of green scales and sinewy muscle. It held a wooden club and stared down at Tik in bewilderment. "Egh?"

Wasting no time, Tik raced ahead under the reptilian's legs, running past him.

"Ssstop!" The lizardman hissed, as he whipped around to give chase.

Tik let out a high pitched squeal, hearing the giant lumbering steps of the lizardman right behind him. Tik's miniature metal feet were a blur, barely outpacing the monster.

The ground shook as the Sleech brought his club down again and again, nearly squashing Tik each time. Tik narrowly avoided the strikes. The impacts were close enough to throw him off balance, making him lose ground. Tik flew down a short corridor and around a corner, but couldn't shake the Sleech. He rounded another corner and—

WHAM!

A meaty smack came from overhead and the next thing Tik knew, the guard hit the ground beside him, unconscious. The club fell from its claws and tumbled in front of Tik.

Tik looked up to see what could have struck the beast.

Jasper was standing over the reptilian, his fists clenched.

Tik whirred with excitement.

Hearing the familiar sound, Jasper glanced down and noticed Tik for the first time. "Tik!"

Tik whirred again, ending it with a small angry hop.

"Are you sure?" Jasper asked with surprise and concern.

A high pitched squeal was Tik's reply, with his arms animatedly thrusting up and down in the air.

"Right," Jasper nodded and picked up the lizardman's club, feeling its heft. "You go get Tok, I'll help Dorothy!"

Tik clicked an acknowledgment and dashed through another doorway, while Jasper charged in the other direction.

Tik soon found himself in a dining chamber with long rows of chipped, stained tables and crudely carved chairs. Most likely where the Sleeches came to feed. Mice scurried about, stealing the spilled food littering the floor.

Tik was in luck, dinner time had already passed and the room was empty. Most importantly, there was a doorway at the end of the room that led outside to where his compassometer was telling him he needed to go. Not only that, but the door had been left open a crack! Tik whirred with glee. He started to move toward it when he heard something shuffle somewhere to his left.

Turning around, Tik saw a crocodog curled up on a pile of hay in the far corner. Its appearance was that of a crocodile, shrunken and squashed down into the shape of a pitbull.

Tik of course had no idea what the creature was or what it resembled. He only knew it looked like a truly vicious, nasty animal.

Lifting its toothy head, the crocodog stared straight at Tik. Its yellow eyes brightened, its pupils drawing into slits.

The sight made Tik freeze in mid-step. His ticking actually stopped in fright.

The crocodog sprang to its clawed feet and bolted toward Tik.

Tik let out a shriek and raced for the door; his ticking now so fast, it threatened to pop a gear.

Through the crack in the doorway, Tik careened out into the courtyard, heading right for the pit where his compassometer was telling him he would find Tok.

KA-RASHHH! The doors swung open as the crocodog barreled outside, hot on Tik's tail.

The pit was near. Tik didn't bother looking back. He could hear the rapid footsteps right behind him. The precise snapping of the crocodog's jaw only inches away…

Tik launched himself at the well's edge, grabbing the stone and without hesitation, flipped himself up and over into the hole.

The crocodog, so intent on its prey, leaped into the pit after him. With one final snap of its horrific mouth, it missed Tik and plunged past him down into the darkness.

As Tik's tiny form plummeted toward the bottom, he saw Tok come into view, hanging from the wall by one arm.

With a squeal of delight, Tik angled himself toward Tok. He landed on Tok's round body with a loud hollow clang and started to slip off. He scrambled for a foothold and managed to snag a rivet, hauling himself up. He climbed onto Tok's back and found his keyslot—his home—and slid inside.

Tik's limbs retracted and then his head. Now in keyform, he sank all the way in until just the top of his head was visible, the butterfly-shaped handle. The handle began to spin, faster and faster, winding Tok back up.

Tik Tok's head lifted and shook back and forth, clearing the cobwebs out. "Good show, Tik!"

Tik whirred from behind.

Tik Tok's metal eyebrows rose in surprise. "The Gen-e-ral you say? No time to spare! We've got to res-cue Miss Dor-o-thy!"

Swinging his free hand up, Tik Tok dug his fingers into the

stone. He yanked his other hand out of the wall and started his long climb back up the well.

CHAPTER 52
THE LION TAMER

"Lion! Fight it! It's me!" Dorothy screamed before ducking away from another clumsy swipe of his claws.

The Lion's movements were jerky and uncoordinated because of the spell he was under. Otherwise, Dorothy knew, there was no way she would still be alive. The Lion was waging a battle against his own mind. She held up her dagger defensively. She hadn't used it on him yet and hoped she wouldn't have to.

"Don't let her do this to you!" Dorothy pleaded once more, trying to reach the Lion's subconscious.

The Lion shook its head, hesitating. She was getting through.

Watching from her throne, Fairuza's eyes were gleaming with anticipation. She was captivated, sitting on the edge of her seat, her wide smile cocked to the side in rapturous joy. Fairuza gestured toward the Lion.

The Lion took a step forward and roared, loudly and ferociously, once more under the spell. Dorothy could feel the air vibrate from the deep throaty sound. It felt like the room trembled and it made the hairs on the back of her neck stand on end.

He lashed out, knocking the knife from her hand. It happened so fast, Dorothy was caught off guard and could only watch as the blade twirled aimlessly away to the ground.

When she looked back at the Lion, she saw that he was losing the battle inside. His eye was cold and dangerous. *It can't end like this,* she thought to herself. Not at the hands of her dear friend.

Something flew past her and smashed into the Lion's chest, knocking him down.

The object fell to the floor and Dorothy saw that it was a wooden club. Both she and Fairuza turned to see where it came from.

Jasper walked into the room with a hint of a swagger in his step. He nodded and winked at Dorothy. "Sorry I'm late, M'Lady."

Dorothy almost exploded with joy. She found herself grinning like a fool. A fool in love.

Fairuza jumped to her feet. "How?!"

"We're the Emerald Knights. The Royal Guard." Jasper had spotted the dagger and now stopped just beside it. "Did you honestly think you could hold us captive?" He snatched up the blade and rushed the stairs toward Fairuza.

The pale Witch stepped back nervously and thrust Glinda's wand at him.

A sparkling ball of energy hit Jasper, throwing him backwards.

"Your authority means nothing here." Fairuza glanced back

at the dazed Lion and snapped her fingers. "Dispose of the intruder!"

The Lion was back on his feet and refocused his attention onto Jasper. They began to circle each other warily.

"Try not to hurt him! He's not in control!" Dorothy shouted, retreating to the edge of the room.

Jasper shook his head. "I'm more concerned about him hurting *me*!"

CHAPTER 53
IT CAME FROM BELOW

A slow, rhythmic pounding echoed across the courtyard. Small animals scampered away for cover.

The noise had drawn a nearby Sleech outside to investigate. Its tongue flicked out, sniffing the air. It smelled bitter danger.

Something was coming.

Something powerful.

The Sleech stepped back into the dining chamber, nervously clutching its spear.

The sound grew louder and louder. Like a hammer being struck against stone.

Abruptly, the sound stopped and a set of copper fingers rose up out of the well and slammed down onto the rim.

Tik Tok appeared, pulling himself up and out. He hit the ground with a soft thud.

The Sleech spat in disbelief and slammed the doors shut, swinging the wooden bar down to lock them.

Outside, Tik Tok charged toward the castle. "On my way, Miss Dor-o-thy!"

The Queen was in trouble and nothing was going to stand in Tik Tok's path, least of which was an old wooden door.

The wood splintered apart as the One Man Army of Oz rammed his way inside. He didn't bother to pay any attention to the unconscious Sleech that had been thrown halfway across the room.

CHAPTER 54
THE CLASH OF THE KNIGHTS

Jasper sailed through the air, smashing into a stone pillar.

The Lion's attack had been savage. There was a ragged gash down the side of Jasper's face. Jasper staggered back, using the pillar for support to get to his feet. He could feel the weight of the knife still in his hand.

"Ow." He looked down at himself. His clothes were torn and there were massive lacerations on his chest. The wounds were already resealing. There was no blood, but it still hurt.

The Lion glared at Jasper, then came at him like a bull.

Jasper dodged at the last possible second, slicing the Lion's arm. The Lion snarled in pain. It was a deep cut. Bright red blood splashed across his tan fur.

The Lion whirled around, grabbing Jasper by the collar, and threw him against the wall. Before Jasper could recover, the Lion slammed him again and swatted the knife from Jasper's grip. The Lion held Jasper up and raked his face with his open claws.

Jasper screamed out in pain.

Dorothy was momentarily paralyzed at the sight.

The Lion raised his hand again, ready to cut Jasper to ribbons. Jasper was barely conscious, unable to raise a defensive arm.

"NO! LION! I AM YOUR QUEEN! YOU WILL STOP AT ONCE!" Dorothy commanded, standing out in the open. The thought of the Lion causing any more harm to Jasper, made her forsake her own safety.

The Lion hesitated, then dropped Jasper, stepping back, confusion clouding his face.

Fairuza would have none of it. She placed her slender hand against Mombi's necklace. "Kill the girl!"

Staring at Dorothy, the Lion's eye flared with renewed rage. He snarled, gnashing his sharp teeth, lowering into a crouch, stalking his prey.

Behind him, Dorothy could see Jasper fighting to get to his feet. He was badly mauled. His body was taking too long to heal and he wouldn't be able to get to her in time. She only had seconds to live. She stood her ground, facing her friend.

The Lion prepared to strike—

CRASH!!!

A heavy oak door exploded into splintered fragments as Tik Tok rammed his way into the room. Several Sleeches that had tried to block him on the other side went flying in different directions, knocked unconscious upon impact.

All eyes turned toward the copper Knight.

"GEN-E-RAL! STAND DOWN!" Tik Tok ordered, seeing the Lion threatening Dorothy. Jasper was on the ground, still trying to get to his feet.

Fairuza's eyes bulged in outrage. She moved away from the throne to the top of the stairs, pointing at the metal warrior. "Stop him!"

The Lion followed the pale Witch's command and swung around to face Tik Tok.

Tik Tok took one look at his Queen's face and knew his course of action. He charged straight at his General. Tik Tok smashed into the Lion, sending him rolling across the floor.

The Lion shook off the hit and lunged at Tik Tok. He hit the mechanical man hard enough to make the Knight's copper body totter backwards. Tik Tok responded with a powerful right hook. The blow sent the Lion down again.

"Par-don me, Gen-e-ral, but you're be-ing un-co-oper-ative."

The Lion stood again, facing his opponent, baring his fangs. A mad look in his eye.

Tik Tok readied himself, striking a combative stance. "I see you still aren't list-en-ing."

Fairuza leaned against the top banister, riveted by the fight, her lips curled into a sneer. She hadn't had this much excitement in years!

Dorothy had retreated into a corner, disappearing into the heavy shadows. She realized the balcony was right above her.

From this angle, there was no way that the Witch could see her. Once she got near the top, the shadows would hide her. At least, that's what she hoped. Dorothy dug her fingers into the grooves between the stones and began to climb up toward the second floor. The sharp edges cut into her fingers and toes, drawing blood, but she ignored it, blocking out the pain. Fairuza was distracted with the battle and Dorothy only had this one chance.

The fight continued. The Lion leaped at Tik Tok, who raced forward to meet him head-on. The two warriors collided, raining blows against the other. Fists punching, claws striking, arms blocking. Several times, each of them were knocked down, but neither would surrender.

Tik Tok finally grabbed one of the Lion's wrists, then the other, grappling with him. "I will not all-ow an-y harm to our Queen! Not by you or an-y-one else!"

At the mention of Dorothy, Fairuza nervously clutched her necklace and tightened her grip on her wand. She leaned over the railing, searching the floor below. "Where is she?"

The wounds on Jasper's face were almost gone now as were the ones on his chest. He leaned against a pillar and saw his two friends locked in battle. He could see the strength being exerted between the two and it was sobering. Any normal man would be dead going head to head with either one of them. But against each other, it was a stalemate.

Movement caught Jasper's eye. Up on the second level, he saw Fairuza's head craning, frantically looking for something. Then he saw Dorothy. And he smiled.

Fairuza noticed Jasper's expression. He was smiling at her. No, he was smiling at something—or someone—behind her. She spun around, already snapping the wand outward to cast a spell at Dorothy who was standing in back of her.

But Dorothy was ready. She grabbed Fairuza's wand hand before it could be pointed at her, sending a whirling ball of yellow magic up at the ceiling where it burst into a shower of sparks. Then she punched Fairuza square in the nose. It was a solid hit.

Fairuza's eyes fluttered as she stumbled back and went over the balcony. Her purple gown rippled around her body on the way down. She was unconscious by the time she hit the ground below.

Almost instantaneously, the Lion stopped fighting and fell to his knees, his arms still in Tik Tok's firm grasp. His head hung low. His voice no longer fueled with rage, now instead trembled with sorrow. "What have I done?"

"Tik Tok, let him go. The spell is broken," Dorothy said softly.

Tik Tok released the Lion, who covered his face in shame.

Jasper met Dorothy at the bottom of the stairs, where she took his hand and gave it a warm squeeze, silently thanking him for coming to her rescue once again.

He nodded. She knew he would always be there for her. They were now communicating on a level where gestures and looks spoke volumes. Her heart swelled with emotions, but she held them in check. There were others that needed attention before she could open her heart to him.

She picked up Glinda's wand and Mombi's necklace, then approached the Lion. His shoulders shook, as he silently wept with guilt-ridden pain. Dorothy rested her hand on his massive back. "I know that wasn't you."

"I had no control, M'lady!" he pleaded.

"I know. You would never hurt me." She stroked his matted fur.

He looked up at her, his one good eye wet with tears. "Never."

She nodded solemnly. "Now do you understand why I didn't allow you to burn the Scarecrow?"

The Lion's single eye widened in horror. His mouth tried to form words, but instead just opened and closed. The realization of what he had almost done to his old friend made his warm blood grow ice cold.

"He's been enchanted," said Dorothy, quietly. "It wasn't his fault either."

After experiencing that kind of enchantment first hand, he knew he would never forgive himself if he didn't try to save the Scarecrow. "We have to go back for him."

She gave him a tender smile. "We will. When our mission is complete. Now rise, General."

The Lion General stood, looking down at Dorothy with a sense of profound love and respect. He bowed. "My Queen."

She smiled and caressed the Lion's cheek, then turned to Jasper. "Gather the others. We've already lost precious time."

Jasper nodded and was off like a shot.

"What should we do with her?" The Lion tilted his head toward the unconscious pale Witch sprawled on the floor.

"We'll have to lock her up. I don't want her causing any more trouble for us." Dorothy looked down at Fairuza, feeling a little bad for her. Dorothy *had* killed her mother after all—by accident of course!—but she was still responsible. And she hadn't meant to steal the slippers. Glinda had given them to her.

Then again, Fairuza's mother was known to be just as wicked as her sibling in the west, according to the Munchkins. The Witch of the East had enslaved the Munchkins and Dorothy had freed them by having her house land on the Witch. *I guess the fruit doesn't fall far from the tree,* thought Dorothy.

She held her grungy bare foot against the sole of Fairuza's purple boot.

"Hmm."

They looked about the same size.

CHAPTER 55
THE SANDSHIP OF OZ

The petrified trees were thinning out. It was mid-day and a warm breeze took the chill out of the air as the group traveled.

Dorothy and her Knights had left the castle before sunrise (after retrieving their weapons and gear), and had made excellent time through the Murky Marsh and the Forlorn Forest.

Now wearing Fairuza's boots, Dorothy had a spring in her step. They fit snugly, but made the journey so much easier. She had also taken the dagger that Fairuza had wanted her to kill the Lion with. Where the Knights were headed, extra weapons wasn't just a good idea, it was a necessity.

The forest soon opened up to a wide open vista. Here, shafts of sunlight were actually breaking through sections of the near impenetrable cloud barrier. The group ventured out onto the shores of an ocean of sand that stretched on and on to the horizon.

"The Deadly Desert," Dorothy said with finality. "Our journey's almost over. In the middle of this desert is the Wild Isle."

"I've never been this far," Wik said, taking in the majestic sight.

"Is it true what they say?" asked Hup, sounding nervous.

Dorothy nodded. "If any living thing sets foot on it, they'll turn to sand and become part of the desert."

Willow eyed the expanse of sand. "How do we cross it?"

Dorothy pointed northward. "Up the coast is Dunes Harbor. We should be able to find a sandship there."

The Lion led the way with the others in tow.

* * *

Traveling up the coast, with no hindrances, they soon saw Dunes Harbor—or what was left of it.

The small town was in ruins. Wooden buildings were burnt down and crumbling. Not a soul was in sight.

The Lion grimaced. "Fairuza's handiwork, no doubt."

Dorothy shook her head. "I've been gone for too long. There's been so much loss."

The Lion walked closer to the banks of the sand sea. "The ships..."

They could see that the sandships had all been destroyed. Blackened and broken, they lay in pieces, waves of sand washing against them.

"Is there any other way, General?" Pok asked, surveying the destruction.

The Lion picked up a heavy plank of wood from a wrecked sandship hull and flung it in anger, roaring at the top of his lungs. The plank splashed down into the Deadly Desert some thirty feet away.

Pok pulled back, giving the Lion space, muttering to the others, "Guess that's a no."

Dorothy's hand drifted up to Mombi's necklace that she was now in possession of. She could feel the magic pulsing under her fingertips. She pulled Glinda's wand from her waistline and it too, hummed with mystic energy. Its crystal tip twinkled in the sun.

Seeing this, the Lion stepped forward with renewed hope. "Can you use them?"

Dorothy bit her lip, thinking about it. "I don't know. I've tried using magic other than the slippers, but… Magic tends to be hard to control. It usually doesn't turn out the way you want it to."

"Look around Dorothy. Do we have any other choice?" the Lion asked in a gentle voice.

Dorothy nodded. "Stand back. All of you."

She gripped the necklace with one hand and held out the wand with the other. She focused, concentrating solely on the remnants of the sandships. She let the magic guide her. Let it find the image in her head of what she wanted and then pull it forth into reality.

The crystal at the end of the wand sparkled, glimmering with a white light.

Wood began to creak among the ruined craft. One of the schooners shifted in the sand, groaning as it tilted into an upright position. Sand poured from its deck like seawater.

Sweat dripped from Dorothy's brow.

Pieces of debris slid across the sand toward the boat, putting themselves back into place, fitting together like a jigsaw puzzle. Planks from other ships hurtled through the air patching holes in the hull. The plank that the Lion had thrown burst out of the sand

and found a position to fill.

Last, but not least, the burnt, torn sails unfurled on the two masts, repairing themselves as they expanded. They bore the royal crest of Oz.

Dorothy relaxed, breathing hard from the effort. She wiped the sweat from her forehead with her wrist.

The rebuilt sandship awaited them. Temporarily patched, with scorch marks across the length of it, it looked strong enough to carry the group. In the golden light of the setting sun, it actually took on a grand appearance.

A rare smile crossed the Lion's face. "That'll do just fine."

CHAPTER 56
THE DEADLY DESERT

The sandship smashed through the crests of the waves, sending plumes of sand skyward.

The morning sun was bright and hot. There was no cloud cover here. No clouds at all in fact. The harsh heat of the Deadly Desert wouldn't allow it. There were no sounds of nature either. No sea life existed in this ocean and no birds chanced to fly over it.

All through the night, Dorothy and her crew had sailed, and now with the sun high in the sky, they were able to see the true majesty and terrifying emptiness of their surroundings.

A vast expanse of sand extended out in every direction as far as the eye could see. They really were in the middle of nowhere.

Thankfully, the winds were strong, filling the ship's sails, propelling them along at incredible speeds.

As the Knights sailed the rolling dunes, splashes of sand

constantly sprayed around them, crashing against the sides of the hull. It was both exhilarating and terrifying and they all laughed, enjoying the thrilling ride.

Dorothy leaned against the railing, smiling, soaking up the warm rays of the sun. It was the first time she had seen Oz's sun since arriving. She wanted to bask in it. It was hot, but it was worth it.

The others were in better spirits too, feeling the heat shine down on them. Willow, especially. She was literally feeding off the light. Her ivy hair shined a brighter shade of green and had become fuller, while her bark-like skin had shifted toward a rich, golden brown. *Amazing what a little sunlight can do for a mood,* Dorothy thought.

The Lion stood at the wheel, guiding the ship.

Pok, Boq, and Bom were at the front of the boat, feeling the wind against their faces, exhilarated at the speed at which they were traveling. Their laughter drifted back to Dorothy, who smiled at the sound.

Wik and Hup were farther back, deep in conversation. They were smiling as well, with their ever present lollipops in their mouths, and from the look on their faces, Dorothy assumed that they were reminiscing about Mik and Kob.

Dorothy felt Jasper step up beside her, leaning both elbows on the railing. She tilted her head, looking at him.

His shaggy brown hair rippled and jumped in the wind. His eyes crinkled as he squinted out into the sun-drenched ocean of sand. A smile was playing about his lips. He was relaxed and peaceful with his fingers crossed, dangling over the edge.

Dorothy gnawed on her lip. She wanted to kiss him. Desperately so. They had kissed in the wispid's dream world, but not in reality…not yet. It had almost happened days ago back at the campfire, then again after escaping the Iron Giant, but both times the Lion had interrupted the moment. She knew they both wanted to. What was she waiting for?

"It's funny," Jasper said, still looking out at the liquid desert, "Here we are crossing the deadliest section of Oz and its been the most enjoyable part of this whole mission."

"I was thinking the same thing." And she had been thinking that, until she felt him next to her. He had wiped all thoughts from her mind, except one. Him.

His attention shifted to her, the look in his eyes becoming serious. "You know this is the last stand for my father. He's weak. He isn't going to back down like before."

His words snapped her out of her reverie. She looked away, nodding solemnly. "I know."

He looked at her with concern. "Are you prepared for that kind of a fight?"

Now it was Dorothy's turn to gaze out at the desert. "I'd rather not think about things like that right now. We've had so few nice moments, why ruin this one."

Jasper nodded, giving her an understanding smile. "Okay."

She continued to watch the sandy waves crest and fall back into the desert ocean. "When I was younger it all seemed so simple. I had two lives, as bizarre as that sounds. My life back home with my aunt and uncle. And my life here. The future was wide open and I was surrounded by people who loved me. Now… there's no one to go back home to. There's nothing holding me there. And here… here… I'm an outsider. I don't fit in."

Jasper leaned on one elbow and gave her a scrutinizing stare, searching her eyes. "That's not true and you know it."

"It is true," she said, turning toward him, "They accept me, but inside, I know I'm not one of them. I really am the false Queen of Oz."

Jasper straightened. "You're wrong. Dorothy, this is your home. *We* know it. You know it too." He gestured to the rest of the Knights who were lost in their own conversations, "There are people here who love you." He held her shoulder. "*Everyone* on this boat loves you."

"Everyone?" Dorothy asked, cocking her head to the side, looking at him slyly. Her shoulder felt like it was burning up where his hand rested.

"Everyone." Jasper said, letting her go, leaning back on the railing. "Some more than others, but I don't want to name names."

She smiled. "Oh, yeah? I have a secret admirer?"

He arched an eyebrow. "I can say no more. Alright it's Hup."

Dorothy burst into laughter.

Jasper shrugged and shook his head. "He's madly in love with you."

"Of course. I should have guessed." She moved closer to Jasper. "Though it's strange how he doesn't pay any attention to me, whereas I always seem to be in *your* arms."

Jasper smirked. "He's shy."

Dorothy started to lean in close to him. "Well, I hope he isn't the jealous type."

Their lips were almost touching.

"I think he'll get over it." Jasper whispered, feeling her light breath against his skin…

"Land!" Willow shouted, pointing to a distant island appearing on the horizon.

Another moment lost, Dorothy cursed their luck.

She and Jasper both turned to look. Directly ahead, the air was rippling with heat. Glimpsed in that mirage like wall, land could be seen. It was the island's enchantment, keeping it hidden from unwanted visitors. Dorothy held up a hand to shade her eyes. The island was emerging from behind the magical veil, much closer than expected, its details coming into focus.

The huge tropical island was shrouded by a lush, dense jungle. In its center rose a snow covered mountain that towered over the tall trees.

"The Wild Isle," the Lion said with apprehension.

Hup squinted, "It doesn't look so bad—"

KA-RRACK!

The sandship shuddered violently, leaning to one side. Dorothy and Jasper were thrown apart, instinctively grabbing hold of whatever was nearby.

"What's happening?" Dorothy shouted in dismay.

"It's coming apart!" the Lion reported, leaning over the side of the boat.

Another loud crack and the ship shuddered again. This time they all saw a chunk of the hull fall away, instantly swallowed up by the waves of sand.

The Lion turned to Dorothy, tension straining the muscles of his face to the breaking point. "Can you stop it?"

Dorothy brought up the necklace and wand in each hand, trying to keep the panic from rising inside her. The wand glowed, but the ship's jerking, sharp movements made it hard to concentrate.

The craft tilted dangerously to the other side, causing everyone to lose their balance and tumble to the opposite edge. They all grabbed hold of railings and posts, almost going over into the deadly sea.

The ship bucked wildly, becoming airborne for a brief second, then came crashing back down into the sandy ocean. The resulting impact shook everyone to their core. It tossed the Knights across the deck.

Before anyone could even try to get to their feet, the boat lifted into the air again, only to smash down into the waves once more.

The impact caused the main sail's boom to break free and it swung loose toward Dorothy.

"Watch out!" Pok was closest to her and saw it coming. He had only a second to react. He dove forward pushing his Queen out of its path. The boom caught the small Munchkin and sent him flying overboard. His short, thick arms frantically windmilling, as he fell into the Deadly Desert.

"POK!" Dorothy shouted in horror.

Pok splashed into the desert ocean. He didn't even have time to scream. He instantly transformed into sand, mingling with the tan waves, getting swept out to sea.

The others were in shock, but didn't get a chance to grieve as the sandship thrust upward again.

A loose end of rope swung into view and Dorothy latched onto it with her free hand. Her other still held the wand. She tumbled towards the rear of the boat.

There was a moment of weightlessness, then the craft fell, crashing back down.

There was another terrible cracking sound—the worst yet—then the ship snapped in half.

Dorothy felt the deck shift and then she was airborne. She saw the railings pass by underneath her, then saw the Deadly Desert looming in front of her.

"DOROTHY!" Jasper screamed, watching helplessly as Dorothy sailed overboard and out of sight. There was nothing any of them could have done to save her.

CHAPTER 57
SPLIT ENDS

The rope Dorothy was still gripping snapped taut, slamming her into the rear side of the boat.

She only had one hand on it. The other was clutching the wand. The sudden stop had wrenched her shoulder. It felt like it was on fire. She slid down a few inches, giving her palm a good burn. Her fingers had an iron clad hold on the rope and she stopped herself from falling into the Deadly Desert, only a foot away beneath her.

From her position, the hull was completely obstructing her view. She had no idea how the others were doing.

She put the wand between her teeth and used both hands to make her way back up the rope. Her shoulder was stiff and her arm muscles were screaming. She didn't have much strength, but her willpower and determination were making up for it.

The weathered old rope began to fray, rubbing against the boat's rough edges. The rope's fibers were popping free, then one full strand snapped apart, leaving only two to hold her weight.

Dorothy saw this and redoubled her efforts. The second strand snapped, jerking her. She was almost there. Directly above her, she saw the rope's last strand was grinding against the edge, wearing away…

Just as the rope broke apart, she grabbed onto a jutting hull plank. There was enough of a handhold to dig her fingers into and she hung there like a mountain climber for a second, catching her breath. There were only a few more inches to the edge of the deck. She hooked her left arm around a railing support and desperately scraped her boots against the sides as she heaved herself up. She pulled herself onto the slanted deck and collapsed, breathing hard. That had been too close.

As soon as the others saw her reappear, they cheered. Although Dorothy saw how relieved Jasper was, she could still see the tightness in his face.

She saw why. She was all alone on the back half of the ship, while everyone else was on the bow section, floating away from her.

The two halves of the sandship were drifting apart. There was no way she could possibly jump across the gap. There was a good thirty feet between them.

At least the rough swells had passed. The waves were returning to normal.

"Use the wand!" Jasper shouted.

Dorothy stood up on aching legs. The deck was still moving, bobbing in the current. "I'll try!"

She grasped the necklace and held out the wand, concentrating, pushing with her mind. Her half of the boat rocked back and forth, then started to float toward the others, but then the broken craft pitched forward at an extreme angle. She had to break off using the magic to grab onto the railing or else she would slide off into the sands.

Without the pushing from the wand, the deck righted itself and bobbed lazily on the rolling sands. She was still too far to jump.

Dorothy let go of the railing. "I can't do it! I can't control it!"

"Alright, don't panic! We can think of something!" Jasper called out to her." He didn't look confident.

There had to be a way. Dorothy looked around, her eyes searching for something that could help. Anything.

There was a loud slap. She stared up at the canvas sail flapping in the wind, loose ropes whipping out into the air. Her gaze traveled up to the top of the mast. The first mast had broken off during the initial separation. The rear one though, was still intact.

Her first thought was to somehow topple the mast and use it to bridge the two halves, but when she glanced back at the bow section drifting beyond her reach, she saw it wasn't long enough. Plus, the only way she could do that would be to use magic, and the chances of getting it to fall exactly where she needed it would be slim. The ropes, however, looked like they might reach.

Dorothy took hold of the rigging and gave it a couple of yanks, testing its strength. Parts of it were broken loose, but it was still firmly attached to the mast. She hauled herself up and began the long climb toward the top.

The rigging was course against her hands. In minutes, she reached the top and tried not to look down. The swaying of the boat was more evident up here and she immediately felt anxious. She grabbed what looked like the longest rope and reeled it in, until she held the very end of it.

The boat tilted crazily back and forth. Parts of the remaining sail kept catching wind, jolting the section in spurts. It could tip at any moment. There wasn't much time.

She licked her lips and hoped this would work. She pulled out Glinda's wand and pointed it at the rope end. It was a smaller object and Dorothy thought it should be easier to control. She was right.

The rope lifted from her hand of its own accord and turned toward her companions on the bow. Like a cobra striking, it shot across the gap, right for them. The end thumped against the deck in front of Jasper.

"Tie it down!" Dorothy called down from above, her voice carrying across the desert in all directions.

Jasper snatched the rope up and tied it down to the ship's steering wheel. "Done!" he called back.

Looking down at the line stretching from the bow's wheel, all the way across the gap, up to the top of the mast she was on, Dorothy wondered if she really might be crazy. She tucked the wand into her waistline again and took off the jacket that Jasper had given her, looping it around the line. She wrapped the sleeves around each hand and took a deep breath.

Then she stepped off the rigging.

She slid down the line, picking up speed as she went, heading right for Jasper, who was standing at the end waiting to catch her. She glanced up and saw the jacket was shredding some. It looked like it would hold though.

Dorothy was almost there. She grinned with satisfaction.

A terrible snapping sound came from behind. She looked back and glimpsed the mast breaking, falling forward into the desert sea. The rope suddenly went slack and Dorothy found herself sliding down toward the sandy waves. She wrapped her hands and jacket around the rope, stopping her fall. She dangled off the bow, just inches away from the desert.

She saw Jasper lean over the side and reach down to her. He was three feet short of her.

"Tik Tok, hold my leg!" Jasper shouted over his shoulder.

Tik Tok stepped forward and clamped his cold, copper fingers around Jaspers left ankle. "I've got you!"

Jasper lowered himself, holding his hand out to her, reaching, reaching…

Still too far. Dorothy tried to climb, but her strength was finally past the point of exhaustion and she could only inch her way up.

The rope began to go taut again. The mast was being carried away by the rolling waves, pulling on the bow's steering wheel, where the rope was still connected.

The bow section gave a mighty creak and slanted down toward the desert sea.

The others had to hold on or else they would slide off the edge.

Hup stared at the rope. It was quivering from the tension being put on it. He looked up at the Lion who was standing near it. "We're going to have to cut the rope."

The Lion had already pulled out his sword. "Not until Dorothy is safe."

Hup nodded and looked over at Jasper and Tik Tok struggling at the edge.

"Lower Tik Tok! Get me lower!" Jasper screamed up to his companion.

Tik Tok was near the edge and the broken planks of the deck were cracking under his weight. He took two steps forward to give Jasper some length.

The broken craft tipped dangerously toward the ocean.

Tik Tok fell onto his side and started to slide toward the edge. Willow dove in and grabbed Tik Tok's free hand, then grabbed a railing, stopping their fall.

Dorothy saw Jasper drop another couple of feet toward her. She reached up for him and this time she felt his strong fingers make contact. His grip was like iron. She wasn't going to slip. She knew he had her.

Jasper wasted no time. "I've got her! Cut the rope!"

The Lion swung his blade down, severing the line. The bow swayed upright, released from the mast.

Tik Tok backed up, hauling Jasper and Dorothy onto the deck.

The bow rocked violently before settling back into the gentle motion of the sea.

Jasper and Dorothy got to their feet and were met with laughter and cheers as the Knights swarmed around them, helping them stand and patting them on the back.

Dorothy waved for the others to quiet down. "Guys, wait. Wait. Don't celebrate yet."

The Knights fell silent.

"We've still got a problem," Dorothy said, gesturing at the Wild Isle in the distance.

The fractured bow of the sandship swayed under their feet, bobbing on the ocean's waves.

They were maybe a hundred feet away from their destination, and yet it might as well be a thousand with the sands of the Deadly Desert between them.

CHAPTER 58
THE WILD ISLE

"We're stranded," Hup said, disheartened.

Jasper was busy wandering around their half of the schooner, examining everything that was available to them—which wasn't much. He leaned over the sides and stopped, eyeing something in particular.

He thought for a moment, then glanced back at Tik Tok. "Tik Tok, would you say you're a living thing or purely mechanical?"

Tik Tok tilted his head and raised a finger, about to answer when Dorothy interrupted.

"Jasper, I don't know what you're thinking, but the answer is no." Dorothy leaned over the side and spotted what had garnered his interest. A few feet below them, the sandship's anchor dangled from its cradle.

"Only living things are affected by the desert." Jasper tilted his head toward Tik Tok. "If he's just mechanical, then he could use the anchor to pull us to shore."

Dorothy shook her head. "I won't let him risk his life to test that out."

Tik Tok stepped forward. "Miss Dor-o-thy, I can as-sure you that I am mech-ani-cal through and through."

"Tik Tok, I don't know what I'd do if I lost you too." Dorothy put her hand on his smooth metal shoulder. The rays of the sun had made his copper surface quite hot. "Please don't."

"I be-lieve Mis-ter Clay-fel-low is cor-rect. There does-n't ap-pear to be an-y al-tern-a-tive." Tik Tok walked down the sloped deck to where the boat had broken in half. Where Dorothy had hung on for dear life only minutes before.

He stopped, seeming to hesitate, then looked back at the group. "If I am in-cor-rect, Miss Dor-o-thy, it was a pleas-ure ser-ving un-der you."

Dorothy's eyes welled with tears. "Oz never had a braver protector."

Tik Tok turned and hopped out into the Deadly Desert. He landed with a solid thud, both feet planted firmly in the sand.

He became completely still. There wasn't even a hint of movement. The group watched with concern. For a long dreadful moment, their worst fears seemed confirmed, then—

Tik Tok swung around and waved to his friends, his mustache tilted up at the ends forming a stiff smile. "All ap-pears well!"

The group clapped and cheered him on. Dorothy and Jasper both laughed with relief and joy.

The Lion pulled a lever and released the anchor. It fell to the desert with a loud plunk, followed by the rattling length of chain attached to it.

Tik Tok picked up the heavy anchor and gripped it firmly in his metal hands. He faced the island with the chain over his right shoulder. "Hold tight!" He took a few steps and the chain tightened with a brief round of clinking. Tik Tok leaned into the next step, grunting from the strain. His copper feet sank into the sand up to his thick ankle joints.

The bow section shifted, following him. He was doing it. He was pulling them to shore.

It took him nearly an hour to reach the island's pebble strewn beach. He pulled the fractured boat up onto land. The hull scraped noisily against the small rocks.

To the group, it was a heavenly sound. They were safe. They all climbed down off the boat and onto the beach, to have a look around.

The shoreline led up to a jungle so thick it was almost impenetrable. The bright green canopies of the trees blocked any view from the outside. The group's gaze drifted up to the snowy mountain towering over the island.

Dorothy pointed in its direction. "He'll be there. In Shiverpeak Mountain."

At that moment, blood-curdling screams rose from deep within the forest, followed by a series of spine-chilling howls. The sudden sounds threatened to produce a few grey hairs on the Knights' heads.

"Be alert. We are entering dangerous lands." The Lion unsheathed his sword.

The other Knights drew their weapons as well. Dorothy pulled out Jasper's dagger.

They all moved forward as one, slicing and hacking their way through the latticework of leaves and branches. They proceeded cautiously, not knowing what lay ahead.

A constant chorus of growls and shrieks pierced the air around them, making them anxious and paranoid. They flinched as a flock of bright orange birds abruptly departed from a treetop, leaving the branches swaying in their wake. This made the group laugh nervously and slightly relax.

The jungle was dense and humid and after twenty minutes of travel, they had worked up quite a sweat. At least Dorothy and the Munchkins did. The Lion's fur was matted and he was breathing hard through his mouth. Not panting exactly, but something similar. Tik Tok, Willow and Jasper weren't flesh and blood, so weren't bothered as much.

If Dorothy wasn't so on edge and wary of the monsters that lurked here, she would have enjoyed the striking, eye-popping colors of the jungle, lit by the golden shafts of sunlight that dappled the area.

The outer ring of trees had been the most beautiful shade of green, but the trees inside weren't limited to simply that one color. There were pink ones, blue ones and red ones. Brightly colored birds and small animals hopped and darted among the forest as the group carved out a path. Animals that she had never seen before and which had no counterpart back in the real world. Some moved so fast, all that registered were their colors. Crimson and violet shapes flapped overhead, cerulean blue streaked between the foliage, while lemon yellow burrowed back into the ground.

Of all the places Dorothy had visited in Oz, she'd have to say that this was the most colorful.

Thankfully, the further they got towards the island's center, the more the trees thinned out, allowing the Knights to travel without having to cut their way through. They stepped over logs, maneuvered around thorny brush, and swatted away vines that dangled in their faces.

The vines, however, slapped back.

The tendrils whipped at the Knights like snakes, coiling around their throats!

Dorothy gagged as she was lifted into the air by the stranglevines. The Lion, Hup, Jasper, Willow, Wik, Boq and Bom all kicked and spun, as they too were pulled up. Tik Tok was too heavy to lift, so the vines were wrapping onto him in greater number.

Jasper, already feeling his feet in the air, softened his clay neck, letting the stranglevines slip through his body. He dropped back to the ground and rushed over to Dorothy, but she was already too high up for him to help.

Tik Tok planted his feet firmly on the ground, while his torso began to spin. Faster and faster his top half whirled around, tearing the vines from their roots up in the trees.

The blood was pounding in Dorothy's head and she knew that in a few seconds she would black out from lack of air. Her friends were swinging to and fro around her, thrashing violently, choking.

Flashes of steel. Glimpses of swords swinging in the air. Dorothy saw the Lion and Wik cut themselves free. She felt around above her head and grasped the vines that were holding her, then brought the dagger up and hacked away at the wretched plants. Suddenly, she was falling. She sucked in lungfuls of air. Her vision was blurred, but she could feel the leaves slapping her face as she fell.

Her fall came to an abrupt stop. It wasn't as hard a landing as she had anticipated. In fact, it was a rather soft one. It took a second for her eyes to refocus, then Jasper's lovable scruffy face came into view. He had caught her in his arms. She grinned at him. "Nice catch."

"Yes, you are." He set her on her feet.

The Lion and his Knights had fallen nearby and were just getting up.

Dorothy did a quick head count. Everyone had made it.

"Move it! Before they try again." The Lion rasped, rubbing his sore neck.

They all raced deeper into the jungle, leaving the severed vines dangling, dripping amber sap.

After their frantic escape, they felt they were far enough away from the region of stranglevines to slow down and catch their breath.

The Lion held up his hand for silence. Everyone seemed to hold their breath, wondering what he was hearing. They didn't have to wait long before they heard it too.

A low rumbling. Then a sound no one wanted to hear—tree trunks cracking and falling. A terrible, wooden popping sound that sent a sharp echo through the jungle.

Something *big* was coming.

They all knew what to do—RUN! They broke into a sprint in the opposite direction of the sound. Behind them, trees continued to splinter and snap apart.

Dorothy hazarded a glance over her shoulder and wished she hadn't. A herd of monsters crashed into view, rampaging through the forest, hot on their heels!

They were shredders. A cross between a triceratops and a great white shark, bigger than the biggest elephant. Horns, claws and teeth. A nightmare on legs! Their rough, wrinkled hide was protected by sharp bony plates and spikes, while their shark-like mouths snapped at the air.

The Knights raced out into a clearing. Before they knew it, they were out in the open, running across a lush field of bright blue grass.

The ground shook under Dorothy's feet. There was no way they were going to be able to outrace these creatures.

One of them was almost on top of her, its jaws chomping at her. It was so close, whenever it opened its mouth to try biting her, she could hear the wetness of its saliva. The clear clicking of its razor sharp teeth. Its hot stinky breath on her neck.

At any given second, she was going to be lunch for this thing. She decided since there was no way to outrun it, she was going to go down fighting.

She already had her dagger in hand. She pulled out the wand as well, then threw herself forward, rolling onto her back, ready to attack!

CHAPTER 59
BEWARE THE BURROWERS!

Dorothy blinked.

She was mystified. The shredder was gone.

The sounds of their stampede had abruptly fallen silent. For a second, she wondered if she had gone deaf, then she heard snorting. She saw that the shredders were all still there. They had come to a halt several feet back and were pawing at the ground panting and grunting, kicking up clumps of dirt and grass.

Dorothy glanced over and saw that her companions had reached their limits as well and had turned to face the enemy with weapons drawn. Bom was helping his father get back up. Boq was huffing and puffing, but still ready with his sword.

The shredders continued to back away, then suddenly turned tail and ran back toward the jungle.

"What?" Hup was perplexed.

"What's going on? What happened?" Dorothy asked between breaths, getting back on her feet.

"I think they're afraid of something," Wik said. He sounded paranoid.

Dorothy and the others all started to scan the area in every direction, but they didn't see anything that could be considered threatening.

They soon became aware of a peculiar sound. It was a muffled buzzing. Or chittering.

The ground erupted between Hup and Dorothy as a fifteen foot monstrosity burst through the dirt, screeching and clicking. It was a blur of bright red and had far, far too many segmented legs.

Dorothy screamed and dove to the side to avoid snapping pincers that suddenly lunged toward her.

The Lion and Jasper both rushed toward it, swords drawn. Jasper hacked off a leg, making it howl in a sharp shrill pitch. Its attention swung around to Jasper.

It didn't see the Lion charge in from the side. The Lion plunged his blade through its giant head, skewering it with a sickly *crunch*!

The monster collapsed with a resounding thump, its antennae quivering in front of it.

Dorothy could see the creature was a hideous combination of a millipede and a maggot. A bright red leathery body, with fleshy ridged ripples down the length of it that was still pulsating and undulating even after its death. Thick spiky hairs protruded haphazardly across its entire form. Six round black eyes the size of softballs stared at her. Dorothy couldn't tell if it had six, eight or ten legs, because part of it was still underground. She didn't like insects to begin with, so this huge beast was giving her a massive case of the willies.

The Lion yanked his weapon out and flicked the gooey dark blood off with a snap of his wrist.

They heard more chittering.

Sections of the ground started to collapse, as if someone had unplugged imaginary drains under the field. Sinkholes were forming all around them.

The group threw themselves into a mad dash as more of the burrowers burst out of their holes and gave chase. The ground sloped down a hill.

Dorothy was running so fast and the incline so steep, that her momentum was carrying her forward, giving her the sensation of flying. She couldn't stop if she wanted to! Dirt exploded everywhere making it hard to tell what was happening. Motion and sound became a blur around her.

She saw Tik Tok ahead of all of them. He had given up trying to run on his short legs and was simply rolling down the hill like a runaway cannonball, mowing down any of the monsters that lay in his way.

Wik and Hup were weaving this way and that, relying more on avoiding the insects than fighting them. They were using Tik Tok's cleared trail to stay ahead of the stampede.

To her right, Dorothy glimpsed the Lion running and slashing and hacking, dropping any burrower that dared cross his path. He was a whirlwind of rage, roaring in a savage, feral manner that scared her.

There was no sign of Boq and Bom. She hoped they were okay.

Dorothy felt like she was in a war zone, bombs dropping near and far. She winced with each eruption, hearing the burrower's horrible high pitched screams as they surfaced, announcing their arrival. Or maybe it was a war cry.

The ground in front of her opened up. A segmented column of scarlet flesh rose up blocking her wild descent.

Dorothy dropped to the ground, rolling to the side. Snapping pincers clacked angrily over her.

Jasper was right behind her. He leaped into the air and brought his sword down, driving it into the creature's head. It reared up in a last death rattle. Jasper dangled in mid-air, hanging on to his sword, which was still planted firmly in the beast. The burrower dropped to the dirt floor, dead. One of its long, hairy legs landed on top of Dorothy, pinning her down.

Jasper ran nimbly down the back of the lifeless monstrosity and jumped off where Dorothy was trapped. He sliced off the offending leg and pushed it aside, freeing her. He took her hand, pulling her to her feet and they both broke into another run.

They could feel the ground shaking under them.

Dorothy was almost in a blind panic. Was that the sound of thousands of the things right underneath, gathering for dinner? She imagined a sea of crimson horror, wriggling and squirming a few feet beneath the dirt. Her blood went cold.

Then the world collapsed under them and she was falling.

She hit soft dirt, landing on her side. Jasper dropped down right beside her with a thump.

Dorothy's head was ringing. She shook it, trying to make sense of where she was. She stood on unsteady legs.

It was darker. It smelled musty. Above, the blue sky beckoned beyond the crumbling edges of the ground they had just been standing on. The edges were out of reach, close to twenty feet above her.

They had fallen into the burrowers' tunnels.

The ground continued to collapse under the weight of the monsters. The burrowers were just as stunned as Dorothy and

Jasper, but were recovering quickly. Their antennae twitching in the air, searching for their prey.

Jasper jumped to his feet and they both tried to scramble up the wall, but the loose dirt just fell apart under their hands. It wasn't firm enough. The burrowers were all surfacing, making the ground unstable.

A burrower screeched, sensing them, and barreled down the tunnel.

Dorothy grabbed Jasper and pulled him forward. "Come on!"

They sprinted through the fallen passage, moving deeper into the burrowers' domain. They were heading downward when they wanted to be going up. Hopefully, Dorothy thought, they would find an exit hole.

Because they were moving further underground, this part of the tunnel was more solid, with few caved-in spots. The limited shafts of light made it harder to navigate.

Glancing behind, they could see that more of the creatures had joined the chase, climbing over each other, pushing and shoving to be the first to get to them. The giant insects were clogging the tunnel. It was more than the soft dirt walls could bear. More and more of the ground above fell in, showering Dorothy and Jasper with sheets of fine dirt, making it hard to see and breathe.

Ahead, the tunnel branched off into two passages.

Without hesitating, Dorothy shouted, "Take the right!" She hoped her instincts were good. *It's a fifty-fifty chance,* she thought, trying to make herself feel better.

They moved toward the passage on the right—

The side of the tunnel ruptured in front of them as a burrower came crashing through!

Dorothy and Jasper both spun on their heels and flew down the left passage instead. *So much for instinct,* she scolded herself.

Another burrower smashed through a wall directly behind them, missing them by inches.

"There!" Jasper pointed toward a patch of daylight shining into the tunnel. A sinkhole with low shallow walls. In a matter of seconds they were at the sinkhole and clawing their way back to the surface. They could feel the tremors of the monsters coming up behind them.

Dorothy and Jasper crawled out, rolled over and popped up onto their feet. Off they went, skidding down the slope.

"There they are!" It was the Lion. Relief was in his voice.

Dorothy threw a glance back and saw the Lion, Tik Tok and the rest of the Knights, charging out of another sinkhole farther behind.

The burrowers came pouring out after them. A wave of red terror. Their angry cries, a symphony of screeches that sent chills down Dorothy's spine.

The creatures were flowing over each other in repulsive waves of rippling, hairy limbs.

Dorothy noted that it looked like her group hadn't lost any more members, thank goodness. She also noticed she still had Glinda's wand in her hand. She felt its power. Like it wanted to be used. Magic seemed like the only way out of this. They couldn't run forever.

The slope leveled out. Now was Dorothy's chance.

She skidded to a halt and faced the burrowers, holding up Glinda's wand and clutching Mombi's necklace.

As soon as the rest of her Knights ran past her, she gritted her teeth and cleared her mind, zeroing in on one objective—saving her friends.

With sick realization, Jasper saw that Dorothy had fallen behind. He stopped and looked back in horror. The burrowers were almost on top of her. She looked so fragile against the wall of giant predators bearing down on her.

Dorothy screamed from the exertion and punched the space in front of her with the wand.

A glimmering wall of magic smashed forward.

At first it was a rush of wind that blew the initial wave of monsters back, but as Dorothy twirled the wand, the winds gathered force, beginning to circle around the creatures. Around and around it went, until it became a tornado, lifting the dozens and dozens of burrowers off the ground, their legs frantically trying to find something to attach to. The blue grass danced in the pressurized air that howled over it, then it too was ripped up into the air, followed by the army of burrowers that were tunneling underground. Sucked up from their holes and tossed into the spinning vortex, they screeched, but couldn't be heard over the roaring winds.

Dorothy snapped the wand outward.

The twister growled upward, retracting into the blue sky, where it ejected the monsters in every direction, then dissipated back into still air.

The Knights watched the bright red creatures sail across the sky, ending up either in the outer reaches of the island or worse—the Deadly Desert. Either way, they wouldn't be troubling the group any longer.

Dorothy was doing everything she could not to collapse. Her own legs trembled, threatening to give way. That spell had taken all of her strength. *Lucky it had worked,* she thought, *because there wouldn't have been a second try.*

Jasper steadied her, holding her up. "I think you're getting the hang of that."

She smiled and wiped the sweat from her brow. "Just don't ask me to do it again."

Using Jasper for support, Dorothy joined the others as they resumed their trek.

The burrowers and shredders had been a blessing in disguise, since they had scared away most everything else in the vicinity. There were no further encounters on the journey to the edge of the jungle, much to the group's relief.

Ahead, lay Shiverpeak Mountain.

CHAPTER 60
SHIVERPEAK MOUNTAIN

It was a white and blue tower of ice with colossal frozen peaks stretching toward the sky.

Blades of ice aimed at the heavens in an act of defiance. That's what came to mind as Dorothy stared ahead at the snow covered mountain. In the middle of the scorching hot Deadly Desert, on a humid tropical island, sat this mountain of ice, refusing to be affected by the heat.

She shook her head and laughed. The edge of the jungle was literally the edge. Without any transition, the ground in front of them was treeless and covered in a heavy layer of fresh snow. She could see the snowflakes swirling in the air just a foot away from her.

The Knights stepped over the dividing line from the muggy temperature of the jungle into a raging blizzard. The Munchkins tightened their coats in a futile gesture to keep out the cold. The sweat on their bodies worked against them when they crossed over, becoming a conductor for the freezing temperatures.

Frigid winds cut across Dorothy's skin. A hard, wracking shiver tore through her body. Her teeth chattered so hard she thought they might shatter. She had somehow managed to save Jasper's jacket back when she used it to slide down the rope, but it wasn't heavy enough to keep out this kind of chill.

The Lion with his fur coat, Tik Tok with his copper body, Jasper's clay form, and Willow with her tough bark, suffered the least from this harsh climate. Though there was a noticeable effect happening with Willow. Her leaves were shriveling up and falling off, one by one, stolen away on the winds.

They all made their way over the tundra, shuffling through the blanket of snow. Approaching the base of the mountain, they spied a cave leading into the interior. With renewed vigor, wanting to be out of the cold, they charged for the opening.

Inside the cave, cut off from the freezing winds, the temperature was immediately fifteen or twenty degrees warmer. Or at least it felt that way to Dorothy.

They headed down the dark cave, its icy walls making it a slippery endeavor. It soon opened up into a massive cavern.

Other tunnel openings led off into areas unknown. It was remarkably well lit in this chamber. Dorothy looked up and saw sunlight shining down from above through more cave entrances and thin sections of ice. Those thinner walls glowed an ethereal blue and white, highlighting the gentle ripples and smooth curves of the ice formations. It was one of the most beautiful things Dorothy had ever seen. And far above them, giant icy stalactites hung from the cavern's ceiling, glistening in the light.

"Which way?" Boq asked Dorothy.

She shook her head. "No idea. I just told him to hide here in the mountain until one of us came for him."

"With all this moisture, he could be rusted up again," the Lion remarked, looking around.

"I made sure he had an oil can. He should still be okay," Dorothy paused, "I hope."

Hup peeked into a nearby tunnel. "I suppose we could split up..."

"No, we've lost too many already." The Lion took a few steps forward, drew a deep breath, arched his back and bellowed at the top of his lungs, "TIN MAN! OUR QUEEN HAS RETURNED! SHOW YOURSELF!"

"I don't think that's a good idea..." Jasper's gaze fixed nervously on the stalactites above them.

Dorothy joined the Lion, "TIN! WHERE ARE YOU? IT'S ME, DOROTHY!"

They all heard it. It was a small snap. A harbinger of danger.

Everyone looked up.

Everyone except Jasper, who looked down. Beneath their feet, the ice floor had developed a nice jagged crack.

He nodded to himself. "Yeah. I was right. Not a good idea."

They all looked down and saw the ice fracturing beneath them.

"Uh-oh." That was all Dorothy had the chance to say before the ice gave way.

They plunged down into another chamber below, hitting the ground hard. Sharp ice fragments rained down after them.

Dorothy sat up. Her body was beginning to feel like one big bruise.

Jasper rubbed his head. "Okay, new rule. No more shouting in here."

The Lion got to his feet, shooting Jasper a smirk. "You might be right."

Hup stood, dusting himself off. "I think I swallowed my lollipo—" He didn't get to finish his sentence. He was yanked off his feet, slamming into the ice floor, then pulled away.

Something whipped out and wrapped around everyone's ankles. This far down, the light was dimmer and things were harder to discern. It looked like a thick, brownish-green tentacle, rough and knobby.

Dorothy barely had time to register the sight when the things jerked her and the others away, dragging them in separate directions. She clawed at the ground—the dirt was slick and iced over, allowing no purchase. It didn't matter because this thing was too strong. The tentacle pulled her toward a dark corner and she saw what she was in the grip of—a huge man-eating flower growing along the wall.

Dark blue on the outside, it was camouflaged against the ice wall, but when it opened its enormous, spiraled petals, a bright orange interior was exposed, revealing a mouth full of needle-like teeth that snapped at her.

A half scream, half gasp slipped from her lips. Her eyes were adjusting to the dimness and she could make out more flowers on the other walls, drawing her friends in for a meal. She spotted some roots, protruding from the ice and grabbed for them. No use. Her fingers slipped away, gouging the bark with her nails.

More tendrils were whipping out, coiling around her arms and body, pulling her in.

Her boots braced against the inner folds of the petals, just shy of its jaws. Its mouth could sense her, smell her. It chomped at the air, trying to find her flesh. Her legs strained, fighting the tentacle's pull.

A large axe flew past her, down into the flower's maw, slicing it in half!

The flower collapsed in two halves to the floor. Dorothy hit the ground, landing on her backside. The pain was secondary. She turned toward her rescuer.

A powerful figure dropped down from the hole above, landing with a satisfying metallic clang. It was the lumberjack of Oz.

The Tin Man.

"Tin!" Dorothy didn't remember him being so…big.

He rose to his full height of six feet. Wide shoulders squaring off his cylindrical torso. His silver colored body, riveted together like Tik Tok's. His face, though hard and angular, was handsome. And intimidating. Yet there was a trace of warmth in his eyes that betrayed his tough exterior. Deep inside, he cared. He loved.

Because of this, Dorothy had entrusted him with the most important part of her plan.

To protect the Ozma.

Her eyes dropped down to the leather satchel resting against the Tin Man's left hip, hanging from a strap that ran diagonally around his barrel chest.

He rushed over to her in two strides, helping her up and retrieving his axe at the same time.

"Hold that thought." His voice was deep and full, echoing within his own body.

Dorothy forgot how much she had missed hearing it.

The Tin Man charged another flower, then another, making short work of them, his axe a blur as he swung away.

Willow was the last to be saved. She pulled away as the Tin Man chopped her loose, coming close to her leg-root. "Watch that axe, treecutter! I won't be another notch on your blade."

"Pardon Miss, but I no longer chop trees." The Tin Man offered a hand to help her back onto her feet. "I save my axe for my enemies."

"Hmph, so you say." She let him take her hand, while she stood back up.

All of the massive flowers drooped lifelessly to the ground.

The Knights had become rowdy and joyful at the appearance of the Tin Man, slapping him and each other on the back. Dorothy couldn't help but smile too.

Jasper shook the Tin Man's hand. "You're a hard man to find." The Tin Man chuckled, then saw the Lion approach him.

The Lion slapped the Tin Man's arm. "Thank you, old friend. It's good to see you again."

"I notice matters have gotten worse," said the Tin Man, frowning, nodding toward the Lion's eye-patch.

"These are hard times, my friend," the Lion said.

The Lion stepped aside as Dorothy walked up to the Tin Man.

The Tin Man grinned and opened his arms for a hug. "I hardly recognize you. You've grown so much!"

She threw her arms around the Tin Man. He returned it with the same affection. Dorothy was surprised that his metal body wasn't cold, having spent all this time here in this icy mountain. He actually felt warm. She remembered why. The heart the Wizard had given him. The love and fondness he had for others would always keep him warm.

"I've missed you!" She leaned back to look up at him, "Do you still have it?"

He winked at her. "Hasn't left my side."

"It's time." Dorothy held out her hand, ready to receive the

Ozma.

That was the moment the world around them fell apart.

CHAPTER 61
THE SHATTERING

The entire mountain quaked violently, throwing Dorothy and her Knights off balance.

A series of sharp pops reverberated from above as several of the icy stalactites broke free and plunged right for the group.

The Knights fell back, diving to the sides as the stalactites smashed into the ground between them, showering them with thousands of ice shards.

Dorothy uncovered her eyes and saw that the stalactites had formed an icy barrier trapping the Tin Man and the Lion on the other side, separated from her group. Through the clear wall, she watched the Tin Man's wavering shape swing his axe into the barrier. It merely chipped it.

He prepared to take another swing when they all heard more pops from above. Several more deadly missiles were on their way down.

"GO! We'll take another tunnel!" The Tin Man shouted, his voice rebounding up and over the blockage.

He and the Lion were gone before Dorothy could say another word. She turned toward her Knights and waved them toward a nearby tunnel opening. "You heard him! Let's go!"

They all rushed inside, just as another round of monolithic stalactites crashed down behind them. Under the impact, the floor buckled inward, creating a widening chasm where only seconds before the Knights had all been standing.

Charging ahead, the group ran as fast as they could through the ice cave. The deafening sounds of destruction urged them onward.

The mountain's tremors were increasing to the point where the group was having trouble staying upright. Dorothy's hand slid over the slippery, corrugated, midnight-blue wall, using it to brace herself. Her fingers glided over the freezing cold surface, too numb to feel the spider-web of fissures spreading across the walls.

The tunnel sloped upward and soon the dark walls began to brighten as light pushed its way through the frozen surface. The translucency allowed them to perceive the crisscrossing ice tunnels around them.

Dorothy suddenly smacked into something, as did Jasper and Boq. "Ouch!" Dorothy rubbed her forehead where she'd hit it. *Another invisible wall?* She blinked. *No. A wall of ice.*

The others stopped in time, before piling into them.

They all stared ahead in silence. The tunnel abruptly stopped, halting any further progress. They could see that the tunnel continued beyond the icy barrier, but there was no way through. They were trapped.

Tik Tok beat his fists against the wall, chipping chunks away.

At this rate, it might take hours to get through the thick ice.

The Knights joined in with their weapons, hacking away at it.

Bom paused, nervously pulling out one of his lollipops, and plopped it into his mouth. He looked up, listening to the mountain shake around them. "What's causing it? Can't be just because of the little bit of noise we made."

Dorothy had an idea of what—or better yet—who, was causing this, but she didn't want to voice her misgivings and make her friends panic even more.

"You ask me, the whole island's against us." Boq said with a nod. He slapped his son's chest with the back of his hand. "Don't be stingy now."

Bom quickly produced another lollipop for his father.

Hup continued to carve away at the ice wall. "I don't care what it is, as long as it gives us time to get through this wall."

Behind the Knights, the floor of the cave started to collapse in on itself. It was falling away into a widening chasm that was expanding toward Dorothy and her companions.

Boq hit Hup on the back of his head. "Now why'd you go and have to say that! You're bad luck, if I ever saw it!"

Heavy footsteps drew their attention to the opposite side. A shiny figure was running toward them from higher ground.

The Tin Man. Followed by the Lion.

The Tin Man jumped down, landing right on top of their tunnel. They watched him pass by overhead and jump down in front of them. He lifted his axe.

Dorothy and the others backed away from where he was aiming. The Tin Man brought his axe down with a brutal swing.

CRACK!

The ice fractured, but didn't shatter. The Tin Man raised his weapon for another swing.

Glancing back, Dorothy saw the chasm was working its way up the tunnel. "Hurry!"

CRACK!

The walls and ceiling were coming apart now too. The mountain was collapsing around them! Their only hope was to get out to open ground, otherwise this mountain was going to be their tombstone.

CRACK!

Big chunks of ice fell from the wall. The Tin Man was almost through. One more hit should do it!

CRASH!!!!

The wall broke apart, sending thick pieces of ice smashing to the ground. Big hunks slid across the floor. The Tin Man reached inside and took Dorothy's hand escorting her through.

The Knights ran through the hole as fast as they could.

The ceiling of the tunnel ruptured down the length of it, ripping itself apart with an ear-splitting, body shaking crack. Cold blue light shined down from the upper sunlit ice walls.

Above them, pieces of the mountainside crumbled away in gigantic chunks, exposing the bright blue sky outside.

The ground heaved up, sending Dorothy and the others sprawling. Sections of ice floor fell away into wide gaps that became yawning chasms.

A blast of hot air hit Dorothy and she could see a bright orange-red glow lighting the walls of the newly formed canyons. Down below, churning rivers of glowing molten rock surged upward.

She and the Knights all froze a moment, shocked at how their surroundings were changing by the second, trying to get a grasp on what was happening. The air vibrated with a sound so intense, that in Dorothy's mind, she pictured a million waterfalls converging during an earthquake.

The mountain gave one last roar and simply fell apart around them, splitting open like a flower opening toward the sun. The gigantic fragments crashed into the tundra, shaking the ground, sending up clouds of snow, ice and pulverized rock.

Somehow, Dorothy and her friends were spared. Seemingly against all logic, the mountain had fallen outward instead of inward.

The barrage of enormous rock and ice chunks had weakened the base of the mountain, forming crevasses. The remnants of the mountain were now sinking into the deep cracks, pulling down sections of ground with it, creating more and more of the lava filled canyons.

The next instant, the ground underneath Dorothy suddenly dropped a few more feet and tilted down at a steep angle. The group spilled over each other, sliding toward the edge, heading for one of the chasms.

With the benefit of having sharp claws on both hands and feet, the Lion was able to save himself by clinging to the frozen dirt. He caught Hup, snagging him with one hand.

The Tin Man swung his axe, slamming it into the ice, lodging it. He jerked to a stop. Willow slid by and he snatched her wrist, saving her. She looked over at him with terrified eyes and nodded thanks.

Tik Tok, being heavier than all of them, was rolling uncontrollably toward the cliff. He reacted by digging his metal fingers into the hard dirt, bringing himself to a halt, then reached out and caught Wik, who grabbed onto Bom. Bom slid to a stop and watched helplessly as his father, Boq, rushed past him, just out of reach. "Father!"

Dorothy, Jasper, and Boq continued to slide to their imminent deaths, their limbs shooting out spastically, searching for a handhold.

Jasper slapped the slick ground repeatedly, unable to find purchase. He saw the edge coming up fast. And beyond that, a long drop into the inferno of super-hot magma, where they would be vaporized. He kicked his legs out, scrambling against the ground, trying to somehow slow his descent. Beside him, Dorothy and Boq were doing the same thing. There was nothing between the three of them and the edge of the cliff to grab onto. Nothing to save them.

Jasper held out his hands instinctively, willing them to stop. Willing something to halt their fall.

To his surprise, the cliff grew outward in spasmodic bursts, extending itself up at an angle, forming a barrier.

Jasper, Dorothy and Boq smashed into the wall of rock, coming to a bone-jarring stop.

Dorothy shot a quizzical look at Jasper. "Did you do that?"

Jasper stared at his hands, flexing them. "I— I think I did."

"You're full of surprises, son!" Boq said with a wink, slapping him on the back.

Dorothy and Jasper shared a glance, realizing that he had inherited some of his father's powers.

"There you are!" boomed a voice from above.

They looked up to see the Nome King standing on a ledge, glaring down at them with angry grey eyes.

A small army of Nomes lined the cliff beside him, weapons at the ready.

CHAPTER 62
THE ATTACK OF THE NOMES

The Nome King smiled with victorious satisfaction. "I thought we'd lost you for a moment in my grand entrance."

Dorothy's keen eye noticed that he appeared older and weaker. He was leaning on one knee, not for dramatic flair, but for support. She also perceived a hint of nervousness in his expression.

"Up we go." The Nome King held a hand out, palm up and slowly raised it.

The ground under the Knights jerked and shifted, lifting itself up. It settled into a more level state, five feet below the cliff on which the Nome King and his troops stood. When the Nome King lowered his hand, the rumbling ceased.

An eerie silence blanketed the area. It had a palpable weight to it. During the mountain's destruction, the assault on Dorothy's ears had been almost painful and now the opposite was happening. It was so quiet her eardrums pounded with her own heartbeat.

The two factions stared at each other in the stillness. The Knights' hands drifted down to their weapons. Fingers tightening around sword hilts.

"Give me the Ozma and you will all live," the Nome King said with a slow measured voice, imparting the seriousness of his offer.

"Never." Dorothy's jaw clenched, preparing for the worst.

"Then I will take it from your dead body." The Nome King pointed at the Knights of Oz. "ATTACK!" he commanded.

On both sides, dozens of blades were drawn from their sheaths at the same time, filling the air with the ringing tone of sharp metal. A cry of rage rose from the Nomes as they charged over the cliff toward the Knights.

The Knights met the Nomes head on, steel against steel, swords clanging and sparking off of each other. The two mechanical men, Ripsaw and Driller stomped forward into the fray, heading straight for Dorothy.

Seeing this, the Tin Man struck down two Nomes with his axe, spilling their sandy interior, then ran to intercept the mechanical men. "Not today, friends. Not while I'm around."

The two mechanical men paused at the sight of the lumberjack.

"Outta' the way, woodcutter!" Ripsaw snarled, his buzzsaw bladed hands whining in preparation for a fight.

Driller's drillbit arms whirred in agreement. "Yeah, Tinny, move it!"

They both rushed the Tin Man.

The Tin Man's axe came down and ricocheted off Ripsaw's

blades. Ripsaw lunged and cut a jagged slice across the Tin Man's chest. With a hearty kick, the Tin Man knocked Ripsaw back, then swung his axe in a short arc, rending part of Driller's shoulder.

Tik Tok flung a particularly nasty Nome over the edge into the magma below, then joined the battle of the metal men. He grabbed Driller from behind and spun him around. "

The Tin Man continued to fend off Ripsaw's spinning sawblades with his axe, while Tik Tok dodged Driller's deadly arms.

Dorothy, not being trained in sword fighting, stood back and used Glinda's wand to zap any nearby Nomes, causing them to burst into clouds of black dust. She knew they were only rocks, brought to life by the Nome King, but she still felt bad about doing it.

The Knights were holding the Nomes off, but exhaustion was setting in. Their journey to this point had taken its toll and the Knights had limited reserves of strength left. They would soon be overwhelmed.

Both the Tin Man and Tik Tok were suffering injuries—dents and cuts that on a normal man would have been fatal, but on them it merely slowed them down. Their opponents were just as damaged. They circled each other, looking for an opening to end the fight once and for all.

Ripsaw lashed out and sliced the Tin Man's leg above the knee, giving him a limp that severely handicapped him.

The Tin Man winced in pain, then responded with a ferocious swing of his axe, embedding it firmly inside Ripsaw's chest.

Ripsaw reeled off to the side, then recovered, coming back at him with his blades spinning. Unable to stand anymore, Tin fell to the ground. The Tin Man was defenseless throwing up an arm to block the approaching sawblades.

Willow's mace smashed into the side of Ripsaw's head, caving it in. He wobbled backward. Willow grabbed hold of the Tin Man's axe and kicked Ripsaw away dislodging the weapon. Ripsaw stumbled over the edge, plunging into the bubbling lava far below.

"I believe this is yours." Willow said, tossing the axe to the Tin Man.

He caught it and smiled. "That it is. Thank you. I don't believe I caught your name."

"Willow Bitterbark," she said, taking out two more attacking Nomes, then stood by the Tin Man, guarding him.

The Tin Man swung his axe, chopping down a Nome that was coming at Willow from behind. "Pleased to meet you, Miss Bitterbark."

She flashed a grin.

Tik Tok relied more on strength then agility in a fight, since his stocky legs weren't very good at maneuvering about. Driller attacked again and again, driving Tik Tok back. One of Driller's thrusts got through and bored deep into Tik Tok's mid-chest. The drill spun until it ground to a halt, stuck in the twisted copper.

Tik Tok groaned.

Seeing this, Dorothy choked back tears.

"So much for the famous one man army," Driller's laugh faded as he tried to free his arm. It was jammed inside Tik Tok. "Hey… let go you lump of scrap metal."

"There's no need for such lang-uage!" Tik Tok drove a fist so hard into Driller's face that it knocked his head clean off his body. Driller's round cranium bounced a couple of times across the dirt then disappeared over the cliff edge. Tik Tok broke off Driller's arm from its headless body, the drill still stuck in his chest. Both he and Driller's body collapsed to the ground.

"Tik Tok!" Dorothy found her way over to him, rushing to his side.

"Don't fret, Miss Dor-o-thy. A m-m-mi-nor wound—k-k-k-k-k-k, at best." Tik Tok's stutter and strained voice said otherwise.

Farther away, Jasper had left the Lion to defend Dorothy while he made his way toward the Nome King. Jasper dispatched another Nome and leapt over his body, gazing up at the grinning Nome King. "Come down and fight!" Jasper shouted at him, with fury in his eyes.

Without thinking, acting on pure emotion, Jasper held up a shaking hand, using his newfound power to connect with the cliff under the Nome King, feeling the solid rock from afar, taking control of it. He yanked his hand down and the cliff came down with it.

The Nome King's face showed shock as he fell with the loose rock to Jasper's level. After the rubble settled, the Nome King rose onto one knee and his eyes flashed with malice. "You've made a mistake, boy."

CHAPTER 63
THE WINGED ARMY

A solitary crow glided down into Emerald City, swooping low, making its way toward the Royal Palace.

It flew through the Palace entrance, into the Royal Hall, then into the ballroom and finally down into the cave where the Wicked Witch of the West was being held captive.

The Witch watched the bird land on a jutting rock. The crow squawked once announcing its arrival.

A wince inducing screech echoed in the hall above. A savage angry scream that anyone in their right mind would have ran and hid from.

The Witch, however, only smiled. An expression that was bone-chilling.

They were coming.

The creatures flew into the room, smelling of musty caves

and soiled fur. Their leathery bat-like wings beating the air as they landed. Their brows knit together and they flashed their sharp teeth in anger at the sight of their master imprisoned in the sphere of water.

The flying monkeys stood at the side of the pool, awaiting their orders. There were more than a dozen of them. They had flown for days from the western reaches of Oz, summoned by the Witch's messenger.

"Hello, my pretties," the Witch purred to her furry minions. "Come."

The monkeys scrambled into the water, some forming a bridge with their own bodies, while others stood on top of their brothers and spread their wings out, piercing the sphere's liquid wall. This created a dry opening in which the water flowed and rippled around the apes' wings.

Clutching her crystal ball, the Witch escaped her prison, stepping through the temporary doorway. She walked across the backs of the animals onto the stone floor beyond the pool.

The monkeys tumbled off each other to watch their master.

The Witch held up the crystal ball. Inside it, the mists swirled into an angry turbulent red cloud, spinning faster and faster. A red cyclone whirled just under the glass exterior.

She threw the crystal ball at the rock wall, where it exploded upon contact in a bright flash of crimson light and orange smoke. When the light dissipated, fragments of the wall fell away, exposing the Nome King's cache. Inside were the Witch's hat and broom as well as Dorothy's magical slippers.

In an instant, they were in her greedy, green hands.

With a sneer, she slid her black-stockinged feet into the slippers then placed the pointed hat upon her head. She grasped the broom like a royal scepter.

"Now, my pretties… we have to hurry or we'll be late for the party."

She turned and exited the chamber, cackling, striking the broom's handle down onto the floor with each step.

The sound reverberated throughout the palace like a death knell.

CHAPTER 64
LIKE FATHER, LIKE SON

In the ruins of Shiverpeak Mountain, the battle raged on.

The Nome King batted away the barrage of sword strikes aimed at him by Jasper. He did so as if they were annoying bugs. He countered by smacking Jasper down with a backhanded swing.

Recovering quickly, Jasper leapt up and sliced his sword across the Nome King's chest. It scraped against his stone skin with no ill effect. The Nome King struck Jasper, sending him sliding onto the ground.

Jasper got back to his feet and smiled. "You're growing weak! I can feel it."

The Nome King hit him again. "I regret the day I spat you into existence."

"Then I'm just another in a long series of failures for you,"

Jasper said, rubbing his jaw. "That's the story of your life."

Bubbling with rage, the Nome King unleashed a steady stream of bone-crunching punches on Jasper, bludgeoning him.

Jasper crawled away, coughing. His face was distorted, literally pounded out of shape. He propped himself up on one arm, while his clay form tried to reconstruct itself.

The Nome King was walking toward him, breathing hard. He'd expended too much energy on Jasper and was suffering for it. "I gave you everything. I gave you the power to be my greatest warrior and you threw it away." The Nome King shook his head with disgust. "I should have drained the life from you once I saw the disappointment you'd become."

Jasper was listening, but his attention was focused on something else. The rock under his hand was humming, had a pulse, like a living thing. He laid down his sword and looked up at the Nome King. "I understand now, Father. I *am* your son."

A spiked shaft of stone erupted from the ground in front of the Nome King, spearing his chest. It carved out an angular crater from his stone exterior. He staggered back, surprised by the attack.

Another shaft burst from behind, gouging into the Nome King's back. He grunted in pain, bending forward. Bits of stone fell from his wounds.

Jasper stood up and summoned another shaft, then another and another, each doing more damage to the Nome King. One of them struck the Nome King in the face crunching against it, sending bits of debris spraying into the air.

The Nome King roared in pain. "Enough!" The ground shook. Jasper was thrown to the floor by the violent quake.

The Nome King spun toward Dorothy, seeing her terrified face staring at him. He frowned and suddenly dissolved into the ground. He didn't disappear. It was as if he was absorbed into the rocky floor, leaving behind only his crown and robe.

In a panic, Jasper jumped to his feet, looking over at Dorothy.

It was just in time to see the Nome King reform directly in front of her, his hand around her throat.

CHAPTER 65
THE OZMA OBTAINED

Dorothy had been too far away to help Jasper and could only steal glances in-between evading the Nomes. She had seen the Nome King vanish only to reappear right in front of her, rising from the bed of rock. Before she knew it, his hand was on her throat, preventing any scream from forming.

He snatched the wand from her and tossed it aside, toward the cliff edge. Next, he yanked Mombi's necklace off of her, flinging it away too. It flew out into the chasm, glittering as it went down into the molten river, where it was eagerly pulled under.

He then stood behind her, holding her close, clutching her neck as he faced the Knights. "This battle is over!"

The sounds of fighting ceased as the Knights turned, shocked that the Nome King had gotten through their defenses.

The Nomes gathered around the Knights, pointing their weapons at them, taking them prisoner, including Jasper.

The Nome King smiled at them, then leaned close to Dorothy's ear. "Now. Where were we? Ah yes... Give me the stone."

Dorothy could feel his cold, hard, fingers digging into her flesh. She could also feel his desperation. His powers were using up his magic. The very thing that kept him alive. Bringing down the mountain had lined his face with cracks that made him look like a weathered seventy year old man. His eyes were glassy and panicked, reminding Dorothy of a cornered animal. This made him all the more dangerous.

The Nome King's fingers twitched, clenching tighter on her delicate neck. "Listen carefully, girl," he said into her ear, "this is the last time I'm going to ask you. Where. Is. The. Stone?"

Dorothy's breaths came in short bursts at this threat, but she remained silent.

His eyes darted back to the Knights. He knew her weakness. "Throw them over the side. Start with the Lion."

The Nomes pushed the Knights close to the edge. The two holding the Lion prepared to push him off into the abyss.

The heat rose to meet the Lion's face as he peered down. He wanted to fight. To savagely attack his captors, but the sharp blade against his throat let him know that action would be futile. His whiskers quivered with frustration.

Held in the Nome King's vice-like grip, Dorothy watched the Nomes push her friends right up to the cliff's edge. She could see the Lion's muscles tensing and flexing, wanting to lash out. The Nomes behind him placed their hands on his back, about to shove him over. The Lion's eyes closed.

"STOP!" Dorothy cried out, unable to take anymore.

The Nome King smiled, pleased.

"The Tin Man still has it. In his bag," Dorothy said softly, defeated.

The Nome King's eyes slid over to look at the Tin Man kneeling on one knee, a hand holding his bag protectively. The Tin Man returned the King's gaze with his own steely stare.

"Bring it to me." The Nome King demanded.

The Tin Man reluctantly tried to stand but the wound in his leg was too deep. His leg bent inward at a wrong angle. The Tin Man winced and fell to the ground, his metal body ringing like a gong. "I can't walk."

"Jasper, make yourself useful for once and bring that to me, would you?" the Nome King said, derisively.

Jasper shrugged away from the Nome holding the sword to his throat. The Nome King nodded and the guard backed off, letting Jasper walk away toward the Tin Man.

The Tin Man kept a sharp eye on Jasper as he approached. Jasper knelt down in front of him. The Tin Man kept his hand on the bag. "You're his son?" he said in a low suspicious voice.

Jasper nodded once, clearly not happy about confirming that fact.

The Tin Man spoke in a soft, deadly tone. "I can tell Dorothy trusts you. If you betray her…"

Jasper met his gaze and didn't waver. "Never."

The Tin Man lifted the bag off his shoulder and held it out to him. Jasper took it with a respectful nod, then stood and faced the Nome King.

"No tricks, boy. Give me the Ozma or I'll snap her neck like a twig." He squeezed her throat tighter to emphasize the point.

"If you harm her…" Jasper warned.

"You'll do what?" the Nome King replied, challengingly.

Jasper didn't respond, but if looks could kill, the Nome King would have fallen over dead at that second.

"You think you have power now, boy? Is that it?" The Nome King leaned forward, irritated. "Let me tell you something. It's but a fraction of mine."

Jasper cocked his head, holding his father's gaze. "And yet here you are, hiding behind a girl, begging us to give this to you."

The Nome King was boiling, barely holding his anger in check. They glared at each other for a moment, all their animosity plainly displayed on their faces.

The King held out his free hand. "No tricks."

Jasper didn't move. His fingers clenched on the leather bag.

"Don't Jasper," Dorothy said in a raspy voice, hardly able to talk through the Nome King's grip. "Just give it to him."

"Yes. Do as she says," the Nome King said, nodding.

Jasper flipped open the bag and reached inside, pulling out a small wooden chest.

It was a light wood, lined with smooth decorative carvings along its surface—elaborate curves and swooshes, much like the designs inside the Royal Palace of Emerald City. On its face was a big bold ***O*** with the letter ***Z*** laid over it. There was no lock, just a brass clasp.

Jasper undid the clasp and gently opened it.

Inside, nested in green velvet, was the Ozma. A breathtakingly beautiful stone in the shape of an angular heart.

He turned the chest to face the Nome King.

The Nome King reached for it, his blocky fingers shaking in anticipation. He licked his gravelly lips with his course grey tongue. He plucked it from its bed holding it up to the light. Sunlight glinted off its edges. A masterpiece of craftsmanship.

He released Dorothy, almost absent-mindedly, letting her

drop to the ground. She rubbed her throat and took in deep breaths. She looked up at him, watching him delight in the emerald's glory.

"It's more beautiful than I imagined." The Nome King examined it from every angle. "Perfection."

Jasper noticed that Dorothy's demeanor had changed. She didn't seem to mind that her arch enemy had just taken complete control of Oz and everyone in it. His gaze was drawn back to the Nome King who was making soft rumbling sounds.

"Odd..." the Nome King said, quietly, almost to himself. His eyes narrowing as he continued to inspect the gem. "This doesn't smell like an emerald."

Dorothy got to her feet and dusted herself off. She caught Jasper looking at her and she winked at him. His confused expression almost made her laugh. She suppressed the urge and looked back at the Nome King, knowing what was about to happen.

The Nome King sniffed the gem, then spun toward Dorothy in a rage. "This isn't the Ozma!"

"No. It isn't," Dorothy said matter-of-factly.

CHAPTER 66
THE THREE CHARMED TRAP

"You—" the Nome King sputtered, so furious that he had trouble forming the words, "—tricked me!" He finished the sentence, spitting it out like it was poison.

"You're right." Dorothy smiled.

He looked back at the fake emerald and was about to close his fist around it, crushing it.

"Wait," Dorothy said, holding up a hand, "You might not want to do that."

The Nome King's gaze creeped sideways, eyeing her with rising suspicion. "And why not?" he growled.

"Because that, Mr. Ruggedo, is a special gift for you, prepared by the late Glinda the Good Witch and myself. She put three charms on what you hold in your hand. The first charm—an illusion. To make it look like the Ozma," she paused, letting him stew, "*That* is an egg in disguise."

His eyes widened, glancing over at the emerald in his palm. He grimaced, uneasy now.

"We all know that eggs are poisonous to Nomes. Especially Grendelgoose eggs, which is exactly what that is," she pointed at him. "We know that they temporarily make you mortal if the yolk touches you."

The Nome King held the gem out further from his body.

"But you've survived an egg attack before," Dorothy continued, "That's why Glinda put the second charm on it—she imbued it with a bit of herself. She gave it a kiss of goodness. One that can't be corrupted. Because of your dark and bitter heart, the inside of that egg will destroy you if it breaks open."

The Nome King was holding it as far away from himself as he could. He turned his hand over and gently tried to drop it to the ground. It didn't move. He carefully gave his hand a shake. It clung to his palm as if glued.

"Part of the third charm—you can't get rid of it." Dorothy smiled. "Ever. It will always be with you."

He threw a hateful glance at her.

"Now comes the fun part. You have to vow to me right now, that you will return to your home and live peacefully, *never* to set foot in the four countries of Oz again." Dorothy crossed her arms. "If you don't say yes—*and mean it*—the egg will burst and that will be the end of you."

Jasper stared incredulously at Dorothy.

"You… miserable, insufferable…" the Nome King grumbled and snarled under his breath.

"Do you understand?" Dorothy said, flatly.

The Nome King's eyes were filled with resentment and disgust. He looked at all of them, giving everyone a blistering stare.

"Well?" Dorothy repeated, sharply.

"Yes. I understand," he said, enunciating each syllable while glowering at her, "Completely."

"And your answer?" she asked.

He stood there staring at her for a good long minute, before giving her his answer.

"No." The Nome King said with a furious certainty.

Dorothy nodded. "I can't say I'm sorry to hear that." She motioned toward the gem in his hand.

The Nome King casually stared down at it. The emerald shimmered and became hazy, then wafted away, revealing a green spotted egg resting in his palm. It quivered violently.

The Nome King watched it, remaining still and icily calm, save for his upper lip which curled in anger.

Before it could burst, he crushed the egg in his fist in one last act of defiance. Yolk splattered down his arm.

As the egg's contents dripped down his forearm, his limb stiffened, hardening. Its grey color lightened to an off-white pallor. It continued along his arm, spreading to his shoulder. Cracks were forming as it went.

His eyes widened and his mouth opened in pain. He grunted and sputtered, but wouldn't allow himself to scream.

It spread faster now. His torso was next, then his other arm and his legs. Then finally up his neck toward his head.

The Nome King couldn't take it any more and howled out one final cry—a mix of agony and rage—before it was cut short as the life drained from him, leaving him frozen in a silent scream. His blank stone eyes stared out in shock. Fissures grew across his face, making him appear ancient. He was now nothing more than a statue representing selfishness and arrogance. His fist held up to the sky, impotent and pitiful.

Everyone was in shock, staring at both the Nome King and Dorothy.

All of the Nomes in the area began to crumble apart, leaving behind piles of rubble and black sand. The Knights were free. The Nome King and his army were no more.

Dorothy moved to Jasper and hugged him. "I'm sorry it had to be this way."

Jasper smiled and shook his head. "Don't be. It was his choice. But I don't understand. If that wasn't the Ozma, then where is it? Is it even here?"

Dorothy gave him a mischievous grin. "Of course. It's exactly where I said it was. I gave it to the Tin Man to protect."

They all looked over at the Tin Man, who stood up, not as injured as he had made himself out to be. He used his axe as a cane, limping toward them.

Dorothy led Jasper over to him. She gave the Tin Man a kiss on the cheek. "Thank you."

He smiled, his silvery face somehow almost blushing. "It was *your* plan, Dorothy. I just did what you told me to do."

"And you did it wonderfully." Her grin shifted into a frown of remorse. "I wish I hadn't kept you waiting so long."

"Couldn't be helped. Besides, how many get to say they carried the heart of Oz as their own?" He reached for his chest and opened up a panel where one's heart would be.

A green glow lit Dorothy's and Jasper's faces.

Inside the Tin Man's chest was a small compartment. The Ozma rested comfortably within it.

It was even more beautiful than the illusion that had fooled the Nome King. The real Ozma not only was shaped like a heart, but actually had a heartbeat. An energy that pulsed and crackled inside the magical gem.

The Tin Man carefully removed it, then held it out to Dorothy. "I believe this belongs to you."

As her fingers touched its surface, taking it into her palm, her eyes sparkled with the same green energy twinkling in the emerald.

BOOM.

The deep hollow sound came from everywhere at once, bouncing off the canyon walls.

What happened next was absolute chaos.

Wisps of purple clouds dotted the sky and the shapes that came out of them were fast, furry and frightening.

And one of them snatched the Ozma right out of Dorothy's hand.

CHAPTER 67
THE WICKED WITCH

It had all happened so fast, Dorothy hadn't even registered who the culprit was.

She had only seen something dark flash by, felt the air swish by her face—carrying an awful smell with it—and felt the weight of the Ozma disappear from her grip. It was only after that did she finally recognize their attackers.

Flying monkeys. A small army of them.

They came from all directions, zipping back and forth, clawing at them, shrieking in Dorothy's and the Knights' ears. The Knights were slashing and hacking at them, trying to drive them back.

The thieving monkey flew high beyond their reach, joining its evil brothers.

Her blood went cold. Where there were flying monkeys,

there was—

A sinister cackle split the air, quieting the screeching apes.

Dorothy spun toward the sound and saw the Wicked Witch of the West stride out of a billowing mushroom of purple smoke that was quickly sucked away by the cold winds. There was a distance of about fifty feet between the Witch and Dorothy's Knights.

The Lion let loose a warning growl.

Dorothy could tell the Munchkins were petrified. With good reason. Everyone feared the Witch more than the Nome King. He had been merely power hungry. Easier to understand and easier to defeat. The Witch, however, was pure evil. She went around hurting things for no other reason than her own pleasure. She was unpredictable and therefore extremely dangerous.

The Witch spied the Nome King's petrified form. She raised an eyebrow, her single eye glinting as it swung to stare at Dorothy. "I didn't think you had it in you."

Dorothy's mind was racing. She hadn't planned for this. The Ozma was still up for grabs and she didn't have Glinda's wand or Mombi's necklace or her Magic Slippers. She was defenseless.

Jasper picked up a sword and stepped in front of Dorothy, motioning for her to stand back.

The Witch glared at him with a broad grin. "I see you're still playing the hero, little brother."

Jasper slowly advanced toward her. "Leave Maghamil, or we'll do the same to you."

"Oh yes. I'd like to see you try. But I'm here for something else." The Witch held out her hand. The monkey clutching the Ozma in its hairy fingers, dived down toward its master.

Dorothy's breath caught, not knowing how to stop the Witch. Then something bizarre happened. Something that took her a full second to even comprehend. Black objects were raining down from the sky.

The Witch's eyes narrowed to slits at the sight.

They were crows. Dozens and dozens of crows were hurtling down, aiming right for that thieving monkey with the Ozma. They struck it head-on, razor sharp talons out, clustering around it in a savage, brutal assault. They drove it back up into the air, where it screamed in terror, trying to flee the birds.

All eyes below were drawn to a darker blot growing larger in the wintery blue sky. Over a hundred crows were descending, carrying the Scarecrow. He dropped down, landing next to a defensive Jasper, who had his sword at the ready. The crows that were carrying him, scattered, engaging the rest of the flying monkeys in a ferocious aerial battle.

The Scarecrow held out a hand toward Jasper to ward him off, while he looked past him to Dorothy.

Dorothy saw that he had patched himself together, his features jagged and slightly off. He was smiling. It was lopsided in an endearing way. Most importantly, his eyes were clear. And friendly.

"Hello Dorothy. Sorry I'm late," the Scarecrow said, with honest sincerity.

It was a pure and simple greeting and apology. The very best kind. And his voice once again had that sing-songy bounce to it that Dorothy had always loved.

She sprang forward and wrapped her arms around him, tears flowing from her eyes. "It's good to have you back."

The Witch's already twisted face, found a way to make itself even uglier as she overheard the Scarecrow. "How *dare* you turn against me!"

They all jumped at her outburst, looking back at her.

The Scarecrow moved ahead of the others, facing her. "You put a spell on me."

A hideous smirk slid across the Witch's face. "I gave you what you wanted. You have your precious knowledge."

The Scarecrow looked at the Lion, making eye contact with him. Saw the eyepatch and the scars on his friend's face. The Scarecrow glared back at the Witch. "At the expense of my friends."

"Everything has its price," she said, in her creaking-door tone, ending it with a cackle.

"Indeed!" The Scarecrow threw his arms forward, commanding the majority of his crows to attack the Witch. The birds smothered her, blocking her from sight.

Using that as a distraction, the Scarecrow pointed at Jasper. "You're pretty handy with that sword. Get that monkey!"

Jasper grinned. *This* Scarecrow, he liked. He could see that Dorothy was a magnet for the good-hearted.

Jasper trained his eye on the monkey with the Ozma. It was still being hounded by a trio of warrior crows. It arced through the air, up and down, spinning, unable to shake its pursuers; screeching the entire time. Some of its fur was dark with blood. The birds were really letting the ape have it. It swung low in front of a piece of the mountain wall. Now was his chance! Jasper pulled his sword back and then hurled it with all his might, sending it slicing through the air.

The sword ripped through the monkey's left wing and sank into the rock wall, pinning the ape. The monkey howled and thrashed around in pain. And in doing so, dropped the Ozma.

"Yes!" Dorothy clapped her hands together in delight.

One of the warrior crows dove and caught the gem in its claws. It soared back up, circling over the area, then came in toward the Scarecrow.

A furious scream burst from the Witch, followed by a fiery explosion that radiated out from her in all directions. The attacking crows were instantly fried, as well as many of her flying monkeys. The shockwaves sent their flaming husks spiraling all over the area. A grim, unpleasant sight.

Any surviving birds or apes abandoned the battle, escaping while they could.

The crow carrying the Ozma was one of the casualties. Both the bird and the emerald hit the ground between the Witch and the Knights, not far from Tik Tok, who lay near a cliff edge.

Unable to move, Tik Tok's eyes irised open, locking onto the prize, just out of reach.

The Lion bolted forward toward the Ozma.

"Back!" The Witch pointed her broom handle at him and a ball of red lightning shot out, striking him in the chest. The impact was like a cannonball, doubling him over and propelling him backward past the others, where he smacked into a rock wall. The red electricity wound around him like a dozen crackling snakes, making every nerve ending in his body feel like it was being torched, until they finally faded away, leaving him gasping on the ground, on the verge of unconsciousness.

The rest of the Knights didn't move a muscle, not wanting that to happen to them. Dorothy couldn't blame them. The Witch would do the same—or worse—to her if she tried to run out to claim the gem.

"Now, straw man. We have unfinished business, you and I." She pointed her broom at the Scarecrow. A stream of fire leaped across the space between them, igniting him like a living bonfire.

Dorothy screamed, wanting to help him, but the heat was too intense.

The Scarecrow flapped his arms wildly, trying to douse the fire that was consuming him.

Willow screamed, retreating from the inferno.

The Tin Man stepped in front of the Scarecrow, letting the Witch's stream of fire splash against his broad back. His metal hide began to redden under the flames.

The Lion, hearing Dorothy's cries, raised his head to see what was happening. The image of the Tin Man standing over and protecting the burning Scarecrow, sharpened into clarity. The Lion watched Bom rip his cape off and tackle the Scarecrow with it, hoping to snuff the fire. The cape wasn't big enough. The anguish in the Scarecrow's screams, forced the Lion onto his feet.

He raced for the Scarecrow, snatching him up over his shoulder and then launched himself up the rocks toward the snowy drifts of the tundra. The burning straw and canvas sizzled into the Lion's fur.

Dorothy's vision tilted and spun. Through tear-filled eyes, everything was happening in slow-motion. She saw the Lion carrying the flaming Scarecrow away, smoke trailing them. Jarring sounds flooded her eardrums: the frightened exclamations from the Munchkins, the horrible wail of the Scarecrow, her own shuddering breaths, and underneath it all—

—the maniacal laughter of the Witch.

CHAPTER 68
THE DUEL

The Witch pulled her broom back, ceasing the torrent of flames and moved toward the Ozma.

The Tin Man collapsed, his torso so hot it was glowing orange and white. "Get back! Don't touch me!"

Jasper stepped out into the open and threw his hands forward. The ground surrounding the Witch shot up, forming a dome of rock over her.

It didn't hold her for long. It shattered apart only a second later. She wore a smug smile as she came closer. "So you have a few of father's tricks, eh, little brother?"

In answer, Jasper thrust his hands out causing stone spikes to shoot out of the ground at the Witch.

Laughing, she snapped her broom out, smashing the spikes in mid-air before they reached her. "That's more like it!" She launched a series of blades at Jasper with a swipe of her broom.

Dorothy fell to the ground, too dizzy to stand. She saw Jasper building stone walls, fending off the Witch's increasing attacks. Each wall quickly crumbled under the Witch's magic. He was spending more time on defense, instead of fighting back. The whole time, the Witch was working her way closer to the Ozma.

Jasper was shouting something to Dorothy, but she couldn't hear him. Probably asking for help. But she was out of ideas. Out of everything. Including her mind. Wasn't it just a few days ago that she was in New York? Or was that a dream? It was all mashing together. All catching up to her. All the years she was gone felt like they were crashing against her shoulders, grinding her down to the floor. Too much pressure, too many people depending on her. Then she saw it—

The wand. Glinda's wand.

It hadn't gone over into the chasm. It was on a cliff's edge hidden among some rocks.

The world around her lurched back into regular speed. Sound came rushing back at her like a flood of water, drowning her.

Dorothy dove for the wand. Her fingers encircled its slender handle. It was white and smooth. It wasn't wood or ivory, but something similar. Whatever it was, it felt warm to the touch, like a living thing. It felt good.

The Witch felt the blast before she saw it. She stumbled back from the impact, then regained her footing in time to dodge the second blast. She scowled at Dorothy, who was facing her, wand out, moving in front of Jasper.

Dorothy didn't take her eyes off of the Witch as she slipped past him. "Stay back, Jasper." She turned toward the rest of the Knights. "All of you, stay back. This is between the two of us."

The Witch grinned. "Yes. Yes, it is." She sliced the air with her broom. Jagged shards of ice materialized already halfway to Dorothy, aiming for her heart.

Dorothy swung the wand out with a snap of her wrist. The deadly projectiles were instantly pulverized into mist. She whipped the wand down.

Directly above the Witch, a huge chunk of rock came loose from the mountain's remains and fell straight toward her. The initial popping and cracking of the boulder's movements gave the Witch enough of a warning to strike her broom handle on the ground, transporting her away in a cloud of purple smoke.

There was a boom and another puff of the purple smoke as the Witch manifested closer to the Ozma, while the boulder smashed into the ground farther behind her.

"Oh, this is going to be fun," said the Witch, cackling with demented glee, "My turn now." She slowly raised her broom as if lifting an enormous invisible object.

Dorothy was ready. Nothing appeared though, which made her worry all the more.

Then the ground shook.

A molten, steaming hand rose from the chasm and slammed down onto the cliff edge. The hand was huge, at least three feet wide and made of oozing magma. It pulled up the rest of itself. A hulking creature made of living lava. It towered twenty feet high and dripped sizzling hot pieces of molten rock as it lumbered toward Dorothy. In its wake, it left irregular footprints burned into the soil.

It raised a bubbling fist, then brought it down, almost hitting Dorothy. She was faster and dove to the side, barely avoiding it.

A bit of magma splattered onto her pant leg, eating through the material. She felt the pain before it even touched her skin. She muffled her cry and rolled away, the cool ground helping to dull the burn. Up and on her feet, she ran toward the open tundra.

The lava thing was big, but slow. It gave her a chance to retaliate. Out of the corner of her eye, she saw that the Witch was watching her. Good. Anything to keep her away from the Ozma.

Dorothy stopped and took a deep breath to calm her mind. She didn't know how to use this wand and was operating on pure instinct. She pointed the wand down, picturing what she wanted to happen, then with enormous effort, yanked it up toward the sky with a strenuous cry.

The ground shook once more.

"C'mon, c'mon," she said under her breath.

A pair of frosted hands exploded out of the snow covered ground, sending fragments of ice and rock into the air. With a moaning groan, an ice creature emerged, standing taller than its molten counterpart. To the side of Dorothy's wintery bodyguard, another snow creature rose out of the ground, followed by two more.

A deep frown spread over the Witch's face.

The four giant snow men stomped their way toward the boiling beast. The molten monster seemed confused by the multiple enemies, swaying from side to side, unable to decide which direction to take.

The first of the snow men rushed forward and smothered its scorching twin. A cloud of steam hissed off the molten man as the ice creature melted on top of him. The second snow monster followed its brother throwing itself on top of the enemy. The third was right behind, disappearing into the wall of vapor that now surrounded the lava giant.

The brisk, freezing winds sucked the steam away, leaving the results of the elementals' combative embrace. The magma monster had cooled off, hardening into a mass of solid basalt rock.

Rampaging past the defeated enemy, the last snow creature thundered toward the Witch.

The Witch didn't react other than to give it an appropriately cool stare. She merely tapped her broom handle down onto the ground.

Small fissures developed along the rocky terrain, spreading outward toward the oncoming ice giant and Dorothy beyond it.

The Witch slammed her broom handle down again.

The fissures widened.

The broom handle came down again. Harder.

With a tremendous crack, portions of the ground fell away. The snow man teetered as the support under its foot gave way, then tumbled over, plunging into the fiery pit.

Dorothy was too busy jumping from spot to spot, leaping across gaping holes as they formed. Once she found a secure foothold, she cut loose. She swung the wand, screaming out in anger and hurled a barrage of glowing blue daggers at the Witch.

These daggers were made of energy and moved faster than the eye could follow. The Witch had no time to dodge or put up a defensive spell, yet her reflexes were such that she was able to weave between the razor sharp missiles. Several of the blue blades sliced by her face, arms, and legs, missing the more vital areas. Only one found its mark, sinking into her left shoulder.

Injured, she bent forward, cradling her wound.

Dorothy was winding the wand back, getting ready to let fly another spell—the last spell. "I told you, I'd never let you win!"

When the Witch looked up at her, there was nothing in her eyes but hatred, in its purest form. "Playtime's over." She jammed her broom handle forward. Seven bolts of pulsing red energy flew straight for Dorothy.

Raising her wand, Dorothy prepared to deflect them, but the energy bolts suddenly split outward, going around her and headed right for Jasper!

They were too fast for Dorothy to react to.

Jasper saw them coming and ran. The red bolts found him, stopping him in his tracks. The energy whirled around him faster and faster, until he was engulfed in a writhing column of crimson fire.

"JASPER!" she cried, leaping over the many gaps to be near him.

The unnatural flames roared, spinning into a miniature tornado. Jasper was completely hidden from view. If he was screaming, Dorothy couldn't hear him over the sounds of the fiery cyclone and her own screaming.

Then just as quickly, the flames died down, revealing a brutally shocking sight. Jasper had been baked into a statue, looking very much like his father, his mouth open in a silent scream. Dorothy caressed his stony face.

"Goodbye, brother," the Witch sneered. She gestured with her broom, causing what was left of Jasper to shatter, his pieces falling over the cliff edges into the molten rock far below.

Falling to her knees where Jasper once stood, Dorothy sifted through the debris, devastated.

CHAPTER 69
THE ONE MAN ARMY OF OZ

He was gone.

Jasper was gone from her life.

A man she had barely met only days ago and now felt like she couldn't live without him. He was her protector, her confidant… her friend.

The ache in her heart was soul wrenching. Her chest felt empty. It was a pain that consumed her from the inside out, leaving her doubled over, sobbing at her loss.

"I warned you, my pretty. You're going to watch them *all* suffer," the Witch cackled, walking toward the Ozma.

At this threat, some small spark ignited within Dorothy and she whipped around to fire off a spell, but the Witch was expecting it. A sharp blast knocked the wand from Dorothy's hand. She watched it twinkle one last time as it spun in the air and then disappeared into the chasm.

Choked with emotion, operating on some primal level, she scrambled toward the Ozma, which was closer to her than the Witch. She didn't get anywhere near it, before a blast of red electricity sent her rolling backwards. The spell felt like a razor cutting along her entire nervous system. Or it would have if her body wasn't already numb. She watched the Witch approach the emerald, a positively smug look on her face.

As the Witch walked past Tik Tok, his hand lashed out and grabbed her ankle!

"That's quite e-nough!" announced the One Man Army of Oz. Unable to stand, he rolled away, yanking her off her feet, slamming her to the ground. He rolled toward the edge of the chasm, pulling her with him.

The Witch clawed frantically at the ground, but Tik Tok continued right on over the cliff, taking her with him.

"NO!" was all the Witch could utter before she disappeared.

Dorothy pulled herself up to the edge. She was farther away and the jagged, craggy cliffs hid them from view, until she saw Tik Tok finally splash into the molten river. His copper body immediately began to melt, dissolving and dispersing on top of the glowing lava.

"Good-bye, Miss Dor-o-theee—" he managed to shout, before he was cut off, his head submerging from view.

Dorothy stared down at the blazing river, shell-shocked. She was losing everyone she cared for.

While Dorothy mourned her friends, something shifted behind a large rock.

Something unseen.

And had anyone been paying attention, they would have heard the faintest ticking sound coming from it.

CHAPTER 70
THE LITTLEST KNIGHT

Hidden from sight and holding the Ozma tightly to his tiny little chest, was Tik!

He side-stepped ever so carefully to the chasm's edge and peeked over. He let out a high-pitched sigh of despair over his companion's death. For what was a winding key without anything to wind?

Tik didn't get time to contemplate that thought (which was much too big for his small, little gears to process) because the Witch's spidery fingers reached back up over the cliff!

Seeing this, Tik whirred in panic, stumbling back, tripping over his tiny feet. He turned and made a mad dash for Dorothy, wobbling under the weight of his precious cargo.

Tok had given him one last mission and Tik wasn't going to fail him.

CHAPTER 71
WICKED TRUTHS

A high-pitched squeal brought Dorothy out of her foggy haze. She looked to her side and saw a very strange sight.

The Ozma was rushing toward her.

No. It was an adorable little mechanical man rushing toward her, *carrying* the Ozma.

The gem was too heavy for it, causing the figure to sway from side to side, like a drunken sailor. To Dorothy, he resembled a miniature, skinnier version of Tik Tok, which brought a faint smile to her face. *This must be his winding key,* she thought.

Her eyes focused and regained clarity. She lowered her hands, cupping them for the little guy as he raced for her.

Swinging herself up onto solid ground, broom still in hand, the Witch glanced about, searching for the emerald. She looked up in time to see Dorothy rise with Tik standing on her shoulder, hand outstretched, holding the Ozma.

Both of the Witch's hands twisted around her broom for support as she screamed out, furious at the injustice of it all.

Emerald energy crackled and flowed over Dorothy's hand, and up her arm, then coursed over her entire body. She had stopped crying, but her cheeks—dirty with smudges, cuts and scrapes—glistened with tear stains.

"It's over." Dorothy met the Witch's cold stare with one of her own.

"Hmph," the Witch sniffed, contemptuously. She tapped her broom handle on the ground. BOOMPH. She disappeared inside her cloud of purple smoke that billowed in the air around her.

Dorothy didn't move a muscle. Her right hand remained extended with the Ozma.

A second later, the purple smoke dissipated, tendrils curling out before evaporating, revealing a very surprised Witch, still standing in the same spot.

Dorothy shook her head. "You're not escaping this time."

The Witch's broom flew out of her grasp and landed in Dorothy's left hand. The Witch gasped in shock. Her stunned expression melting into one of absolute hate.

When Dorothy threw the broom over the side into the chasm, the Witch's one eye bulged briefly, almost popping out of her skull. "Agh!"

"I want my shoes." Dorothy snapped her fingers and pointed to her own feet. Instantaneously, the gleaming magic slippers appeared, replacing Fairuza's purple boots she had been wearing.

The Witch lifted her black robe enough to see that she was now wearing Fairuza's boots. She dropped the edge of her robe back down and glared at Dorothy. "You foul little thing. I despise the day that old fool brought you here."

Dorothy was thrown by the remark. "No one brought me here. I came by accident. The tornado."

The floor around the Witch began to fracture and fall away. The Witch acknowledged the fact with a glance, but didn't react. Instead, she laughed at Dorothy. "He kept you in the dark as well."

"Who?" Dorothy asked, now curious.

"That devil in disguise! The Wizard! A pox upon this land since the day he was born." The Witch spat to the side, showing her disgust at the mere mention of the man.

"You're insane. He's not from Oz. He's like me. Came here by accident. In a balloon." Dorothy thought the Witch was either crazy or trying to deceive her.

More of the ground near the Witch fell away, leaving her standing on a lone pillar of rock with the lava below surrounding her on all sides.

The Witch paid no attention. "That's what he told you?" She cackled again. "Who do you think started the Witch Wars? He divided the land, playing us against each other. We were the only threat to him and he knew it. He brought you here to finish the job."

"More lies." Dorothy said.

"No point to lie, is there, dearie? You've won, haven't you? All of us Witches are dust now." She looked down into the fiery chasm, then back up at Dorothy. "Or soon will be."

Her words had the ring of truth to them. Dorothy didn't respond, sorting through her memories, hearing bits of the Wizard's tales echoing in her mind. Images were flashing in the back of her brain that she couldn't quite focus on. Slippery memories like when she had been under the amnesia spell.

Memories that didn't want to be found.

The Witch pointed her long finger at Dorothy. "You were his special weapon. Hidden away from us until you came of age."

Dorothy started to falter. Her hand, holding the Ozma, lowered a fraction.

"Didn't it ever strike you as odd that you were the only outlander to enter Oz, besides the Wizard?" The Witch arched her one good eyebrow. "Only Ozblood can stay here."

Dorothy's eyes widened. Thoughts were warring inside her. *Was* everything she knew a lie? How did the tornado bring her here? Why only her and no one else? She remembered her last encounter with the Wizard in the sanitarium. How he liked to avoid direct answers, play games and sidestep the truth.

The Ozma lowered further, almost to Dorothy's side. Her mind was jumbled and racing.

The Witch nodded knowingly. "Your blood is pure and true, one hundred generations strong. Royal blood."

Dorothy's stomach dropped. A cold nugget of uncertainty in the pit of her gut. She felt dizzy. The images in her head began to sharpen. Her mom and dad. Holding her, caring for her. They were wearing *crowns*. A King and Queen.

A chill rippled up Dorothy's arms, then down her back.

More images. A man falling to the ground. Blood on his head. Her father. Then someone screaming. Her mother. Crying over him. Trying to protect a baby in her arms. *Me*. Then a terrible thunk and her mother was suddenly silenced.

Dorothy was stunned. Her parents had been murdered. The King and Queen killed.

The final images swam to the forefront of her mind. A man standing over her. Holding a cane with an emerald handle. *Blood* was on the handle. The man wiped it off, then picked Dorothy up.

The world blurred after that.

"You remember now, my pretty. I see it on your face." The Witch was enjoying this. "He'll return one day, mark my words. And he's going to want his power back. All of it, including yours." That disgustingly sinister smile of hers creased her craggy face. "With the rose, come the thorns."

Those words and that face renewed Dorothy's resolve. She raised the Ozma once more. "I can't let you go. You know that."

"Do what you must. I'm satisfied knowing that I've taken away what you're heart has grown fond of." The Witch's crooked smile brimmed with spite. A portrait of evil if there ever was one. She burst into a boisterous cackle.

Dorothy slashed the air with the Ozma. A quick, violent movement.

An ear-splitting crack pierced the air and the pillar of rock crumbled apart under the Witch. She fell, laughing the whole way down, until she was snuffed out and swallowed up by the lava with a satisfying hiss, ending her reign of terror once and for all.

Standing alone on the precipice of the chasm, Dorothy stared down, feeling the waves of heat washing up against her face. She had done it. She'd defeated the Nome King and the Witch and reclaimed the Ozma for Oz. But she felt no joy in her victory. In the process, she had lost too much that was dear to her.

Jasper, Scarecrow, Tik Tok, Mik, Kob and poor innocent Pok. All were gone.

"Dorothy?"

The voice was weak, but she recognized it instantly. The Scarecrow.

She turned to see the Lion and Tin man propping him up, helping him to walk over to her. He was blackened and scorched, but *alive*. Behind them were the Munchkins and Willow, her ragtag

Knights.

She ran to meet them halfway and hugged the Scarecrow tightly, "I thought I'd lost you too."

"He saved me." The Scarecrow nodded toward the Lion. "Though I wouldn't have blamed him if he hadn't."

"I couldn't let that happen," the Lion said gruffly.

Much of the Lion's fur had been singed during the rescue. There were a few patches where there was no fur at all, only reddened, burned skin. Dorothy wondered how many *more* scars her friend would have.

"Thank you." She stood on her tiptoes to kiss the Lion on the cheek. He still had to bend slightly to let her reach him.

She stood back and looked at all of them. Her three friends, wounded, but still together. Willow and the Munchkins—Boq, Bom, Hup, and Wik—who fought for her and for Oz, that sacrificed so much to get her here. She couldn't let them down. There was still so much to do to bring the land back from the brink. She still had work ahead of her. "Thank you all."

The Munchkins bowed, then started pulling out lollipops as a token of victory.

It was hard for Dorothy to look at the Tin Man, because out of all of them, he was the one most in touch with the workings of the heart. The one that understood. She could see it in his expression. The sad smile. The pained eyes.

The Tin Man put his hand on her back, consoling her. "I'm sorry. I know you cared for him."

And that was it. She leaned against him, sobbing uncontrollably, needing his comfort. He held her close, his metal cheek resting against her forehead.

The rest of her friends lowered their heads and mourned for her loss.

CHAPTER 72
THE SCARECROW'S GIFT

Against the brilliant blue sky, Emerald City sparkled like a jewel in the sun.

Once the Ozma had been brought home, its energy had started to bleed out into the land, reviving it. Rejuvenating it.

The recurring storms had receded. The ever present grey clouds finally broke apart, letting the populace feel the pleasure of warm sunlight again. Clear skies had appeared with puffy, cotton-shaped white clouds drifting lazily overhead.

Colors saturated the landscape, twice as vibrant as before to make up for the lost years. A lush, vivid shade of green had spread across the grass, then into the gently swaying trees. Flowers had bloomed in every color imaginable and some that couldn't be imagined.

The land was alive again.

The Munchkin citizens had returned and were thriving, happily working the grounds, rebuilding walls and roads, repairing the damage their beloved city had endured under the Nome King's rule. Once news of the Nome King's demise had reached them in the Southern lands, the Munchkins had packed up and left their sanctuary, returning home as fast as their short legs could carry them.

Dorothy stood in the Royal Study, leaning against the wall, looking out the window, watching them work and play and cheerily sing songs as they liked to do. The upbeat, bubbly melodies made her smile.

Her fingers absent-mindedly caressed the smooth silky fabric of her gown. It was an exquisite green dress with gold trim. A high collar showcased her delicate neck, while her slim sleeves, which ended just past her elbow, made her arms look long and graceful. It wasn't too flamboyant—she had told the dressmakers to keep it simple—but it was obviously a gown that befitted a Queen.

On her head was a crown. Simple, elegant and studded with emeralds.

And around her neck was the Ozma, fitted to a golden necklace. She could feel its magical heartbeat against her chest, letting her know all was well.

On her feet were the magic slippers, always glimmering, always changing color depending on what angle you were looking at them. At the moment, they were a ruby red. Then Dorothy moved away from the window and they shimmered a deep blue.

Toto, her faithful old terrier, was sleeping next to her feet. When Dorothy left the window, Toto woke and trotted beside her, his nails lightly tapping on the marble floor. He was much older, with spots of grey in his black fur, but as lively as ever. Hearing him, Dorothy laughed and knelt down, ruffling the fur on his head.

"Good boy. I missed you too." When the Munchkins had returned, they had brought back Toto, much to her delight. Toto hadn't blinked once that Dorothy was so much older. He ran right to her and welcomed her like no time had passed. He was just overjoyed to be with her again. To walk by her side.

Tik sat on Dorothy's right shoulder, looking down at the dog. The tiny mechanical man had been polished up and looked brand new. His left hand held onto Dorothy's collar, his head leaning to the side every now and then, inquisitively watching the world around him.

Toto noticed him and raised his snout, coming in for a sniff. Tik pulled in his legs. Undeterred, Toto pushed in closer. Tik whirred a warning and kicked his small foot out, shooing the dog away. Toto took the hint and turned aside with an insulted snort, leaving him alone.

Dorothy giggled and stood back up to look at the room. It was still in disarray from the Nome King's occupation. The Munchkins had wanted to start work on repairing and cleaning the palace as soon as they arrived. Dorothy had told them that it was more important to rebuild the city and their homes first. The palace could wait.

She flipped through some of the books that were strewn about. Some were about Oz history, some about magic, while others were simply farming information. The Nome King didn't strike her as much of a reader. She guessed that he had probably had a tantrum or two in here, throwing the books around or at his minions. On the walls were maps of Oz, tacked on at haphazard angles. *This must have been his base of operations*, she thought, *trying to track down the Ozma. Or me.*

She gazed around the room, feeling the sadness creep back. Her eyes stopped on a mirror sitting on a round table, propped up against a stack of books. It was oval with a decorative frame. Nothing special. Probably from one of the palace's guest rooms. It had a light layer of dust on it, which she wiped away. Her fingers caressed the glass and she wondered to herself why the Nome King would want to take the time to stand it up like this. In this room.

Her own reflection stared back at her. Dorothy saw how unhappy she looked. The weary expression. The sad circles under her eyes from the lack of sleep due to nightmares and sudden, unexpected bouts of sobbing. She was about to turn away, unable to look at herself any more, when the reflected image faded—

—and was replaced with a view of a small room. One that looked familiar.

Dorothy's jaw clenched.

The image in the mirror was of a bed in a stark room with an I.V. stand nearby, tubes dangling down to the floor.

A polite clearing of the throat finally drew her attention away from the mirror. It was the Lion General, standing just inside the room. His singed fur was starting to grow back, but there were some spots where his skin had been burned that were still scarred and hairless. There was a softness in his expression now that the war was over.

"M'Lady," he said, with a slight bow of the head.

"Please. Don't." Dorothy gave him a pleading look.

He chuckled. "Sorry. With that crown and dress, it's hard not to revert to formality."

She sighed. "I told them it was still too much. I'm a simple girl. I think I'll go back to my T-shirt and jeans. What do you think?"

"I'm sure you can find a middle ground," he said.

"I suppose." She smiled. "That was a very diplomatic answer, by the way."

"Such is the life of a General." He gave her a slight grin and gestured toward the door. "He's waiting."

Dorothy stayed where she was and pointed to the mirror. "Look."

The Lion glanced down at the room in the reflection.

"That's the Wizard's room. Back in Kansas." She had recognized it instantly. It was Oscar Zoroaster's room at the Plumly Sanitarium. The Wizard of Oz. And his bed was empty.

The Lion's eyes narrowed.

"The Nome King was in contact with him." She didn't want to believe it, but there wasn't any other explanation.

The Lion crossed his arms and stroked his furry chin. "Hrm. It would appear that way."

"The Wizard was watching me," she said with certainty.

He looked up at her. "You don't know that for sure."

"I do." She placed her hand over her heart. "I felt it. Whenever I was near a mirror. Thought I was just imagining things."

"It might have been the Nome King. Watching both of you," the Lion said hopefully.

Dorothy shook her head. "No, it was him. He was spying on me. For the Nome King."

The Lion nodded, then placed a hand on her elbow. "Thoughts for another time. Come, Dorothy. He's waiting."

She nodded and let him escort her out into the Royal Hall. Toto trotted along beside them.

As they made the long walk toward the throne room,

Dorothy picked up the conversation again. "Have the engineers found the plans yet?"

He nodded. "They'll start rebuilding him at once."

Tik whirred happily.

Dorothy glanced at the Lion. "He won't be the same."

"He'll be loyal and brave," said the Lion, with confidence.

"But he won't have his memories," Dorothy added, sadly.

The Lion gestured toward the little fellow sitting on her shoulder. "Tik will fill in the blanks."

Tik proudly whirred again, nodding.

Dorothy laughed, reassured. She tapped Tik gently with her finger. "Of course you will."

Tik whirred softly, sounding like a purr.

They turned a corner and entered the throne room. Sunlight poured into the majestic chamber through the emerald lenses in the arched ceiling, flooding the area with an amazing soft green glow. The gold trim decorating every doorway and ledge, caught the light, adding a warm yellow into the mix. All of this light hit the polished marble floor, and reflected it up at the mirrored walls in shifting patterns, creating the dreamlike atmosphere that so many Ozites marveled at.

Near the back wall was the throne, more gold than emerald, making it stand out in the room.

In front of the throne was the Scarecrow, looking slight against the room's grandeur. He looked healthier, having been restitched with fresh stuffing and new clothes. His smile was still slightly lopsided. He was wearing the uniform of a Knight of Oz.

The Lion led Dorothy up to him, then gave a nod to the Scarecrow, before walking away, leaving the two of them alone.

The Scarecrow fidgeted, finding it hard to look her in the eyes.

"You wanted to talk?" Dorothy asked softly.

He stared down at the floor. "I don't know if you'll ever forgive me, but—"

She interrupted, smiling and held his shoulder. "There's nothing to forgive. I know it wasn't your fault. The Lion knows it as well."

If a scarecrow could blush, this would be the moment. He shook his head. "I don't know if I'll ever be able to forgive myself."

She placed both hands on the sides of his face and stared him right in the eyes. "Dear Scarecrow. Please don't be so hard on yourself."

Metallic footsteps echoed across the floor.

Dorothy turned to see the Tin Man and Lion walking toward her, with Chalk in the rear. They were carrying a huge chunk of dirt on a stretcher constructed of a tarpaulin and wooden poles. The Tin Man and the Lion each had a pole over one shoulder, while Chalk held the other end of the poles via a crossbar clamped between his teeth.

The Tin Man had been repaired, polished and was gleaming. The welding scars on his chest and leg were barely noticeable.

Behind them were the rest of the Knights. Willow, Wik, Hup, Boq and Bom. Dorothy noticed that Willow was carrying the Tin Man's axe—they had been spending a bit of time together lately, much to Dorothy's delight. The Tin Man had a big heart and Dorothy was glad he was finally able to share it with someone. And she found it fitting that the lumberjack should fall in love with a tree.

But her attention was quickly drawn back to the hunk of dirt they were carrying.

Dorothy looked at them all in confusion. "What is this?"

Without a word, they lowered the gurney before her, then stood beside the Scarecrow.

"I hope you don't mind," the Scarecrow said nervously, crossing and uncrossing his hands, "I—I learned a lot under the Witch's control."

Dorothy was at a loss. "I don't know what you're talking about..."

"I thought, for once... maybe that knowledge could be put to better use," the Scarecrow said earnestly. He held out his hand and presented her with a small piece of broken rock resting in his palm.

"I was able to rescue a piece of Jasper," he said softly.

Dorothy took a step back.

The Scarecrow held it up higher toward her. "You can bring him back..."

Her breath caught. Her eyes welled up with tears.

The Scarecrow pointed to the chunk of dirt on the floor. "I've already mixed and prepared the clay."

Hesitantly, she took the small rock from him, cradling it in her shaking hand. "What do I do?"

He pointed to the Ozma hanging from her neck. "Use the Ozma to give it the spark of life. Then insert it into that clay."

She stared at the fragment of rock in her palm, entranced. "Is this really him?"

The Scarecrow nodded.

With her free hand, she touched the Ozma resting against her chest. It glowed brighter, sending the now familiar green energy crackling down her arm, to her hand and into the rock resting on her palm.

She knelt down and pushed it deep into the chunk of dirt.

Moments passed. She looked up at the Scarecrow with tear

filled eyes. Disappointment clouding her face. She couldn't go through this heartbreak all over again.

But the Scarecrow smiled and pointed at the clay.

When she looked back down, she saw a piece of dirt fall to the floor. She stopped breathing.

Another piece fell away, clunking to the hard marble and breaking apart into fine particles.

Human fingers poked out from the main portion of the chunk of clay. They were slowly moving.

At the sight of that, Dorothy couldn't contain herself and began tearing into the clay, ripping chunks out, exposing more and more flesh underneath.

Then she saw Jasper's face. He moaned.

Dorothy's fingers were shaking as she brushed the dirt away and cradled his head. His eyes opened and he sucked in a huge lungful of air. He sat up coughing, getting out the last traces of dust and dirt. He looked around the room with wide searching eyes.

His gaze landed on Dorothy, who was bursting with Joy. He just stared at her seemingly not recognizing her.

Her chest started to tighten. He didn't remember her.

Then he blinked, as if getting the sleep out of his eyes and focused on the Ozma around her neck. He looked back up at her and grinned. "What did I miss?"

She laughed and cried at the same time. "Shut up and kiss me!"

"Yes, M'Lady." They embraced and he kissed her longingly.

The Tin Man patted the Scarecrow on the back. The Lion grinned, his eyes moist.

"About time," Chalk muttered under his breath, chuckling.

Dorothy lost herself in the moment, melting into Jasper.

She had found her prince—soon to be King—and she could live happily ever after.

EPILOGUE: I
REFORGED

In a dark sweltering room, sparks filled the air as molten copper was poured into the waiting molds.

In time, the glowing metal was pulled out, the jagged edges trimmed and made clean.

Once cooled, the pieces were assembled, connected to an intricate armature.

Hundreds of gears were carefully put into place, interlocking and rotating around each other in a delicate dance of mechanical precision.

Rivets were hammered into the metal plates, fitting them in place.

The word "***OZ***" was engraved into the front chest piece with great care.

There was one last piece needed.

A tiny metal figure, having watched the long process, now slipped into a keyhole in the back of the round copper form, transforming into a winding key.

It began to spin inside…

* * *

On a palace balcony, a Queen and King stood, making plans to rebuild their cherished land.

Hearing a familiar sound, they both turned to see a figure stomp into view behind them, its copper form shining brilliantly.

The stocky, round mechanical man walked up to the Queen and bowed deeply before her.

"At your ser-vice, Miss Dor-o-thy." The mechanical man's voice was deep and staccato.

The Queen's eyes filled with tears of joy and she welcomed him home with a warm embrace.

EPILOGUE: II
THE MAN BEHIND THE CURTAIN

It was mid-afternoon at the Plumly Sanitarium and the day was bright and sunny with a November chill in the air.

Even under these cheery conditions, the building was a blight against the landscape. A dark brooding block of red brick that siphoned all the joy around it.

Kids in the neighborhood gave it a wide berth on their way to the nearby park. They would often take the longer route using the next street over, just to avoid seeing the place.

Inside, the hallways and common rooms were empty—or so it seemed.

The sanitarium's staff lay on the floor, unmoving. Unconscious or dead, it was hard to tell.

Oscar Zoroaster stepped over them as he walked along the hallway.

Dressed in a dark green business suit and a green derby hat, he looked quite dapper. He no longer appeared frail. Old and wrinkled, yes, but the way he moved showed no hint of age. In his hand, he carried his aluminum foiled communication rod. He tore at the foil and copper wire, revealing a straight cane with a marvelous emerald stone for a handle.

A cane that Dorothy would remember had she seen it. There was no trace of blood on it this time.

Entering the front lobby, Mr. Zoroaster made for the exit, passing the short, round nurse that Dorothy and Jasper had met during their visit. "Good day, Miss Mulligan," he said, with a jaunty tip of his hat to the woman.

The nurse, surprised by the warm greeting, nodded and smiled, giving him an equally buoyant reply, "Well, thank you, Mr. Zoroaster—" The nurse did a double-take.

Mr. Zoroaster walked out the door without breaking his stride.

Miss Mulligan jumped to her feet and rushed after him. She threw the doors open and stepped out of the heated building into the cold Kansas air, scanning the area.

She had a clear view in both directions and there wasn't a soul in sight.

"Mr. Zoroaster?" She glanced around uncertainly, taking a step back. "Mr. Zoroaster?"

And with that, the Wizard of Oz was gone.

Acknowledgments

I want to thank my Mom and Dad, and Carolyn, who have always encouraged and supported me in all of my crazy creative endeavors and for putting up with me during the hard times.

Thank you dad, for being the best father a man could be. You're my hero. Miss you, pops.

Thank you to my sister, Monica, who opened my eyes to the idea of being a writer and showed me the way, leading by example.

Also thank you to Serena, Sabrina, Aaron, Zach & Samantha, who have all given me so much joy (especially when I needed it most).

And of course, thank you to L. Frank Baum for creating the wonderful world of Oz.

You can contact me here:
www.ndamon.com

ABOUT THE AUTHOR

Nick Damon is both a writer and artist, having worked in various industries over the years. He sculpted action figures for the toy market, did production design for several themed restaurant projects, created a line of collector monster masks, and had the privilege of freelancing for both Disney's California Adventure and Tokyo's DisneySea theme parks.

In-between all of those jobs, he was also secretly writing, toiling away in his fortress of solitude. Numerous screenplays later, his first film was produced in 2010, titled "Hunter Prey". Having accomplished one dream, he set his eyes on another. To write a book. "Shadow of Oz" is his first novel.

Made in the USA
Charleston, SC
07 May 2013